SOMEPLACE
GENEROUS

SOMEPLACE GENEROUS

A ROMANCE ANTHOLOGY

edited by

ELAINA ELLIS and **AMBER FLAME**

Generous Press

AN IMPRINT OF ROW HOUSE PUBLISHING
BELLINGHAM, WASHINGTON

Because we at Generous Press and Row House Publishing believe that the best stories are born in the margins, we proudly spotlight, amplify, and celebrate the voices of diverse, innovative creators. Through independent publishing, we strive to break free from the control of Big Publishing and oppressive systems, ensuring a more liberated future for us all.

Library of Congress Cataloging-in-Publication Data Available Upon Request

ISBN: 9781955905626 (TP)
eISBN: 9781955905633 (eBook)

Printed in the United States

Distributed by Simon & Schuster

Interior design by Pauline Neuwirth, Neuwirth & Associates, Inc.
Cover design by Becca Fox

Image and logo by Reesa Beesa

Photo of Elaina Ellis by Heather Posten
Photo of Amber Flame courtesy of Amber Flame

First edition
10 9 8 7 6 5 4 3 2 1

How are we able to love under duress and, when we can't, what distorts love for us? How can we negotiate the various claims and loves we choose in order to make them include ourselves—the love of the self that is not narcissistic, not simply selfish—and also something bigger than ourselves, something that is not martyrdom, something that does not mean setting one's self aside completely?
I'm interested in negotiating between those two extremes, to get to someplace where the love is generous.
—TONI MORRISON

I want to be generous, to spoil myself beyond measure, to understand that my flesh is worthy of extravagance . . .
—AKWAEKE EMEZI

Your traveled, generous thighs
between which my whole face has come and come—
the innocence and wisdom of the place my tongue has found there—
—ADRIENNE RICH

Contents

Epilogue

Dear Reader

Thank you for picking up this book. *Someplace Generous* is the first-ever title in the Generous Press catalogue. This is how it begins.

At Generous Press, our mission is to publish lush, high-caliber romance fiction written by brilliant BIPOC, queer, and disabled authors. Our intention is to bring more joy and pleasure to this hurting world, and to reflect the vitality of our interconnected communities. That's why the theme of our first book is, in a word, *yes*. These are stories that heal through generous consent.

At the heart of Generous Press is a series of meet-cutes. When Deputy Publisher Amber Flame met Publisher Elaina Ellis back in the mid-aughts, we became friends, briefly flirted, made art, and (fast-forward twenty years) launched a press together. When Generous Press met Row House, a proudly disruptive publishing house at the intersection of social justice and literature, it was love at first Zoom meeting. Now, our first cohort of authors meets our growing community of readers. May this be the first of many happy encounters. May we change the face of romance fiction together.

The epigraphs that begin this anthology—words from Akwaeke Emezi, Toni Morrison, and Adrienne Rich—are, collectively, our namesake. The name of our imprint holds the wisdom and music of these writers and many more. The title of this book is a nod to Morrison's vision of a balanced love: a love that is neither selfish nor self-harming. This is the place we want to get to. It's where we want to help one another go. Someplace generous.

Love,
Elaina & Amber

A Word About How to Navigate This Book

Someplace Generous is an unusual volume of romance fiction. The love stories here are written by twenty-two brilliant authors who have applied twenty-two fantastically distinct perspectives and writing styles to the theme of generous consent. There is a gorgeous, wildly diverse ecosystem of creativity and storytelling herein.

Speaking of consent, Reader, you have some choices ahead.

CHOOSE YOUR OWN ADVENTURE:

If, Reader, you prefer to know what kind of story you're reading before you begin—things like spice-level, subgenres, and basic plot points—flip to page 306 to reference our content descriptions.

If, Reader, you're in the mood to be surprised, you can move through this book in any way you like—reading the anthology from beginning to end or flipping until you find a voice that speaks to you today. You might choose by eyeballing the length of a story—one piece in this book is a single poem-like gem of a paragraph, while others span thirty-plus pages.

If you come across a word or concept that you're unfamiliar with—perhaps in a language you don't speak or from a subculture or fandom you don't belong to—turn to page 297 to check out our author-generated glossary. It's not an exhaustive list of terms by any means, but it's a beautiful resource for the curious.

REGARDING ENDINGS,

The stories in *Someplace Generous* depict a lot of wonderful beginnings. Meet-cutes, first dates, second chances, brave connections. In the middle, there's mess and sex and darkness and humor and sweetness and intimacy and the hand of fate. The romance genre defines itself by the guarantee of a happy ending, but in the span of a short story, there's only so much an author can show. Sometimes the future happens off the page. Sometimes you get to close the book and wonder, *what further happiness will bloom between these two?* And maybe that helps you to ask, *what happiness will bloom for me?*

Let's delight in imagining the ever after.

SOMEPLACE
GENEROUS

PROLOGUE

For the Love of Sky and Smoke

MAVIS L. JOHNSON

Clove leaned back in Poppy Smoke's chair, just to feel him. The leather was soft, warm, and buttery. She could feel his hug in it. If she turned her head just so, she could catch the smell of her grandfather's neck—a heady mix of sugar and spices. To-night, she needed to remember what Poppy Smoke and Nana Sky told her so long ago, back when they used to hold court in the Lounge every Saturday night. She closed her eyes to recall Nana Sky's sensual presence, her ease and flow, the way she would slink through the kitchen door, lean over the bar, and slowly trace her index finger around the rim of a highball glass.

She wanted a love like theirs. One that was smoky, sensual, and left a sweet and spicy taste on the tip of the tongue. She settled in the chair, her own highball glass filled with her best whiskey, and breathed in the scent from the kitchen. Tonight, Clove—or Baby Spice, as they always called her—was ready for them to whisper again to her heart and spirit. She was ready to listen.

Baby Spice, back then everyone called your Poppy "Toke." He owned the West End Lounge on the corner of Third and Lee. My cousin CeeCee and I went there on the weekends, and sometimes on Wednesday nights if they were cooking oxtails and playing spades. West End served the best whiskey in town. I liked the whiskey. A LOT. CeeCee (God rest her soul) liked the men. A LOT. If I walked in and smelled smoke from cigarettes, cinnamon, cloves, and sugar, I knew Toke was there. He was always cooking sugar. The men CeeCee liked a lot would laugh and yell back to the kitchen, "You're gonna kill us with all that smoke." I liked the smoke. It made me remember.

Clove laughed to herself. Nana and Poppy would switch up right there every time. He would reach up, stroke Nana's cheek, smile, and keep the story going.

Baby Spice, your Nana told us to call her "Treetop."
The men who were always running behind CeeCee didn't talk to Treetop. CeeCee was tiny and could fit in the crook of a man's arm. They liked that. It made them feel strong. They didn't like looking up to a woman who wasn't even trying to pretend that she wanted to fit into such a small space. One said it hurt his neck to look up to the sky. They did like the fine view, particularly going south. I liked looking up, and, hah, I LOVED going south. I saw forever in every inch of her.

That Saturday night, CeeCee was tucked into the crook of Johnnie Tate's arm. I guess Treetop figured she would follow the smoke. I looked up and saw her in the kitchen doorway. She asked me about the cinnamon, cloves, and sugar. No one had ever asked me about that before. We walked to the back. I showed her the bags of sugar stacked up by the boxes of whiskey. I told her about Jamaica. She told me about Georgia, about the cinnamon, cloves, and sugar on her grandmother's stove. I stirred the pot. She dipped her pinky in the pot, put it on the tip of her tongue, then softly traced my lips with that same sweet and smoky pinky. She said, "Thanks for the taste, Smoke."

Then she walked right back to the lounge. I called out, "You're welcome, Sky."

This was the part when Sky always chimed back in, joining Smoke. Clove's favorite part. As if on cue, the two would look at each other—they still had that heat, after all those years—and say it together.

That night, we knew.

Clove opened her eyes and raised her glass to Nana Sky and Poppy Smoke. She remembered now, who she was—descended from a legacy of smoky, sensual, sweet, spicy love, by way of Jamaica, Georgia, and the West End Lounge on the corner of Third and Lee. She was the inheritor of half a century of stories about romance, luck, and living. Right there in Smoke's chair, she renewed her faith in love.

BEGINNING

Sofia

EJ COLEN

Most versions of the story start with my mouth on hers in a corner booth of a bar in Portland. I will, of course, have gotten there early with a book so that I can watch her walk in. So that I can see what she looks like when she is unsure, watch her scanning faces to look for me. She has only seen me in a few small images on a tiny screen. I will want the upper hand.

The bar is quiet. It's a Sunday. A boy in his late twenties, perhaps, sits at the L-curve of the bar with a book and a drink.

So, I can't have the bar, I think.

"What are you reading?" I ask him.

"Vonnegut," he says.

And so he turns the book over and thumps down a few rungs in age. He can't be more than twenty-two to be reading Vonnegut.

"Does that work?" I ask.

"Work?" he says.

"Never mind," I say.

I order an old fashioned from the bartender. For the cherry and the squat glass. I want a Manhattan, but want to be drinking something in a stemless glass, masculine. I hate that I'm thinking this way. I want to swivel that fat ice cube around in the glass. Something for when the conversation lags, though I'm not here for conversation, and I'm not really nervous. Not yet. This is my fourth date this weekend. I'm trying things out. I'm trying to find out what it means to not get invested. Fifty first dates, I've told myself. Fifty first dates with no second dates. I'll be up-front about this, of course, at some point in the stream of things this evening. I've just gotten out of a thing that wrecked me. I don't want to get into another thing that'll wreck me, not for a long, long time. The fact that the woman who's meeting me already has a long-term partner changes the risk factor for wrecking a little, I think. But only a little. I am a serial monogamist trying things.

I choose the booth and set down my glass. Set down my book and go into the bathroom to check my hair and my face. I got through an entire date on Friday with a streak of dirt on my chin. My last haircut was a few days ago and my sides are close-shaven, a clean fade that leads to the curly, though curated, mop at the top. Nothing on my face or in my teeth. I don't check my breath; the whiskey will take care of that.

I would like to say I get lost in the book, but I spend twenty minutes traveling over the same four pages. I get to know them well. I get to know the chatter of the bartender well. The boy at the bar, the back of his head, the shape of his hands turning pages. Two women come in. I clock them as straight. Two men, the same. The men cue up a pool game within sight of the booth, and I watch them play. At forty-two I am old here. The men are in their late twenties. I think about whether they will think the show is for them. I don't think this is a gay bar. I have let her choose this place. She too is in her late twenties.

I am in a bar in Portland, a few hours from getting on the road to drive 250 miles back home, my dog in the car parked right out front, windows rolled down, the street bluing and cooling out there.

She comes in. My heart skips a beat, though I don't want it to. I'm not going to fall for this girl. *Fuck*, I think. She hasn't seen me yet. *Fuck*. I have never been with a girl like this. "Fancy," my friend J will say when I show him a picture later. She looks like she gets anything she wants. Like no one has ever said no to her. They couldn't.

SHE DOESN'T HEAD TO THE bar first. I see her looking around. There is hesitation in her glancing, perhaps, but confidence. I wanted to be reading when she came in. I look down at my book, not reading, but turning the page. I feel her walking straight toward me. A swirl of heat and light getting closer. And then there she is.

"It's you," she says.

I smile up at her. My look lets her know that I can fuck her in a way that no one ever has. This is what she will tell me later. That my look said I can take control of her body, that I can make her understand anew what her body is capable of, that I can leave it better than it was.

"It was supposed to be," I say.

I don't know what either of us means, and I like that maybe it's awkward, that maybe her footing is a little off here, I think. If that's possible. That mine is a little off.

I get up and hug her, a little clumsily. Our arms find their places eventually. She smells like everything I've ever wanted to devour. Her hair is soft against my cheek, and suddenly I'm in junior high. Or rather, I am letting my junior high self have something of this moment. I reach back into time to tell my young self how lucky I'll be when I'm older. In this moment, I have no heartbreak. In this moment, the world is wide open.

"Sofia," she says, backing up and holding out her hand.

"I know who you are," I say. I do the thing where I take her hand as though to shake it and I bring it to my lips, which seems overkill and ridiculous, but she seems to like it. I try not to inhale too deeply.

"Can I buy you a drink?" I ask.

"Finish your page," she says and walks back to the bar.

I MARK MY PAGE AND I watch her. Perfectly fitted pants cradle her ass. Her tough leather jacket that somehow makes her seem softer in her attempt. And I'm still staring when she turns back around. One side of her mouth pushes upward, a half-smile that travels all the way to her eyes. She holds my gaze the whole walk back to the table.

She sets her drink down and sits across from me.

"I was convinced you weren't real," I say.

"How so?"

"I could not believe that you would be who you were in your photos."

The photos had looked professional. Something pulled out of a magazine.

"What about my mouth?" she asks.

"Oh, you went there," I say. We both laugh.

On the app, I had messaged her, *I'm just passing through this weekend. But all I can think about is kissing your beautiful mouth.*

She had sent back a gif of a woman coquettish, but alluring, in false surprise.

IN ANOTHER VERSION OF THE story, my ex texts me on my way to the bar and says she wants to talk. I cancel with Sofia and get on the road and spend another year and a half figuring out that this thing with my ex will never work. I think occasionally about the girl with the mouth whose name I will not remember because I have deleted the app.

In another version of the story we go right to her apartment. Her girlfriend is out. Sofia makes a drink for herself that sits sweating on the kitchen counter for the next two hours. She tells me the bedroom is off limits, and I look around the kitchen and living room and back to her and say, "I don't think that will be a problem." And she laughs and I laugh and we take it from there.

In some versions of the story, she isn't allowed to bring other lovers to her apartment. In many versions she is.

Another version of the story involves me texting a Portland friend and asking if I can spend the night on her couch. I'm too tired to drive and despite my one-date plan I want to try to see Sofia again tomorrow night. Of course, she has plans. I get shy for asking and never text her again.

In one version of the story a man playing pool gets a black eye. In another version, the black eye is mine. Caused by her elbow in the backseat of my car. Both of us laughing.

Some versions of the story involve me getting home at two in the morning, three hours after leaving the bar, three hours after the last long kiss, and texting:

> I don't want this to make you nervous,
> but I want you.

| Oh?

she texts back after only a few moments.

> Naked and on all fours. |

| Ohh.

Just that extra h. This girl.

IN MOST VERSIONS OF THE story, she sets down her drink and sits on the opposite side of the booth.

I smile and she smiles, and I am feeling every stereotype of butch-femme right now. Not as though I put it on for play, but as though everything depends on it. The electricity that starts the hazy lights of the bar. The sleepy, easy feeling in the alcohol in every bottle. The scaffolding to keep the building upright. The soil that keeps the city from slipping into the river. The spin to the Earth. Gravity. The stars in their places. And all is right in the universe.

"It doesn't make any sense that I'm sitting all the way over here." She pushes her drink across the wide table and slides in next to me.

How to Open a Door

SAMMY TAUB

I daydreamed a lot about what Hax might be. I knew she wasn't a real werewolf, but that was about it for biodata: I didn't know her age or gender, if she was married, what she did during the day. I thought about it a lot, but mostly I needed our mutual anonymity more than I needed whatever lay on the other side of the door.

Until the anniversary of The Event started coming up.

What do you do when you feel scared? I'd texted Hax. We had started playing *In the Woods* online together months ago, and had started texting via anonymous messenger only recently. She was the only person I used the messenger app with, and when it made its particular sound, I got a Pavlovian thrill.

Is something frightening you, Hax responded a beat later. (For all I didn't know about *who* she was, in our disembodied space I knew *how* she was: reliable, blunt, hungry, rapt.)

It would be quicker to talk about what doesn't scare me.

Hm, typed Hax. *You seem pretty brave to me.* She continued: *Tell me one scary thing.*

My heart started to thump. This was the door, and Hax and I had done so well within the present limitations of our relationship. I could back up now and say *snakes,* or *I'm afraid of the dark,* or *earthquakes,* and we'd discuss that normal-human-person fear, then stay on the safe side of the door—texting each other, sacking video game villages, and having voice-changed phone sex a couple times a week. Who knows how long we could keep it up? Maybe a long time.

But I put my hands on the phone and watched my thumbs start to type: *There's an anniversary vigil I want to go to.*

ALTHOUGH, DID I REALLY WANT to go? Earlier that week, my therapist had tried to talk about the upcoming anniversary, and I'd tried to talk about the erotic meaning of werewolves.

"I know being into werewolves is totally uncool," I'd said. Jeanne and I both knew that I had no social life anymore, but I liked to maintain the concept of coolness, the possibility of embarrassment.

"Mm-hmm."

"But where do you think the hotness of the werewolf *comes* from?" I said, a weird feeling in my belly, waving my hands just outside the video frame in an attempt to communicate that which could not be said. "What do you think its source is, like, psychologically, mythologically?"

Sometimes my questions made Jeanne redden—just at the tips of her ears—which I never mentioned in case it was a therapist faux pas, but this day she had great facial composure.

"Well, monsters didn't used to be sexy, any more than cooped-up chickens found foxes sexy," said Jeanne, her voice warbling for a moment as our video connection faltered. "But for our ancestors, I think monsters did an important, helpful job: They helped people know where their fear belonged."

Keeping fears in place was one of Jeanne's recurring themes: The importance of having an organizing principle for your fear, so it stayed where it was supposed to.

Only, following The Event, my fear was anything but contained: It was like a crystal lit from within, fracturing and spilling everywhere, filling the world with terrifying objects, weathers, qualities of light. So far, I had failed to find an organizing principle that would let me comfortably leave the house.

In the end, we never got back to what it means when you're hot for a monster.

THE NIGHT BEFORE I MET Hax, I had bad dreams I couldn't quite remember that left me feeling violent, impotent. I wished I could go out, get really fucked up, and maybe see a punk show—you know, noise, bodies thronging, a momentary slice of oblivion.

So, I was gaming, playing as a woman, racking up XP in the back of a giant stone library, when my console started to emit the loud shrieking that meant werewolves were in the lobby. My screen told me that the number of players in the library was plummeting; those alive were either outside or racing for the egresses.

I found myself just standing there, though, and soon a female werewolf rounded the corner. She was a player advanced several levels beyond my own, dark brown, a few scarred patches; strong. One paw dripped shiny-wet with digital blood.

The wolf paused. "You're not going to run?"

The timbre of her voice made it clear she was using a voice changer. At her words, I felt my first glimmer of okayness that day—an upwelling of something, maybe the blackout ecstasy of the animal who plays dead. For so long my only desires had been negative—I wanted to hide, to forget, to run away. Suddenly I felt a great hope that someone else could do the wanting.

I didn't want to get away from this feeling. I made my avatar shake her head no. She crowded me up to the bookshelves. My real body shivered.

"Take me," I said, and waited to see what the werewolf would do.

HAX CAME TO ME AT a time when my real world was dead. My real world had shuddered and shrunk, and Hax was life.

When I told Hax about The Event that day over text, I didn't get much into facts. (It's common not to remember traumatic events in a precise or tolerable fashion. And if someone wants the facts bad enough, they can read about it in a newspaper: the make of the car, the name of the terrorist shitbag, the names of the people who died.)

I told her what my brain actually remembers: the cheesy popcorn I'd just bought; the smell of cheese powder; the look of tiny little grains of salt; the rainy summer sky and the smell of wet sidewalks; the sudden flash of noise, pain, horror. A girl crying, and blood, then nausea. I couldn't stand to remember more.

Hax carried me back to her den that first night in a firefighter's carry, like booty. Her den opened onto a clearing next to a cliff drop, and someone had built a bonfire in the clearing—a place with meat curing on racks, a place for people to join and tell ghost stories.

She dropped me next to a rock, and our avatars sat and faced each other, the digital fire crackling, our bodies rocking in that tiny rhythmic motion that game designers use to symbolize the restless nature of living bodies.

"I'm going inside now," Hax said. "You can escape down that rock face; I won't chase. But if I come out in five minutes and you're still here, you're my captive." She stood, then, and entered the cave.

. . .

I REALIZED I DID WANT something: to get mauled, destroyed, obliterated. I didn't know why I'd ever played as a wolf when being consumed was obviously the outcome I'd been waiting for. I imagined how I'd look at her face, how she'd look at mine, if we were in a space where we had physical faces, and I blushed. Then the wolf was gone and both my avatar and I went delightfully blank, just staring at the fire.

JEANNE SENT ME PAMPHLETS ABOUT PTSD and agoraphobia. I read about thought distortion after trauma. Two common distortions are that the person thinks they are a terrible person, or that the world is very dangerous.

"But I actually am terrible, Jeanne," I said. "And there is a war in the cities. An actual war on."

"I know you can see the conflict," said Jeanne. She didn't call it "war" like I did, despite the fact that the driver who hit me admitted his act was political. She didn't call it "war" despite the constant acts of chaos bedeviling our nightly news landscape. "Of course, you can see the conflict, but can you also see the peace?"

AND ACTUALLY, IN THE WIDE, fat, night hours, something besides war had indeed begun to seem possible. Hours unfurled before me like a secret landscape, wide dark expanses spread out like jars of jam and slabs of butter, and all for me.

Hax and I started to play together a few nights a week. I used voice so we could talk in real-time; I rode on her back; we sacked cities. By the end of the night there was sex in the air.

When I thought of Hax, my brain produced streams of images: grapes growing in the air around us, their leaves curling around

her like a crown; me turning into a giant eagle and covering her
with my wings; her roaring and rolling me on my back, biting my
feathers.

THE TRAUMATIZED SELF REMEMBERS ITSELF as all-responsible
for what happened. (Taking all the responsibility means you fan-
tasize you won't let it happen a second time.)

The werewolf, on the other hand, symbolizes being fevered,
ravenous, controlled by powers in the sky.

Every night I turned on the console, seeking the end of hyper-
vigilance, seeking "I get taken over by the moon."

"Get on your hands and knees," said Hax. "Imagine my teeth
at the back of your neck."

A thrill flashing down my spine. The werewolf and I as one.

A NORMAL WEEK PASSED AFTER my disclosure to Hax: I pretended I wasn't waiting for her to ghost, and she pretended that
nothing transgressive had happened.

And then she texted: *i sent you a package.* (*In the Woods* has an
internal post service, allowing players to send and receive packages
through a blind drop.) *Let me know when it gets there.*

What was it: A sex toy? A condolence card? I went straight to
the front door each morning to see if the package had arrived.

Days later, I held a white box about the size of a toaster. Trembling, I sliced it open, looking at the slashy black handwriting that
said the package came from El Cerrito, thrilling to be holding
something she'd touched and marked.

She'd sent me a pair of black-rimmed video-link glasses—the
type that spies in the movies use to send streaming video back to
their secret HQ.

I took a photo of the glasses and sent it to her. *Spy glasses!* I
wrote.

camera glasses, Hax replied. *there's an earphone speaker in them too.*

Cool, I wrote, like everyone sends camera glasses to their gaming slash sexting partners.

I thought, she typed and stopped for a moment, *if you wanted to go somewhere and felt scared. This way I could go with you.*

I COVERED THE MIRRORS IN my apartment to keep my face private, and then we tested the glasses. She could see what I saw, and I could communicate with her silently if I wanted, just by nodding or shaking my head.

i like your balcony, she wrote.

We spent a lot of time over the next couple days on the balcony, just sitting "together" and listening to music, looking at the lights of the city. The sex got weirder, dirtier, more like falling into a vortex; I wasn't sure whether this was because of the addition of streaming video, or because we'd transgressed the boundaries of our previous silent agreements, or both.

I was high on the whole thing and felt strong. Like the bravery of drunks.

Even though the anniversary was still hovering.

"Are there going to be people who care about you there?" Hax asked through the earphone.

My mind opened and closed like a fist. Yes, there would be. Jeanne. My brother. My old friends.

"Ah," Hax said, not bringing up how alone I'd previously told her I was. "Good."

"And you'll be there too."

"Yes. Of course. I will."

WE DECIDED TO START WITH some less charged outings: a visit to a park, a visit to a library.

The night before my first outing—to an ice-cream parlor—Hax and I stayed up super late in a haze of fucking. I don't know if it was fear coming out sideways, but I hadn't been able to get enough.

You don't have to get ice cream tomorrow if you don't want to, typed Hax as I laid there, panting. (I still liked to use messenger sometimes. It can be easier to say things that way.)

I know, I wrote. *Hey, if I survive this, wanna someday swap IRL names?*

You will survive, Hax wrote. *And yes.*

I ROLLED IN BED THAT night, tossed by dreams that weren't quite nightmares, my nervous system jangling with this question of the door, and what could lie behind it.

Then morning finally came to find me standing in front of it. Keys and money in my pocket, glasses on.

"I'm here," said Hax.

I liked that she didn't say *you can do it*; a new wave of fear was piercing through the exhaustion and arousal of last night, and I didn't properly know that I could. Do you remember the first time you got on a high dive and looked down, then split in two—half of you gunning for a midair leap, and the other desperate to go backward down the ladder?

I stood a moment in that "maybe" space, looking at my hands, which were shaking. And then I took a deep breath and looked up, so Hax and I could watch together as my hands reached to open the front door.

The Boiler Room

MAX DELSOHN

Frank had been the front desk assistant at the Temple Beth Shalom for the past two years. His duties were, broadly, to unlock the front door for visitors and greet accordingly, answer the phone, prepare and mail out the yahrzeit letters, refill the water cooler, maintain and update the events calendar, and assist managers with various data entry projects upon request. There was the weekly standing staff meeting in the sanctuary lobby on Thursdays at 11 o'clock, just for the office workers, though Frank could leave at any time if the doorbell or the phone went off or if Ruth, the executive director, asked him to perform some other time-sensitive task. Today she had asked him to team up with Lucas, one of the new facilities workers, to get the extra music stands out from behind the main sanctuary's stage and store them in the boiler room.

"Of course!" Frank said.

It wasn't really Frank's job to move the extra music stands down into the boiler room, but such was the nature of working at a nonprofit. Plus, he hated the weekly standing meetings. He had chosen the illustrious career path of admin assistant so he could sit around and do mostly nothing all day, not stand.

"Thanks, Frank," Ruth said. "Lucas should be in the conference room downstairs, cleaning up this morning's Torah study."

"Thanks, Ruth," Frank said back. He liked Ruth well enough. She was thin and short, a few inches shorter than Frank, and seemingly owned a high-end pencil skirt in every color. Ruth was a compulsive schmoozer in the way only EDs of nonprofits are, but she always got his pronouns right, back when he was actually trying to get people at the Temple to use they/them. He'd stopped requesting that and put he/him in his email signature instead; it was close enough. In fact, it fit better than it used to, the whole he/him thing. He was finding his sweet spot, he/him-wise. Plus this was easier than constantly negotiating the misgendering, the elaborate apologies, the questions about grammar. He at least passed well enough, now, to avoid any she/hers, except from the IT guy, Sean. Sean accidentally slipped a *she* in when referring to Frank once or twice—only after learning Frank was trans, of course.

Frank walked down the stairs and into the open door of the conference room, where a man not much taller than Frank had his back turned. He wore a pale blue T-shirt and gray jeans; his hair was black and tucked loosely behind his ears, falling around his shoulders. He was tying a knot in a garbage bag full of paper plates, plastic forks, empty cream cheese containers, and half-eaten bagels.

"Hey, Lucas?" Frank said. Lucas turned around.

Since starting testosterone four years prior, Frank had come to accept his newfound attraction to men, particularly cis men. It was a thing that happened to a lot of trans guys, Frank initially reasoned; no big deal, he was single, he had successfully dated women before, so how hard could men be? It made Frank cringe to think now of his bravado early in his transition, this distinctly *lesbian* bravado, he considered it, a lesbian bravado that had always taken cis men and their customs for granted, a lesbian bravado that assumed years of carefully cultivated sexual competency with women would just easily *transfer over*. He went on Tinder, Grindr, Scruff, Sniffies; the sex was always somewhere between fine and bad, romance never on the table. He'd never gotten past a first date, in part because he never gave the interested guys a second chance, for reasons Frank himself still didn't entirely understand. Whatever his hang-up was, his lesbian bravado was to blame, he was sure of it.

But what Frank felt at this moment, standing in front of Lucas—compared to his initial sparks with women he'd been with previously; even women he'd *loved*—this was an anomaly. Frank wanted Lucas on sight.

First impressions came rushing at him, faster than Frank could process. Lucas was also twentysomething, with an easy smile and an eyebrow piercing, a thin mustache and a patch of hair on his chin. He had a bright, open face; his eyes were brown, almost black, and lit up as he told Frank *hello!* He was gay, Frank was certain, though he was not particularly flamboyant in dress or in gesture—something about his smile, his genuinely friendly greeting, like he wasn't afraid to show that he cared about saying a nice, normal hello to someone, like he had nothing to hide.

What Frank said was, "I'm Frank." But what Frank thought was *oh fuck*.

THE BOILER ROOM WAS ON the other side of the Temple, underneath the school building the Temple shared with the magnet school Portland Arts and Sciences College Prep. To get there, you had to go through the main entry to the Temple, then take a left down the stairs and toward the big prep kitchen the Temple used for the latke dinner and the usual b'nai mitzvah fare, which was a room off PASCP's gymnasium. Walk through the gymnasium and you're in the hallway with all the ground-floor PASCP class-rooms, and, bizarrely, the Temple gift shop; take a left from there until you find the boys' restroom, where there is an unmarked, locked wooden door across from the row of sinks. Unlock this door and go down a set of dirty, cramped, spiraling concrete stairs cluttered with traffic cones, for whatever reason, and enter into the vast gray expanse of the boiler room.

"In two years, I've never been down here before," Frank told Lucas as they approached the boys' restroom.

Frank and Lucas had agreed they would find the boiler room first before carting the music stands down.

"But I'm not surprised I have the key. Look at this ridiculous ring Ruth gave me." Frank produced a ring of a dozen or so faded keys of various golds and silvers.

"You think that's a lot of keys? Oh, Frank," said Lucas. He then pulled from his pocket what must've been at least sixty keys of every size and shape Frank had ever seen, plus several other key shapes he'd never seen before.

"Is this, like, a key to Rabbi Cohen's diary?" Frank said, pulling out an ancient looking key with a red jewel set in the top.

"I have no idea what any of those keys do," Lucas said. "Except the card key—this opens all the main doors, right? Sean said he'd show me the rest next time he was in."

"That guy sucks. And he never comes in," Frank said. He was fitting a round, gold key into the lock of the boiler room door; it was an old lock, and it gave him some trouble.

"Oh, good to know! Why does he suck so much?"

"Uh," Frank said. He stopped wiggling the key in the lock and looked at Lucas. He hadn't meant to be so candid with Lucas, being a new employee and all, you never knew who might rat you out. Jews talked. But Frank trusted Lucas instinctively—there was an intelligence to the way they spoke to each other, even though they knew almost nothing about the other's life. Did Lucas know Frank was trans? Frank hoped so. The thought that he might be prompted to come out as trans to this extremely beautiful cis guy in this disgusting boiler room made him shudder.

"He's just an evil nerdbro type," Frank said, which was true and did not contradict Sean's misgendering habit. Still, better to change the subject. Frank turned the key in the lock and the door opened.

"So, why'd you take this Temple job?" Frank asked as Lucas followed him down the stairs. "Have you worked in facilities before?"

"I was a janitor for a school once, yeah. Such are the prospects for a bachelor's in art history. Plus, I thought it'd be a nice way to get in touch with my Jewish roots."

"That's so cool," Frank said. "Not many of the facilities people are actually Jewish, they're just looking to pay the bills. You'll meet Mandy, she's Catholic of all things. I told her I was Ashkenazi once and she asked if that was the same kind of Jewish as Seth Rogen."

"Yikes," Lucas said. "My mom is Catholic, actually. That's the Japanese side. My dad is Jewish. He's kind of terrible, unfortunately. We don't really talk. Wow, this is fucking huge!"

The boiler room was huge. Two giant gray tanks, pipes all over the ceiling, panels and switches Frank couldn't navigate if his life depended on it.

Lucas walked into the center of the room and raised his arms above his head. "This place is its own planet!"

Frank tried not to blush as Lucas's pale blue T-shirt raised ever so slightly to reveal a smooth strip of his stomach and the top button of his jeans.

"This is bigger than our break room!" Frank cried. His voice echoed off the walls; Lucas and Frank smiled gleefully at each other. He would never associate the word *disgusting* with this boiler room ever again.

"Our break room!" Lucas shouted, delighting in his own words bouncing back at him.

Lucas's shout was deeper than his speaking voice, which Frank hadn't expected. It was useless to repress it; Frank felt blood rush to his little dick. Outside of an explicit sexual counter, a man hadn't made him hard like that before. He could imagine what it looked like in his pants right now, the top of his clit-dick broadening, flushing red. He wanted to tell him he was trans, right then and there—put all of himself in the room. All of his body.

"We should take our breaks in here," Frank said. Then he spun around, as if he had heard an unexpected sound, but he was actually so shocked by his own audacity that he could not watch Lucas respond to it.

"We totally could," Lucas said. "We could just hang in here, post-music stands. Man, who ever comes down here? We could decorate."

"No one comes down here. No way."

"Make it our own little world!" Lucas shouted. The echoes washed through Frank, soaked through his skin.

There were fifteen music stands that had been stored in the back of the sanctuary stage for G-d knows how long. Apparently Moshe Goldberg had been saying he wanted to pick them up for G-d knows what reason and finally admitted to Ruth last Shabbat that he wasn't going to commit. This was in part inspired by one of the Schoenbergs donating new music stands to the Temple, but

Ruth never wanted to throw away anything. The boiler room was the last chunk of real estate not already cluttered with boxes of prayer books or old Purim decorations.

Just as Frank and Lucas were about to begin moving the first of the stands, Lucas got a text message from Ruth on the facilities team cell phone asking him to stop by Ruth's office.

"Start without me," Lucas said, "I'll be back ASAP."

FRANK CARRIED TWO OF THE music stands all the way into the boiler room alone, but after he'd reemerged, he decided to take a bathroom break, which would just happen to take him past Ruth's office, where his appearance might prompt the two of them to end their meeting and let Lucas join him in the boiler room again. Then Frank would come out to Lucas, there in that giant gray dreamscape, their own little world.

Frank made sure his shoes slapped loudly on the carpeted hallway as he approached Ruth's office door, which was open. Lucas was standing while Ruth sat at her desk—a good sign. That meant the meeting was casual and/or almost over.

"Right, well, I'll let you get back to Frank," Ruth said to Lucas, though she was looking right at Frank. "I knew Moshe was never going to get those music stands."

"I did, too," Frank said, giving a small wave from the doorway. Ruth and Lucas laughed. Frank smiled sheepishly. It felt unreasonably good to make Lucas laugh. It was a full-throated, deep laugh, indulgent.

"Oh, Frank, that reminds me," Ruth said. "Lucas doesn't have his own email address, so he might want to hear this too. I saw you changed your email signature to he/him, rather than they/them. I asked Sean about it, and he said he had no idea what pronouns you were using these days—I told him it's important we at least try to be accurate! He can be such a jerk sometimes. So, which pronouns would you like us to use around the office? He/ him? Or is that just with the congregants? Personally, I think switching back and forth like that sounds like a headache, but it's your gender journey, not mine!"

Frank's body surged with cold. His face felt tight. He couldn't help it, he had to look at Lucas. Even if his coming out had been wrested from his control, Frank still wanted to know what Lucas did with the information. Was he going to laugh? Freak out? Never talk to Frank again? The worst outcome was, of course, the most likely outcome—Lucas would keep talking to Frank but never again meet his eyes, never again look at him with his face bright and open. He'd start carrying himself in that friendly, distant, vaguely apologetic, classically cisgender way.

Frank looked at Lucas. Lucas was looking at his feet, saying nothing.

Something inside Frank crumpled; he tried not to show anything on his face. The silence had been long, and it was, apparently, his job to fill it.

"Oh," Frank said. "Right. Whatever is fine. I mean he/him is fine."

Ruth sighed in relief. "Oh, good," she said, "that's much easier for all parties! Thanks, Frank. You two carry on!"

"I'll join you in a moment," Lucas said to Frank, but he was looking at Ruth. "I just need to use the men's room."

Frank watched Lucas walk out. Frank didn't want it to be true, but he had heard that wrong note, that subtle but unmistakable discomfort, the way Lucas had said *men's*.

No longer eager to interact with Lucas in the boiler room again, Frank started carrying down the rest of the music stands on his own. He was just about to enter the gymnasium when he heard Lucas jogging up behind him, two music stands in hand.

"Hey," he said. "Sorry, I'm here now."

"No worries," Frank said meekly, continuing to walk with his head down. He would do anything for his shift to be over right now. Eat only matzoh for a year, convert to Catholicism, *anything*.

"So . . . that thing with Ruth was weird," Lucas said slowly, too carefully.

"Yeah. Ideally, I'm the one telling people I'm trans, not my boss," Frank said. He was shutting down, pivoting to humor. That's what he did when these things happened, it's what he was good at, how he'd made friends, kept friends, kept his jobs, kept alive.

"That was really fucked up," Lucas said.

Frank let himself look at Lucas. He wasn't looking at the ground now. He was still walking, but he was staring straight into Frank's face. He looked remarkably serious, like he wanted to make sure Frank knew that he meant it.

"Thank you," Frank said. "Thanks."

He was touched by this genuine display of concern, but his shame only rooted itself deeper. He could feel it already, their dynamic turning into exactly what Frank had feared—the righteous anger, the pity. The well-meaning ally. The big, strong human being lifting the fallen baby bird back into the nest.

They arrived at the locked door in the boy's bathroom. Frank hated being in this boy's bathroom, this *men's room*, with Lucas, who surely no longer thought of him as a man, who could now see all the ways in which any given *men's room* was fraught for him. He fished the ring of keys out of his pocket.

"Is there . . . anything I can do?" Lucas said, still eyeing Frank intensely.

Yes, Frank wanted to say, tell me you think I'm the sexiest man you've ever met. Kiss me in this boiler room. Put your hands on my chest.

"I guess not," Frank said. "But thanks. You're sweet."

He let himself look at Lucas again, sadly, then used the key to unlock the door. Lucas shifted around, searching for what to say next.

"Here, let me take those for you."

"What?"

"The music stands. I can carry them."

"Why?"

"I don't know. I just want to do a nice thing for you."

For a second, Frank let Lucas grab the music stands. Then he narrowed his eyes.

"Dude, I got it."

Lucas frowned. "Okay . . . dude."

"Yup. Thanks," Frank said.

He took his music stands back and carried them down the stairs. Then he grabbed Lucas's music stands from him, too.

"I don't need your help," Frank said.

"Come on," Lucas said, "you don't have to—"

"Just let me," Frank said. Lucas put up his hands.

Frank took six steps before tripping over the base of one of the music stands and tumbling down the rest of the stairs, onto the boiler room floor.

The metal stands clashed loudly around Frank. He landed on his stomach. After the clanging and clattering finally stopped, he rolled onto his back. He was looking up at Lucas, who was still halfway up the stairs above him, looking down on the scene in horror.

"Ow," Frank said mildly.

"Fuck, you're bleeding," Lucas said. He rushed down the rest of the stairs.

Frank brought his hand to his knee, which stung. His jeans had torn in the fall and now revealed a cherry-red line of blood and clusters of dirt.

"Shoot, these pants actually fit," Frank said.

"It's so gross down here," Lucas said. "Your wound is dirty. How many fingers am I holding up?" Lucas held up three fingers.

"I'm not concussed," Frank said. "Three."

"What about now?" Lucas said. He gave Frank a thumbs up.

"One thumb up," Frank said. "Fifty percent of thumbs. An F in thumb school."

Lucas smiled. Frank felt his dick pulse again. He was turned on right now? Now?

"If you're not concussed, let me look at your knee. Can I touch your leg?"

Frank almost laughed in surprise. He was shocked by this small, thoughtful question.

When had a man ever asked him how he wanted to be touched? While he was injured on a boiler room floor, no less?

"Yes," Frank said. "By all means."

"Great," Lucas said. "Just want to look."

Lucas put his hands on either side of Frank's knee. Frank's heart was beating so fast, he was afraid Lucas would somehow feel his pulse in his leg.

"I think I'm fine," Frank said, after a long, silent moment of Lucas looking intensely at Frank's knee. "Just an arrogant dickhead."

"You *are* fine," Lucas said. Frank's heart went even faster. Fine like healthy? Or fine like *fine?*

"Glad we agree on that," Frank said.

"You just let Nurse Lucas get you all cleaned up."

There was no possible way Lucas could see Frank's two-inch dick through his pants right now, but even so, Frank had to resist the tremendous urge to cross his legs. There was something different in Lucas's face now—focused, like he was honing in on a target. His hands were still on either side of Frank's knee.

"So, you'll kiss it and make it all better?"

Lucas looked at Frank in that very serious way again. This time, Frank saw that it was not just genuine, it was more than that—it was present. Lucas was there in the room with him, responding to Frank's actions, what he said, how he moved.

"You want me to kiss you?" Lucas said. He hunched forward.

Frank nodded vigorously.

Lucas climbed on top of Frank. Frank's blood was pounding. Lucas lowered his mouth down until it was inches away from Frank's mouth and said, "Where do you want me to start?"

The Séance

Peace lilies were dramatic bitches. If left unwatered for too long, the tall elegant, white blooms skirted with voluptuous green foliage would droop and sag and hang their heads over their pots like drunk and disgraced Southern belles hung over pleasure boat rails, their hair in their faces as they puked their guts into the river. Funeral flowers, Laurel's mother had called them. Dramatic and constantly going on as if they were dying. The one in Laurel's room at the Grand Isle Hotel had been a gift from a client, one Laurel had accepted with all the false graciousness they could muster. It wasn't uncommon for happy customers to give them gifts along with or besides (but never to replace) payment. Still, Laurel preferred their tips cold and glittering over living and green. They had a black thumb, both literally and figuratively, and had never understood other people's obsession with trying so hard to keep things in their homes alive that didn't belong there. In their opinion, if the damn plant couldn't survive on its own in the Mississippi sun of their hotel room balcony, it didn't deserve to survive at all. Of course, if more people thought that way, Laurel recognized they would probably be out of a job.

Instead, they were considering providing future clients with a list of acceptable gifts as they all but drowned the lily with tap water poured from an empty hotel ice bucket. They even nudged the pot into the shadier corner of the balcony before stepping back. Couldn't have it looking all droopy and pathetic in front of clients. That would've been embarrassing. Bucket in one hand, they fanned themself and wiped beaded sweat from their forehead with the other, looking out over the city and, distantly, the Mississippi River snaking its way elsewhere. Somewhere cooler, perhaps.

The air rippled with heat, wet heat, liquid heat. It was going to be a scorcher today. It was already hot enough to have them feeling wilted themself, loose-fitting cotton shirt and skirt sticking to their dark brown skin.

Laurel wanted nothing more in that moment than to get another bucket of water and dump it over their own head, or at least strip off a few layers of clothing, but there wasn't time. They set the bucket down, tightened the red kerchief covering their tightly braided hair, and stepped back inside. They were meeting a new client today.

The decor of their room at the Grand Isle Hotel reminded Laurel of places they'd stayed while visiting New York. All gold filigree, wood paneling, and soft shadows. The sort of room in which you'd expect to meet a jowly, cigar-smoking, balding fat cat with more money than sense. It even smelled slightly of cigars, a familiar, acrid scent set deep into the velvet curtains and carpet. At once affordable and presentable with a staff who knew how to be discreet, it was the only hotel they used when staying in Mississippi, had been for years. They traveled often to meet the needs of clients. For someone like Laurel, who gained clients primarily through word of mouth and kept them by ensuring privacy and comfort, presentation and consistency were everything.

They left the balcony door open for airflow, pulled the folding screen by the bed straight so it mostly hid the plushy four poster from sight, and had a tea tray brought up, smoothing the white tablecloth with their hands to soften the creases. It was all perfectly presentable, like the woman they were preparing to meet. Mrs. Felicity Wilbur, wealthy philanthropist, former socialite, and recent widow. Before she'd contacted them some weeks ago, offering the names of current and former clients as references, Laurel had never heard of her.

They'd nearly turned her down for that alone, but Mrs. Wilbur had been persistent, and Laurel had found her name and picture in the society pages when they'd looked. Dated mostly before her husband's death, said appearances had usually been in support of some charity event or another. Nothing scandalous enough to warrant attention or wariness. Even her husband's death from a heart attack, though front-page news (Laurel thought he'd been an oil baron or something similar), wasn't all that exciting. People died, even rich ones.

They had heart attacks and died and left behind rich widows or widowers or children or aggrieved mistresses or business partners. It was the ones left behind who interested Laurel. It was those left behind who were their bread and butter. They assumed Felicity was the same. It was easy to assume.

When the knock at the door came, Laurel rose and opened it, greeting the woman on the other side warmly but without surprise.

"Welcome, Mrs. Wilbur. Come in. Would you like some iced tea or water? It's quite hot today."

"I'll have neither, thank you."

The widow edged her way into the room, barely responding to Laurel's small talk. All wary eyes and uncertain steps, she was a handsome woman, no matter the fact she had to be pushing near her mid-sixties. She had the sort of face that looked both younger and ageless all at once. Dark brown skin, a strong nose, her black hair coifed and pinned beneath a church hat. Laurel smiled and gestured to an armchair.

"Shall we sit?"

She agreed, and they took a seat together on opposite chairs, the tea table between them. Laurel poured themself a cup of tea, sweetening it with two sugars and a spoonful of honey, sipping, waiting. They found it helpful to see how a person reacted to silence.

Mrs. Wilbur was a starer. She stared at Laurel, which Laurel pretended not to notice. She stared at the floor, at the ceiling, at the folding screen where, through the gap Laurel had left, you could just see the pillows on the bed. Laurel sipped their tea and sat back in their chair.

"You were referred primarily by Mrs. Pembrook, right?"

"Yes," Mrs. Wilbur replied eagerly, jumping on the new topic of conversation. "She recommended you quite highly. As did several of her friends."

"But?" Laurel prompted, hearing the caveat the widow had yet to speak aloud.

Mrs. Wilbur's expression tightened. "They talk about you in hushed tones like you're some sort of miracle worker, but none of them could or would tell me exactly how it is you do what you do."

"Well, that depends," Laurel said. "I have many talents and different people have different needs."

"What talents?"

"Why don't we start with why you're here?" Laurel said. "And go from there."

Mrs. Wilbur frowned, but didn't argue. "All right."

Laurel sat forward, setting their drink aside. "Why are you here, Mrs. Wilbur?" they asked. "What is it you need?"

The widow swallowed, shifting in her seat, avoiding Laurel's gaze. "I told you on the phone, I need to contact someone," she said finally. "Someone who's . . . passed on."

Laurel nodded. "You said as much on the phone. The séance is one of my most popular services. Who is it you'd like to contact? Great aunt? Old business partner? Husband?"

"No," Mrs. Wilbur shook her head. "Someone else. She . . . her name was Winnie. Winnie Forrestor."

Laurel felt surprised, though they tried not to show it. Widows were always coming to them looking to contact dead husbands or rich family members, but there was something about the way Mrs. Wilbur said the name that didn't sound like how one would speak about a distant relation. There was something soft and aching in her voice.

"Do you think," Mrs. Wilbur continued. "Do you think you could reach her?"

"Did you bring what I asked?"

"Yes. Of course." The widow's vulnerable expression wavered, then hardened. She opened her clutch, pulling out her checkbook and a fancy metal fountain pen.

"Not that," Laurel said. "Not yet, anyway. The personal item belonging to the deceased. Did you bring that?"

"Oh, yes." She dipped back into the clutch, this time pulling out a slim, woven bracelet. It looked fragile, woven from some kind of dried grass and strands of what looked like hair. "This was hers, ours. She made it for me."

"It's lovely." Laurel held out a hand. "May I?"

Though somewhat reluctant, Mrs. Wilbur handed it over. Laurel gently examined the dried, cracking grass, and the hair—it *was* hair, they concluded, pulled so long ago from its roots that it too was beginning to fray and fade. They brought it to their nose and caught the faintest whiff of honeysuckle and wet earth. "The hair is hers?"

Mrs. Wilbur nodded. "A piece of her to carry with me, she called it."

"Should do nicely." Laurel slipped the bracelet carefully onto their own wrist. "Something made by or with a special connection to the deceased makes the connection easier to forge in the absence of a blood relation," they explained, catching the widow's questioning look. "Now, is there anything else you want me to know before I reach for her?"

Surprise flashed across Mrs. Wilbur's face. "You're going to do it now? Just like that? We don't need . . . a sacrifice or a circle of people holding hands?"

"I see you've been to a séance before," Laurel said with a laugh, twisting the bracelet on their wrist so it wasn't too snug. "Tell me, did any of those séances work? With the circles and the crystal balls?"

"No," Mrs. Wilbur admitted, flustered heat rising in her face.

"This one will."

"How?"

"How isn't important," Laurel said. "What's important is what you want with Winnie. When we spoke on the phone, you asked for the full service. Is that still what you want? To touch and talk to and feel her?"

"I . . . I do," the widow said. "So much. But . . . but what if that isn't what she wants? What if she doesn't want me? It's been so long. I've changed. I won't be the way she remembers me—"

"Felicity," Laurel cut her off, taking her hands, bridging the space between them. "Breathe. Think. Why wouldn't Winnie want you? Why wouldn't anyone?"

"I loved her," Mrs. Wilbur said, near tears. "But I married An-
drew. I wouldn't let us be together. I was too afraid."

"Are you afraid now?"

"No. Yes."

"Do you want to leave?"

Mrs. Wilbur heaved in a deep breath, her head hanging like the
peace lily, top heavy and wilted. Then she looked up, eyes glassy
wet, knuckles white around her clutch, held between them like a
shield. "No."

THEY LAY ON THE BED together, hidden from the balcony, the
door, and the world by the tall folding screen. Laurel let Felicity
undress them first. Lifting each limb to allow her to peel the sweat-
sticky clothing from their body until they were completely nude
atop the blankets, save for the bracelet. Felicity stared at them still,
but there was less wariness than wonder in the stare this time.

"How does it work?" She asked, voice soft as Laurel undid the
buttons of her fine silk shirt.

"The item connects me to the spirit and, if it's a willing spirit, I
can open a door. Or maybe a window. Or a moment. And they
can step in."

"Into your body? From where? And why?"

"I don't know where from, or if there is a where," Laurel said.
"It feels like . . . reaching through the mist for a hand you simply
know is there. As for why, well, the dead don't have a body of their
own anymore, do they?"

They slid the shirt down Felicity's arms, letting the garment fall
away before moving down to unzip her skirt. She lifted her hips
for them, heels and clutch abandoned by the side of the bed.

"So, it will be Winnie, but in your body?"

"It'll still be me," Laurel said, voice firm. "I'm still here. It's still
my body. Winnie and I will just be sharing for a while, that's all."

They tilted their head, sliding their hands over Felicity's waist, up her back and down again, until their fingers were resting on the waistband of her underskirt. "Is that okay?"

Felicity's hair was falling out of its coifs and pins, and her skin had become flushed and warm beneath Laurel's hands. "I don't mind, if you don't," she said shyly. "And if Winnie doesn't."

"I don't mind," they said.

Slowly, Felicity trailed her fingertips up Laurel's arms to their shoulders.

"Can I . . . touch you?" she asked, and Laurel nodded, laying back with a smile, closing their eyes as Felicity felt their body. She was careful at first, too careful, barely touching them at all. The hairs on Laurel's arms rose, goosebumps prickling as Felicity brushed her skin against theirs. They peeked through their eyelashes, and the sight of the woman bent over them—dark skin aglow in fading sunlight—struck Laurel as beautiful. Not just beautiful, but also right, right in a way that came from beyond this moment. Like they'd seen it before.

The touching grew more brazen, fingers and then palms rolling over their legs, their waist, their chest and nipples, then down between their legs. Laurel arched into the touch just slightly, focusing on that sense of right.

"Tell me about Winnie's hands," they said, their voice rough from effort and arousal. A familiar something was uncoiling beneath Felicity's hands. Something cold and slippery and just out of reach. Felicity paused at their request, but only for a moment, and then her hands continued their exploration, massaging, squeezing, and curling into their wetness.

"She had long hands," Felicity said. "Long fingers, you know? Like a musician's. That's what they say, but her hands always reminded me more of birds. They flew and fluttered when she talked, up and around in the air. They weren't always soft. She gardened and did laundry for a living, so the work left them lined, but she kept them clean, kept the dirt from under her nails. They smelled sweet, like earth and soap."

"Honeysuckle," Laurel breathed out, hips moving in time with Felicity's fingers, small lifts off the bed, their body pulling her closer even as the coil in their center spread its own slick fingers through their veins.

"Yes," Felicity said. "Honeysuckle. She always smelled like honeysuckle."

Laurel breathed out and opened their legs, wrapping them around Felicity's waist. They lifted themself, kissing her before pulling back.

"Keep going." They prompted, half in her lap now, hands searching for the clasp of Felicity's undershirt, palms ghosting the breasts beneath. "Keep going."

At their prompting, Felicity continued to describe Winnie's body, her arms and shoulders and legs and torso and hair, and finally, her face, building an image in Laurel's mind. A séance of memory shared between two people could never be perfect, of course. Memory was a fickle, shifting thing. A game of telephone with your own mind. Still, imperfect as a memory was, if you gave it a spirit, the gaps would close.

Laurel felt it come together, felt it coalesce in the space between their and Felicity's body. Felt Winnie accept their invitation, felt her arrive. She slipped beneath their skin as Felicity slid over it, fully nude now, not just her fingers but her body, wrapped around them as she pushed her way deep, deeper inside them.

Winnie's wrists had been slenderer than Felicity's and were slenderer than Laurel's. Felicity's bracelet fit her more loosely. She was shorter, too, about Felicity's height. Laurel felt their bones creak as they shrunk down a few inches. She'd had a full body, broad shouldered and wide-hipped, freckled and golden hued, scarred from years in the sun. Years she'd spent running wild in the backwoods of Mississippi, with parents too busy or drunk to mind and only Felicity for company. A friend she'd loved and then loved more, loved differently. Loved even after life and fear and death had separated them.

Laurel didn't always enjoy the flood of memories and emotions that came along with inviting another soul into their body, or the physical changes that invitation brought with it. But Winnie's soul rested easy against theirs. And their bodies weren't so different. This was manageable. Comfortable even.

Felicity noticed the changes. How could she not? The two of them were almost a single person themselves at this point. This was the point that Laurel enjoyed the most. Looking at them now, the widow's eyes were wide, her breathing ragged from both exertion and emotion.

"Winnie?"

"I'm here." Winnie's voice was honey and all spice, an after-tang to it, an accent Laurel hadn't tasted before.

They—Laurel and Winnie both—slid their hands down Felicity's body, cupping her breasts, smoothing their fingers down her back. It was their turn to stare at her, drinking in all her skin, every wrinkle and spot. She'd grown, aged, changed in ways Winnie never would and Laurel hoped to, but right now it didn't matter.

Time meant nothing to a ghost or to love. Felicity was still Felicity. She had paid Laurel through the next several hours. They kissed her, hard, tasting her tongue with their tongue and though she froze for a moment, it was only a heartbeat. Then Felicity kissed them back, hard, teeth and tongue and hands moving. They wanted to taste every inch of her. They'd missed her. For now, that was all that mattered.

Why Won't You Die?

JESSICA P. PRYDE

1. THE ASSASSIN

Kill the reporter, they'd said.

Should be easy, they'd said. But D was calling bullshit.

This was her seventh attempt at knocking off *that woman*—a frail, flighty journalist who defied logic. Somehow, the reporter snagged the best scoops in town, regularly brought down diabolical criminals, and managed to dodge expert attempts on her life.

The first three times, D had tried to make it look like an accident. Freak elevator crash. Cut brakes. Electrocution. Her kills had been works of art for fifteen fucking years, and she had wasted three of her best connections on one stupid woman who had luck on her side in a major way.

So, the assassin tried the hands-on approach. Robbery gone wrong. Pushed in front of a bus. She'd even tried to shank her in a club, but D had apparently left that particular weapon out in the rain or something, because it shattered in her hand. And Minerva Stanley kept on dancing.

Short of two in the chest, one in the head, she couldn't think of an elegant way to eliminate the target. Had she lost her edge?

Maybe she wasn't trying hard enough. Or was she trying too hard? After the attempt in the club, she decided to step back and take a break, give herself time to figure out what the heck to do. She had plenty of per diem funds left; her superiors were willing to keep her on as long as possible.

What am I failing to notice?

She watched now as Minnie—that's what her friends and colleagues called her, this infuriating wisp of a woman—walked into her apartment, chatting into a smartphone tucked between her ear and shoulder as she closed and locked the front door. Didn't she have wireless headphones like everyone else in this city? She was going to get a crick in her neck that way.

The assassin huffed silently to herself as she counted the locks: Minnie engaged one, two, three locks before turning to enter her home. So, she had *some* sense, some awareness of danger, at least.

Minerva smiled as she spoke, kicking off a pair of nude pumps and plopping into an armchair that faced the window. She crossed firm brown legs underneath her, letting the skirt of her red dress with white polka dots cover them.

Really, Minnie? Red with white polka dots? What a cliché. D checked her watch. Typically at this hour, the woman would already be in her bedroom, changing into a witty T-shirt and lounge pants before settling in for the evening. The assassin had become accustomed to a chuckle and eye-roll during this part of the routine; not that she'd admit it to anyone, but she looked forward to seeing which punny slogan her mark would be wearing on any given night. Next on the schedule should be Minerva messing around on her laptop or watching some vapid teenage drama on her tiny television. But not tonight—tonight she was chatting away.

This conversation must be important to her. Was it a lead for a new story? Or her silver-haired mother back in Kansas, currently serving as mayor of a dying town built during the first Great Migration? Or—D furrowed her brow—was Minnie chatting with a lover?

At the thought, the assassin heard a crack. Pulling her binoculars away from her face, she saw she'd been gripping them so hard with her metal hand, she'd broken the casing. She wasn't born with a metal hand; she'd woken up ten years ago with the damn thing, after an explosion that had killed her entire team. She'd worked alone ever since. And she had learned well enough how to pull her punches over the years. But not here. With a grunt, she flung the binoculars onto the blanket she was using as a gear table and pulled a new pair out of the bag on her other side. Between the hand, quick reflexes, and the intensity of her work, it wasn't unusual for D to break things. Here and there. But this was ridiculous. She'd gone through so many pairs of binoculars on this one job, she should have bought stock in the company six months ago.

No, Minnie didn't have a lover. Of that, she was certain. If she was seeing someone new, D would be the first to know.

The assassin sighed. Sooner or later, she was going to have to face an ugly fact. *Yep,* she mumbled to herself, *I've finally done it.* She had violated the number one rule of the elimination racket:

Don't get attached.

Don't.

Get.

Attached.

At first, she'd been watching Minerva to figure out how the hell she'd survived not one, but two tried-and-true methods of Making It Look Like an Accident. As a professional, D had to gather information about this elusive target—had to learn about her habits, her friends. Did this woman have covert contacts in the very department that was trying to get rid of her? Did she use back entrances or take secret meetings at her home and place of work?

Places of work, the assassin corrected herself. Plural. Not only did the reporter have a posh office at *The Sun, Moon, and Star*, but she occasionally worked at a nearby coffee shop that had amazing gluten-free doughnuts.

The assassin knew which restaurants Minerva frequented, and her preferred rotation of meals. She knew what tea she made in the morning (Irish Breakfast) and drank on her walk to work. Twenty-five blocks there and back, and never a hair out of place, not a bead of sweat in sight. D knew that her mark had an irritatingly charming collection of colorful A-line dresses and three pencil skirts in black, gray, and brown for her more formal workday needs.

D knew that, academically, Minerva Stanley had been at the middle of her class in high school and college. She wore glasses out in public even though she saw perfectly well in the comfort of her own home, and did her best not to stand out in most situations.

She knew that, when Minerva thought no one was looking, she would fix little problems—return a runaway dog, give directions to someone looking lost. And Minnie was fierce, as much as she took pains to appear otherwise. Small as she was, she could give a boy in her neighborhood a *Look* and he'd turn right around and pay for the candy bar he'd just lifted from the corner store.

This woman put on the front of being flighty and careless—flinging a tote bag into someone on the walk to work, scrambling her words as she asked a question, spilling a drink, breaking a heel—but she regularly stumbled her way into "accidentally" stopping questionable people from doing questionable things, wherever she happened to be. The assassin had watched her casually apprehend multiple criminals at a nightclub. Once, she even sacrificed a dozen cupcakes to stop a fleeing robber, dropping the pink box directly into his path when she got her skirt stuck on a fire hydrant. He'd slipped and slid and eventually fallen face-first at her feet.

Afterward, Minerva had been very sad about those cupcakes. But to her delight, she received the exact same dozen at the office later that day. Origin unknown.

And since D had bought them with her own money in order to avoid explaining *that* in her per-diem paperwork, she took the opportunity to watch Minerva select a chocolate and strawberry concoction with covetous joy and devour it in her office before offering them up to her colleagues.

Shaking her head to wipe away an embarrassing smile and regain focus, the assassin realized she had been *thinking* about her mark rather than *paying attention* to her mark. When she went to look through the new pair of binoculars—she always carried a spare now—Minnie was gone.

Instead, her binoculars found a note, taped to Minnie's window. The same window D had been watching her through.

"Meet me at the café."

Of course, this woman had to use a proper accent mark and punctuation in a hastily scrawled note to—

Fuck. Fuck. FUCK.

She'd been made. That note was pointed exactly in the direction of her rooftop hideout. The assassin felt every muscle in her body tense, and there was a roaring in her ears. How long had Minnie known she'd been watching? Was she confusing her on purpose? She was a top assassin, incredible at what she did, and now *she* was being played? What was happening?

WHAT IS HAPPENING?

She had gathered her gear, preparing to make a run for it, when a thought stopped her in her tracks.

This woman—this insufferable, unkillable woman!—was one of the best investigative journalists in the world. *Of course* she'd notice if someone was following her, let alone trying and failing to kill her. So, why hadn't she called the cops? Why hadn't she enlisted the support of her connections in every known and unknown branch of the military?

The café could be a trap, but D doubted it. If Minerva wanted her would-be assassin arrested or otherwise disposed of, it would have happened already—and in a much less public place. She could have easily snuck up on her on the rooftop, taking her down before D even realized she wasn't in her apartment anymore. Honestly, Minnie could have just pushed *her* into traffic. So, why the note? Why meet face to face?

Well . . . why else would a reporter, especially one like Minnie, risk her own life to meet the person who was obviously trying to kill her?

It seemed that Minnie was . . . curious. Well. So was the assassin.

FIVE MINUTES LATER, SHE WALKED into Minnie's favorite café, which was open late for the working and dating crowd. She felt a bit out of place wearing her black tactical jacket and single black glove, but at least she'd taken the time to grab her cap. Minnie could see who she was, but it would be harder for others—including the security cameras—to make a positive ID.

"I wasn't sure you'd come," the other woman started, picking up one of two mugs of tea that steamed on the table.

The assassin joined her, slowly lowering herself into the seat directly across from her. She noted that Minnie had chosen the centermost table in the room. Strategic choice for maximum visibility? Maybe, but she didn't know why the woman had bothered. Obviously, D wasn't going to kill her here. She picked up the cup in front of her and took a confident sip, figuring likewise that if

Minnie wanted her dead, she would have placed them somewhere out of view.

Earl Grey with lemon. What she ordered whenever she watched Minnie in this very café. Apparently, the assassin wasn't the only one who'd been watching. Or taking notes. She put the cup down, offering a nod to the tea with a smirk.

"Color me curious."

Minnie snorted, a quick intake of breath through her nostrils that was way more charming than it should have been.

"Me too, my friend. So, what should I call you, Ms. Rhythm Nation?" Her eyes glanced at D's black cap, then down to her metal hand. "Misty Knight? The Equalizer? Winter Soldier?"

"The latter might be appropriate. Would that make you . . . Miss America?"

"If I remember correctly, Miss America is a teenager, hardly aware of her own strength. I would rather be the Captain."

Minnie took another sip of her tea, then waved the barista over, whispering a request before sending them back to the counter. With a smile, Minnie turned to look at the assassin and leaned over her mug.

Is she trying to seduce me? D wondered, and then pushed the thought away. The smell of chamomile and vanilla wafted across the table, and Minerva's playful expression suddenly hardened.

"Why are you trying to kill me, Bucky?"

The assassin caught the appellation just as she was gulping down a sip of her own tea, leading to a brief coughing fit that Minnie made no attempt to help her with. When D finally caught her breath again, she found that she was laughing aloud. How in the world did a high-stakes meet-up turn into a Marvel Cinematic Universe joke?

She could have taken the bait, offering the obvious response— Who the hell is Bucky?—but instead she blurted out the one thing that could get her killed. The one thing that proved her own guilt.

"Why won't you die?"

2. MINERVA

Oh, dear, Minnie thought. She'd just had to ask that question, hadn't she?

Instead of answering her question with deflection, humor— weapons they'd both used in the banter of those first exhilarating moments—this tall, quiet, stunning assassin had just bluntly asked her why she wouldn't die. Should she tell her?

Would the assassin even believe her?

After six months of watching this poor woman continue to try and continue to fail, Minnie had started to feel sorry for her would-be murderer. By the fourth attempt, it was clear this person's heart just wasn't in it anymore. And yet, she kept going. The real question was—why? Was this dark and dangerous stranger being paid to eliminate Minnie? Blackmailed? Did she work for some shady government agency?

Minnie had brought far too many unwanted truths to light, written too many stories that she couldn't with any conscience let remain untold. And she knew plenty of powerful people (and institutions, for that matter) weren't particularly happy about it. In a recent heart-to-heart, a friend—the one who always gave a tiny wink when explaining that she "works for the government"— had sternly advised Minnie to find another job. For her own safety.

But Minnie was determined to save the world through her reporting, righting wrongs by exposing one billionaire oligarch or corrupt policy at a time. Sure, theoretically she could go about things a different way, using what some might call her gifts. She shuddered to think of the other names people might use to refer to her abilities. Minnie had read lots of comics and seen all the movies, and she understood this was not the world in which to come out as indestructible. Not her, not here. She already had to navigate the other kind of Coming Out, again and again as daily life demanded. She did not feel like adding one more thing to the list of reasons ignorant people had to hate her, just for existing.

She did little things to help the community and deter any true harm that she could prevent—knowing she wouldn't die was quite a perk when it came to assisting folks who needed it—but she wasn't about to stitch an S on one of her dresses. She couldn't just go around helping damsels in distress, even if that was her thing. Those people would as soon call the cops on a fat, Black woman trying to help them as they'd offer her thanks.

It wasn't like Minnie could fly, anyway. So, what was the point? For the time being, she was satisfied knowing that the people who wanted her gone weren't going to get rid of her easily.

And so, back to the question at hand.

Why won't you die?

"I have the feeling you already know, Queen."

Minnie felt her cheeks flush as the word *Queen* left her lips; was she flirting with her would-be killer?

Yes. Yes you are.

The woman laughed, slow and crackled, like she didn't do it very often. Hearing her throat clear, Minnie guessed she didn't talk much either.

"You have . . . a feeling."

Bucky's voice (Minnie laughed internally at the nickname, the joke they already shared) was quiet, intense, but full of command and authority. This was a woman who knew what she was doing. A woman who had taken lives but probably saved them, too. Bucky was a killer, but she was still somehow gentle. Generous.

Minerva had observed her small good deeds: holding a door open or helping an elderly woman with her rolling cart after following Minnie to the grocery store. Offering small assists when Minnie helped someone out on the way to work.

She smirked. Bucky probably thought Minnie didn't know any of this, including where those cupcakes had come from.

Speaking of cupcakes. The barista returned with two on a plate: one strawberry, one chocolate, both with vanilla frosting.

"I've seen you try both; wasn't sure which one you liked more."

The stunned look in Bucky's eyes proved she'd had no idea that Minnie had been observing as much as she'd been observed. The silence that followed was somewhat expected.

"How about we split them both. A little Neapolitan action, yeah?"

Minnie went to readjust her glasses, only to realize she didn't have them on. How had she become so comfortable, so unguarded, with this nameless assassin? She hadn't even made an effort to wear her one safeguard to their meet-up; she wore those glasses like armor. They influenced her whole demeanor, her personality, when she had them on. It was easier to look unassuming, weak, and unthreatening in an unfashionable pair of glasses. In her glasses, Minnie could blend into the background, be spacey and clumsy. She could make people forget her, a simple barrier keeping the onlooker from seeing straight into her soul.

She didn't have that barrier right now. But Janet Jackson over here had just silently taken a bite of the strawberry cupcake with a fork, then one of the chocolate. The poor woman was going to have to steal the mug and the fork if she didn't want to leave DNA behind.

As the assassin chewed, contemplating, Minnie asked a question that had been on her mind for a while.

"That first time—on the elevator—my neighbor could have been killed if I hadn't been able to stop it. After that, you only went after me when I was alone. What happened?"

The assassin continued to savor her double-bite. Her lips were full, the severity of her look eased by the constant motion of chewing. Her eyes were closed, either to enjoy the food or to concentrate on a thought. Or maybe just to avoid the question. She put her fork down and idly stroked the long brown braid that hung over her shoulder.

"Something was telling me that collateral damage wasn't worth it," she said, her voice husky and quiet. "I don't like taking out anyone but my target, but they wanted it to look like an accident. I'm very good at making it look like an accident."

Her eyes blazed from under her plain black cap as she looked from her mug to the cupcakes to Minnie's face.

"But then, you just . . . wouldn't . . . die. I've had to give up ten planned jobs to stick with you, and I'm beginning to think I can't finish this contract."

Minnie, agape, closed her mouth with a snap. Ten jobs. Ten people the assassin would have hunted down and . . . eliminated. She picked up her mug, her appetite gone.

"Well," Minnie started, wrapping both hands around the mug in search of its comforting warmth, "at least I've saved ten people. The ones you would have targeted if I hadn't been so . . . hard to get."

"These aren't people you want alive, believe me," Bucky said quietly. "And I thought you were some kind of threat to democracy or whatever kind of bullshit they told me."

Minnie snorted. Truly, this was getting out of hand.

"But it's clear to me—you're kind. Considerate. Hard working. You believe in something, and it must be something worth preserving. Because I don't botch jobs. What I'm saying is, there must be something larger at play here. You'd be dead by now if you deserved it."

The woman's voice had become more audible, more passionate. Minnie couldn't look away. The fire in those dark eyes, the energy pulsing from her—Minnie wanted it for herself. And the words Bucky was saying, about Minnie's ethics, her mission. How could someone know her so well without knowing her at all?

"Okay, Stalker," she laughed, trying to dispel some of the intense energy. "I want to trust you. But I think we need to talk about next steps in a more secure environment."

"Next steps?!" Bucky was wrapping the cupcakes in big paper napkins, instead of getting a takeout container like a normal person.

Minnie downed her chamomile, waiting for her companion to do the same. Bucky tucked the cupcakes into a zippered pack slung at waist height.

Minnie lowered her voice to a whisper, leaning as far across the table as she could.

"We're going to take out your clients."

3. D IS FOR . . .

The assassin reeled at what she'd just heard. Minerva Stanley was an undeniably beautiful and intelligent woman, but was she *completely bananas*? This wasn't a television show, no matter how ridiculous her antics were becoming. This was real life, with real people—who could *really kill her.*

D walked with Minnie back to her apartment, deep in contemplative silence. She had to admit, she liked the feeling of walking at this woman's side this time—not fifty feet behind her. They took the infamous elevator up to the fifth floor, jumping a bit when it gave a little hop on arrival. She didn't know it had been doing that; she would have thought the building's owners would have replaced the hydraulic apparatus after she'd disabled it. But it looked like they'd only repaired it, leaving it open to a future failure.

Minnie should move out of this building. It was dangerous.

As Minnie let them into the apartment, the assassin took in all the little things she hadn't been able to see from across the street. The Vashti Harrison art prints on the walls between the windows, little girls with big stacks of books and even bigger imaginations; the second couch underneath the bay windows at the front, plush and well-used; and the king-sized bed she could now see through the open bedroom door.

"Have a seat, Killer," Minnie called over her shoulder. "I'll be right back."

The assassin flinched.

"Don't call me that. Please." But Minnie had already disappeared into the bedroom.

She needed a plan, a way to maneuver Minnie out of this dangerous idea of hers. But the only way forward, D feared, was to gain this woman's trust. She wasn't sure why, but she wanted that anyway. She wanted too many things, she realized with a small shake of her head, from this woman she knew inside and out, but had only met less than an hour ago.

She realized she was still standing in the middle of Minnie's living room, and turned to take a seat on the couch, hand returning to the comfort of her braid. She pulled it over her shoulder, giving it full, long strokes as though it were a pet to soothe or be soothed by.

"What should I call you, then, Queen?"

Minnie emerged now, clothed in black leggings and an oversized tee that said "Lois Lane Saves Herself." She nestled into the other cushion on the couch, one knee up and the other swinging down the side. Her expression was open and inviting, like she was enjoying being seen by someone, anyone, even her assassin.

Queen, she thought. *Why does she keep calling me queen?*

She continued to stroke her braid as realization struck. *Oh. Like Queen Latifah. The Equalizer.* D certainly resembled the rapper-turned-actress, with her stocky build and long hair. But she wasn't a friendly neighborhood anything.

"What should you call me?"

D took a deep breath and sat forward, trying to mirror Minnie's position. Taking both of Minnie's hands, she rubbed a gloved thumb over the woman's knuckles, wishing she could feel the skin. She looked from their entwined hands into Minnie's eyes, steadily and bravely holding her gaze.

"You can call me Dee," she started, still holding onto that part of herself that was hers alone.

But really, what use was keeping it to herself? She wanted Minnie to trust her, and she wanted to trust Minnie in return. What better way to start than to reveal her true name, the one that nobody had called her since she was a child? She shook her head slightly, as if to loosen the harshness that had been programmed into her.

"Actually . . . it's Dream. That's my name. So. Call me Dream."

The smile that Minnie offered in response broke something in her. Somewhere deep inside of her a giant iceberg cracked and began to melt. But that was nothing compared to hearing this woman say her name, one she hadn't heard in almost twenty years—

"Dream," Minerva sang, slowly and (truly) dreamily. "How can a trained assassin have such a lovely name?"

Dream scoffed. *Lovely.* "It's not like my colleagues call me that. Or even my clients. It's usually my call sign. Or The Assassin."

Oh, wow, she had definitely said too much. Minnie wasn't the only one more comfortable inside these well-appointed walls, apparently.

"Don't ask me what my last name and call sign are, please. I've put you in enough danger."

"Dream. You're a skilled assassin. You've been trying to kill me for six months. Maybe more? How much more danger could I possibly be in?"

Dream looked into Minnie's honest, wholesome eyes. This woman, who fooled the world into thinking she was weak and timid, wanted to go up against a force she didn't understand. To do what? Break a story? Stop an underground system from doing the dirty work no one else would?

Of course, if taking Minnie down was part of that dirty work, Dream had to second-guess the other missions she'd been fed. Who else was in the Company's sights when they didn't deserve to be? What if she was hired to take out someone else fighting for Truth, Justice, and a Better Tomorrow, all for someone who claimed to be fighting for the American Way? Would they get lucky like Minnie had? And you know what—her question still hadn't been answered: how had this woman survived six attempts, anyway?

Regardless of the answer, Dream was incredibly happy—more so every moment—that she'd been unsuccessful. But it didn't make sense. Every single move she made had been expertly taken.

"Minnie," she started.

Their eyes held. Minnie's thumbs were the ones doing the soft stroking, now. How the hell could she get the information she needed, without sounding threatening, without ruining the moment?

"Why? How . . ." Dream cleared her throat, trying to push that little bit of indignation back. It didn't all go away. "How are you not dead?"

It was the best she could come up with. Less accusative, more curious. She braced herself for Minnie's response—she expected anger, hurt, offense that her would-be killer would insist on this conversation. Or perhaps Minerva would pretend naiveté, with a shrug and some bullshit answer, like, "just lucky I guess." What she didn't expect was to catch a falling body as her companion crumpled into hysterics. Was Minnie crying?

As Minnie pushed herself off Dream's shoulder, she wiped her eyes, but she was smiling. She let out a light giggle. It was a high-pitched and cute sound, so different from the lower pitched, warm tones of her speaking voice.

Dream was relieved—Minnie was shaking with laughter, not sobs. She laughed with no fear, no shame, no restraint. How was this woman real? And what was with the laughing?

"Your confusion, Dream. It's . . . cute."

She giggled again, turning to lean back against the couch, facing forward in her seat. Dream was befuddled. She regarded her companion—head back, neck exposed, face glowing in joy and trust. Minnie presented the perfect opening. What if she just . . .

The assassin's hand itched for a blade—a switchblade or karambit. Something that would take the other woman out quickly and with little pain. Her bag was still on the roof, though. She would have to strangle or smother her.

No. Dream blinked away the thought. She didn't want to cause that kind of death. Not to this delightful person. She didn't deserve it.

"I can feel you thinking about ways to kill me, you know."

Minnie's eyes were closed now, but Dream could feel all of the woman's focus on her.

"It's in your heartbeat. The rush of your blood. The smell of your endorphins. I can tell, now, that you've got murder on the mind."

Heartbeat? Endorphins? Some kind of extra-sensory something going on. Dream scanned what little she knew about creatures who resisted death and sensed life, stuttering through her next question. There seemed to be only one answer that might make any lick of sense.

"Minnie . . . are you . . . a . . . vampire?"

There was that adorable snort again, and a giggle, but Minnie's eyes were still closed.

"You'd have been closer with werewolf, probably. But no. No supernatural affliction of any kind." She fluttered her eyes open, and gave a laughing nod toward the television across from them. "Sam and Dean aren't coming after this gal."

Sam? Dean? Who were they and what did they have to do with this? Dream let her gaze linger on the flat screen and imagined a different possibility, a different conversation. She couldn't shake the image of them relaxing together, watching a show, sharing inside jokes, and cuddling together on this plush couch without a care in the world.

It wasn't something she could ever have. Such was the irony of her given name.

A shout of laughter startled her from her thoughts.

"Oh, honey, your face. I take it you didn't watch much *Supernatural*." Minnie reached over and gave her leg a light pat, like she was offering her some kind of condolences, before returning to the subject at hand. "I do have sensitized hearing, vision, and smell."

Dream snapped her attention back to Minnie, who was holding something sharp and gleaming in her direction.

It was a knife. How had she gotten a knife so close to her without Dream realizing? How had she moved that quickly and stealthily, directly under Dream's nose? Dream made a quick move to push it away, but Minnie somehow resisted, keeping her arm outstretched. She didn't relent until the assassin grabbed the knife with her gloved left hand.

Minnie was incredibly strong. She'd apparently been faking or caught off guard when she'd been pushed. And when she'd stepped into that puddle of water with the live wire. She'd definitely broken Dream's knife in the club.

"It was you—you broke my knife," she said, dazed and full of wonder.

"You want to know who I really am? Try it, Dream. Stab me. Slit my throat."

Dream shook her head, resting the paring knife in her lap.

"Why would you trust me with this, after all you've done to evade my attempts?"

Minnie smiled softly, running a hand up Dream's covered arm.

"Babe, I'm invincible. I can stop anything you throw at me. You might as well call me Superman. Except I don't have a Kryptonite. That I know of, at least."

Dream stared, wide-eyed and quiet. What could she possibly be saying?

"Think of the things we could do together, you and me. I'm not going to put on a spangled suit to rescue babies from burning buildings—I can jump real high, but I can't fly. Yet. But we could change things from the inside. As long as we can trust each other."

If there was anyone who could break through Dream's walls, it was this woman. This magical woman who lived to fight injustice and stopped to gently coax a frightened cat down from the tree while she was at it. Who would never get the recognition she deserved for her job or the other good deeds she did, because Black women might save the world, but they would never be rewarded for it.

Lifting her flesh hand, she slowly moved it back toward the pair of soft but durable, medium brown hands sitting folded in Minnie's lap. She picked up the woman's right hand and gently tugged, inviting her to slide forward. The assassin wanted closeness. She needed to know if the other woman yearned for the same thing.

Minnie answered silently, scooting closer until the two sat with their knees meeting, noses mere inches apart.

"I'm not built for trust," Dream whispered, sliding one finger up and down Minnie's forearm. "But I might be able to change that, with you."

She felt a light touch on her face. Minnie had once again by-passed Dream's defenses, placing a warm hand against her cheek.

"That's all I'm asking for, at the moment," Minnie whispered back, just as quietly. Her eyes were glistening, and Dream wondered if now the woman was actually going to cry.

"My mom called me today, out of the blue. She said it was to catch me up on the news back home, but we both knew why she really called me. She's been begging me to move back to Freedom, where it's safer for me." She huffed. "Safe. Like I care about being safe."

Dream watched in agony as Minnie wiped a stray tear from her cheek.

"I care about being seen. You see me, Dream. You know me, in the strangest way possible. You know more about me than anyone—probably even my mother. I've been so alone. I don't want to do this alone anymore."

Making a rash decision, wanting to offer reassurance to the woman who looked so open in front of her, Dream moved her face forward, just one inch.

Sometimes one inch is a vast field that, once crossed, changes the nature of a relationship entirely.

Their lips touched for barely a second, and Dream's eyes shut at the softness, at the spark that burst through her blood from that one brief touch. The plush heat of the other woman's lips filled her with a euphoric feeling that she could never hope to re-create outside of this room, away from this spectacular person.

She expected to hear a sound of regret or disgust as they parted—or maybe to see Minnie covering her face in horror. Dream chided herself. *Why did I do that? What am I going to do now?*

When she finally realized her eyes were still closed, she opened them cautiously, only to find a look of adoration on the other woman's face—a sweet, half-raised curve of her lips; wide, liquid eyes; dimples that only revealed themselves when Minnie truly smiled.

This was the first right thing Dream had done in six months. Now? Well, they'd just have to see what could happen from here.

4. THE DREAM TEAM

"Why won't you *die*?"

This white nationalist dude was just like all the other white nationalist dudes. Her skin, her size, her smarts—everything about her made him uncomfortable. And when he was uncomfortable, he got violent.

He should be able to understand, by now, that she remained tied up as a courtesy to him, to give him a false sense of ease and plenty of time to tell her all about his evil plans and goals. But just like so many others before him and countless to come, he couldn't see what was right in front of him.

Minnie could do without him messing up her hair, though. She had a date tonight.

"Before you dump my head in this giant barrel of water, I'd like to remind you that it will not be any better than the other ways you've tried to kill me. You might as well take a break and soliloquize just a little bit more."

The two goons stationed on either side of the steel door, one with an AR-16 and the other with a police baton, shared a look, and then looked at their boss, waiting for instructions. He opened his mouth to respond.

Yes. YES! They were going to get to the good stuff—but just then, a loud bang sounded.

Minnie heard a heavy lock clank to the ground, having been shot off of the door from the outside. The door flung inward, revealing a tall shadow in black. A black tactical mask covered the lower half of the figure's face, and their eyes were glazed with purpose from below the lid of a black cap. Fast as lightning, two hands moved in unison—one a smooth, brown hand made of flesh, the other a steel alloy that Minnie still hadn't pushed for the history of. In each hand a pair of fancy weapons straight out of *Star Wars* were pointed and ready to fire, but Minnie wasn't afraid. The newcomer took out each of the goons in quick succession, using a pulse that would knock them out but not kill them, and then aimed both guns at the back of Soliloquy Guy's head.

"Untie the lady, would you?"

As he leaned forward obediently, kneeling in front of the restraints around her ankles, Minnie broke her bonds and grabbed her captor's head, kneeing him in the face—hard enough to send him to the floor while keeping him breathing. This bastard was going to jail, but only *after* he finished revealing the top-level governmental and oligarchical bigots who were funding his operation.

"Dammit, Dreamy, we were almost there!"

In the darkness, Minnie could practically see Dream rolling her eyes as she used the goons' own zip ties to bind their wrists and ankles.

"Please. The minute you asked him to soliloquize a little more to keep him from messing up your hair, I knew it was time to step in."

She helped her lover out of the folding metal chair the men had tied her to, leaning in for a quick kiss and using her free (and flesh) hand to give Minnie's backside a little massage. Minnie moaned a little; those creeps could have at least gone with wood or plastic! Her ass was killing her, and she was invincible, *for chrissake.*

"I'm sure," Dream smirked as she leaned back, "that you've got plenty of information. These guys aren't going anywhere for a while. We'll come back and get the big answers tomorrow, after you've submitted your story."

With one more kiss, she grabbed Minnie's hand and led her toward the door, gingerly stepping between the unconscious men littered around the room and in the hallway beyond. When they emerged from the brick compound, Minnie saw that they were surrounded by woods, and wondered how she'd missed this detail. Blindfolded, she hadn't been able to tell they'd left the city. She should have been able to identify the change in temperature, in sound, in atmosphere, but she'd been so focused on the people driving the van they'd thrown her into, she hadn't kept her due diligence.

Dream would still have to teach her a few more things if they were going to keep doing this together. And they were. No doubt about it.

As they approached the old pickup that Dream had probably "borrowed" to cover the terrain surrounding them, Minnie wished once more that flight had been included in her little collection of powers—the powers that made her the most dangerous person in the world. Dangerous to the ultra-rich and corrupt, the ignorant and armed.

They couldn't silence her. Not even the best assassin in the world could take her out.

Well. That wasn't completely true.

"Step on it, Babe. We've got reservations to keep."

True to Your Heart

BRITTANY ARREGUIN

ll I see is red.

Not blood, thank goodness. Just the sight of paper lanterns draped from the ceiling of the elder care home my grandmother recently moved into, after selling the house she shared with my grandfather for more than twenty years. I usually come here once or twice a week, to make sure she's not feeling lonely since my gong gong passed. Twice a week is kind of a sweet spot, because I don't know how comfortable she is here yet. She seems to like it. She walks around the complex every day, racking up a lot more steps than I do, and frequents the mahjong tables instead of watching whatever Chinese drama is on the television in her room. Yay for slight socialization! I just worry about everything, especially this time of the year, with the Lunar New Year right around the corner. My entire family is full of busybodies who don't know how to chill, so it's like pulling teeth to comb through our respective planners and figure out who is available to visit. My job is hybrid, so I get to work from home a few days out of the week. It seems to alleviate some of the added responsibility on my

parents for me to handle regular visits, since they are already doing a lot for their own jobs.

I knock on the door to her room before trying the handle to see
if it's open. It is, so I slowly peer into her room and call out her
name.

"Por Por?" I step inside, greeted by her tidy living space lightly
decorated with Lunar New Year wall decor, with tangerines and
dried fruit candies on the dining room table.

"Hiii, Daphne!" She walks out from the hallway with cleaning
gloves on and sleeves hiked up as I take off my shoes and place
them on the shoe rack. Must've been tidying up before I got here.
"Sorry, I was scrubbing the toilet. Sit down! Are you hungry?
Thirsty? There's juice in the fridge and jook in the slow cooker. No
egg, just for you!"

Por Por hates feeling stagnant; she needs to be constantly doing
something to feel some sort of fulfillment in her life. Even in her
old age, standing still can get tiresome quickly. I love that she still
finds enjoyment in activities like cooking and cleaning; I'm definitely not as enthusiastic about chores. I look over at the TV my
parents bought her when they moved her in, silent and dark, and
the remote on the coffee table that is encased in a plastic bag like
it's brand new. I wonder how she can be so content without enter-
tainment; I bet she'd like the new, hot K-drama on Netflix that I
watch with my parents.

I call out: "Thank you! I'll grab some right now." I head to the
kitchen and grab a bowl from the cabinets—built lower to the
ground to accommodate Por Por's height (and mine, because ge-
netics favors us to stop at five-feet tall)—and scoop jook, a.k.a.
congee, a.k.a. rice porridge, into a bowl. It's the perfect comfort
food for me. Warm, easy to eat, easy to add flavors catered to your
liking, but whatever secret seasoning Por Por puts in makes it
flavorful on its own.

"How's work?" she shouts as she makes her way back through the hallway. "Still busy?"

"Yup!" It's the busiest it's been in a while. I work as a software engineer for a new company called Double Happiness, a dating app for Asians, created by a Chinese woman with a mostly Asian team, including me, that does the coding and design. It's very much a start-up that goes through start-up problems, but we're on our third round of funding and already have more than ten thousand sign-ups on our app, which means we're becoming more known in the dating app universe: an extremely saturated and competitive place.

"You know, I was playing mahjong with some of the ladies and told them my granddaughter works for a dating app company. They asked me if you found someone on the app yet and I didn't know. Did you? I'd be upset if you didn't tell me!"

I shake my head. She's an incredible sleuth when it comes to our lives. I'm pretty certain that I couldn't keep a partner a secret unless I fled the country, and I would never move away from her or the rest of my family. "No, I haven't found someone on the app. I don't use the app for myself. Just if I need to test things."

Despite the company I work for, I don't want to find my soulmate on an app. If it works for others—which I know it does, because our marketing team seeks out those success stories to sell our app—then great! I am secretly an old-fashioned romantic inside. I want my love story to be like one that people read in a romance novel, with a meet-cute, a chance encounter. I want to fall in love with someone who will sweep me off my feet on our way to a happily-ever-after. I can't see myself finding that on any app that people use as a "u free 4 a hookup?" method of dating.

"So, you're still single?"

"Yes, Por Por. I'm still single." Sadly single at twenty-nine, internally struggling to come to terms with the possibility that I might never feel a connection to someone that's greater than the connection I have to my work. Work is busy, so I haven't been out there searching for my person.

"You should try looking on the app for someone," Por Por gently insists. "Maybe see . . . How does that saying go? What fish are in the sea?"

"That is a saying," I say with a laugh. "But I don't know when I'd have time to date. I work, and I want to make sure that I'm still here on my visiting days. I don't want to feel like I'm committing to too much."

I love Por Por, but we grew up in two different generations. She was married by nineteen because she was lucky enough to fall in love with my gong gong, a.k.a. the boy bagging groceries at the corner market a block from her parents' house. I can confidently say I frequent the grocery store near mine, and there has yet to be a bagger that's caught my attention.

"I'm just saying," she adds, "I love spending time with you, but I am always looking for more friends. We can teach him how to play mahjong, he'll learn to cook, and we'll become fast friends."

I will my eyes to not roll, because then she's going to think I'm disrespecting her, but it's not that easy. I'm not looking for someone who will give me a good time for a day or two. Before I'd introduce anyone to my family, my person would have to be interested in committing to the long road, and I'm very selective of who I would let into my life to even consider the option. These hypothetical potential partners Por Por is drumming up in her head to manifest in my life are like buying lottery tickets. You only have a one in a billion shot to hit all the right numbers, or else the payout is less than what you should be settling for.

There's a knock at the door, and I get up to answer it. When I open the door, my jaw drops. I close my mouth quickly and blink.

The man in front of me, with "Leland" written on his name badge, is hot. He's young, probably around my age; although given how nicely Asians age, he might be older. His skin is flawless. His dark hair is neatly combed and gelled, and he's smiling with the deepest dimples I've ever seen on a man. I can't seem to avert my gaze.

"Hi, I'm Leland, one of the care nurses. I'm here to check on Ruth Ma?"

"Over here!" my grandma shouts. "Oh, I was told I would be getting a new nurse, but no one told me how good-looking he would be!"

I quickly turn back to her, embarrassed by her unfiltered mouth. "Por Por!"

She scoffs. "What? He looks good—he should be honored to receive such a compliment. Are you single? This is my granddaughter, Daphne. She's a software engineer at a company called Double Happiness."

"Oh!" His eyebrows perk up. "I've used the app before. The dating app for Asians. That's cool!"

My stomach sinks a little bit. I wonder if that means he's in a relationship. Maybe he found his girlfriend through the app. I manage a weak grin. I just want to keep him looking at me, and I can't think of anything smart to say. I babble about work.

"It's a fun job, and we're doing well right now. We just passed ten thousand profiles."

I know nothing about the guy, other than he's a care nurse here, but suddenly I want to abandon everything to spend more time talking to him. I didn't know I was capable of being so singularly focused.

"That's awesome! Yeah, I went on a date with someone I matched with on the app, but it didn't lead to anything more."

"So, you're saying you're single?" Por Por interrupts, with a wink. "Funny, so is Daphne! Isn't she beautiful?"

Oh God. I want to stick my head in that piping hot slow cooker and drown out the sounds around me with porridge.

"Por Por!" I moan. "I'm sorry. Please do not feel like you need to listen to anything she's saying."

"It's okay," he chuckles. "Good thing her granddaughter *is* beautiful."

Oh my God. My heart beats loudly. *Is this really happening?*

Por Por's mouth opens up into a wide grin, and she grabs my arm from her spot on the couch.

"Wow! What do you say to the nice man, Daphne?"

"Thanks," I blush. "That's very nice of you to say."

She gasps, like a lightbulb went off in her head. "You two should arrange for a date! It's the least you can do after he calls you beautiful, Daph."

"Is it?" I'm not sure I'd even be able to carry on a conversation with him.

"Yes yes! Go on, talk a little more. Go get me a lemon square or something from the cafeteria. You'll show Daphne where the cafeteria is right, Leland?"

"Uh, sure, I wouldn't mind."

"Por Por," I stammer, looking for an out. "I can't just leave you alone here. And didn't Leland knock on the door to do a checkup on you?"

"It's fine," she swats away my hand. "Leland, I took my meds. You can check. And to make you feel better, Daphne, I will just sit here and watch some television, so I don't injure myself. Go on! Talk for a little bit, get to know each other!"

"She doesn't like being told no, does she?" Leland murmurs at me.

"No." Neither did I, for that matter, but I knew I wouldn't win against an eighty-year-old Chinese woman who immigrated here by boat.

Leland looks Por Por up and down, as if he is assessing her health with his eyes. When she winks at him, he nods. "Come on," he beckons. "Let's go grab some lemon squares."

"Have fun!" Por Por yells as we exit her room. I can't believe I just got set up by my grandmother.

"Did you know she pushed her nurse response alarm?" Leland asks with a grin as we make our way through the lantern-strewn hallway.

I genuinely gasp, then laugh. "Ha, nope! She got that one past me. She must have heard a rumor that her new assigned nurse was an eligible bachelor." I blush. "It's no real surprise. She's a little . . . *preoccupied* with the idea of me meeting someone. She just wants me to be happy. Apparently, she thinks my happiness is being married, like everyone else in my family is. That or she doesn't want me to get more of her lei-see."

That gets a chuckle out of him, and I go warm at seeing those dimples again. "She's been giving you money for too long!"

"Longer than my parents and brother before they got married." My parents married at twenty-two and my brother at twenty-six.

"So, they think you're a late bloomer at the ripe old age of—how old are you?"

I shrug. "I'll be thirty next year. And yeah, I guess so. My family's so obsessed with my lack of a dating life, but what they don't realize is that there's a lot more to me—my job makes me happy, my friends. And spending time with Por Por—"

"Sure," Leland nods, matching my pace as we walk past one of the home's living spaces, where residents are mingling, sleeping, or watching variety television. "I get that too, from my mom. Though, it's not like I haven't tried. I was in a close relationship a few years back. We were engaged, had set a date, started looking at venues, but we hadn't lived together yet, and I got placed in a program close to home. She was adamant about wanting me to move to SoCal, where she was from. After a lot of thought and conversation, we decided that was just the start of the ways we were misaligned. I broke it off."

"Wow," I frown. "That must've been hard."

"It's all right. I wish her nothing but the best. We rushed into things, and she decided she wanted to take some time to discover herself. I think she's in Seattle now."

"That's cool. I've never been to Seattle, but it seems like a fun place to live."

"I couldn't!" he laughs. "The rain would put me in a funk."

I find myself strangely relieved to hear that he doesn't want to share a city with his ex.

We reach the cafeteria, which is mostly empty, save for a few tables. Dinner isn't served for another two hours, and I think now is the time that most of the residents like to take naps. Leland escorts me to a table next to the serving area that has some leftover desserts on it. Sure enough, there are some lemon squares left over from lunch.

"So, when did you start working here?" I ask Leland, reaching for a lemon square with an old Christmas napkin. "I assume not long ago, because the last nurse my grandma had was this cute Filipino lady named Crista who would lead tai chi in the living room."

Leland chuckles, leaning on the dessert table. "I just started last month. I've been training for most of that time; they just started assigning me to residents. Crista's still here. Still teaching tai chi."

"Funny I've never seen you around," I say mid-bite. The lemon square is surprisingly good. Maybe another grandma made it. Grandmas are the best at making any baked goods. "How do you like it here? Is this your first elder care home?"

He nods. "I used to work at Highland. I mean, it's less fast-paced here, but you grow connected to the residents in a different way. These people know they don't have much more time. One day you're laughing with someone, and the next, they're gone. Sorry, that took a really morbid turn. But that's the hard part about working where I do. You'll lose someone more often than most people do."

"Yeah," I nod solemnly. "We put my por por in here a little under a year ago, after my gong gong passed away."

"I'm sorry," he says. "What'd he pass from?"

"Pancreatic cancer. He fought it, but it only came back stronger. I miss him a lot this time of year, when we think so much about family and gathering. I wish he could live forever, but he accomplished a lot. Immigrating to this country, working his butt off to send his kids to college, supporting us at the inevitable piano recitals my parents forced us into as kids. I don't think my grandmother will ever really get over him being gone. That's why I've been working remotely here with Por Por when I can, instead of at home or in the office. I make sure to visit as often as I can. I know some of these residents have no one, which makes me sad."

"It makes me sad too," Leland replies. He looks around the room at the residents who sit quietly and alone.

"I'm sure they're thrilled when you go to check on them—a bit of conversation, even if they might not have family." I instinctively reach to put my hand on his.

The smooth, cool surface of his skin causes my own skin to tingle, and I pull back, embarrassed. I probably crossed a boundary. I just met the guy ten minutes ago.

"Shit," I murmur. "I'm sorry. I got in my feels, talking about sad, elderly people—I'm so sorry, if you don't like being touched by strangers."

"Daphne," he says, placing his hand on my arm and looking confidently into my eyes. I'm wearing a long-sleeved shirt, but his touch is electrifying through the cotton. "You don't have to be sorry. And you're officially no longer a stranger. It felt . . . nice. You feel nice."

I try to make a sound come out of my mouth. "I do?"

"Yes," he smiles, his gaze making my stomach churn with butterflies. "I haven't known you for long, but I've felt . . . *warm,* ever since we started talking. To be honest, I can't really think about anything right now except when I can see you again. Outside of here. Can I . . . take you out? On a date? Somewhere I can treat you?"

His hand stays on me, and I feel the warmth he mentioned. It's filling my veins, red heat racing up my limbs and flushing my cheeks. My lips turn up in a smile. The smile widens into a grin when I think of how Por Por will never stop gloating. She will want full credit for the match.

"Sure," I say. "I think I'd like that a lot. But Leland, can I ask you a question?"

"Of course." His look is serious, like he's bracing himself for what I might ask.

"In my line of work—"

"The dating app, right? You want to know more about my dating failures?" Leland groans.

"No! I mean, unless you have some good stories to tell."

He laughs, so I continue.

"It's just that developing software for the app means I'm always crunching numbers, looking at the odds. And I have to tell you, the odds of this happening—" I gesture to the space between us.

"Our meeting, you mean?"

I nod. "Right. I show up to visit my grandma in her nursing home, just before the new year, and run into you? This is entirely against the odds. So, I have to ask—Leland, do you play the lottery?"

He looks at me, and once again, I see red.

Late afternoon light seeps into the room and shines through the lanterns hanging from the ceiling. Glowing. It radiates around Leland's face. The whole scene makes my heart beat faster, like it's about to burst.

"I've never bought a Lotto ticket, but—" He grins slowly. "I'm pretty sure I just won."

Luna × Noura

AYLA VEJDANI

Noura, 41
she/her, woman
1 km away 📍

Palestinian. Social Worker. Cries during *The Voice* auditions. Will Insta-stalk all cast members post reality show binge. Shares food but hogs the blanket. Teach me how to play poker and I'll teach you how to make rummaniyya.

Height: 5'5"
Sun Sign: Cancer
Moon Sign: Libra
Rising Sign: Leo

Okay, that's a start. Right? I can do this. What's next?

"Looking for" . . .

Ugh, what am I looking for? Casual? . . . I'll leave it blank for now.

"Status" . . .

*Single? I guess. Divorced is more accurate. Not a label I love . . .
Blank for now, too.*

"Children" . . .

Is that something I actually have to share?

I leave the app and pop open the group chat.

> NOURA: Do I have to tell people
> I am divorced with children?

> CLEO: You don't have to tell anyone anything you
> don't want to.

> NOURA: Is it lying?

> CLEO: You don't owe anyone your personal
> information.

> DANI: Do what's comfortable for you. You're just
> getting your feet wet.

> CLEO: Hopefully your feet aren't
> what's getting wet. 💦

> NOURA: Kill me.

> GAYA: Later, if you connect with someone, then you
> can decide if you want to share more.

| GAYA: Also, I'm proud of you!

| DANI: You're doing it! 🐱

| CLEO: 💦💦💦

I switch back to the app.
Okay, I got this. What's next?

| "Sexuality" . . .

Good God, I don't got this! What the fuck do I say here?
I promptly return to the group chat.

NOURA: What do I say for sexuality? |

| DANI: Pansexual?

NOURA: That sounds like an Olympic game. |

| GAYA: Bi?

| CLEO: What do you want to say?

NOURA: I don't know. Like I literally do not know.
I want to try and date women. But I never
have. How do I know? I don't. I
don't know anything. I'm spiraling. |

| DANI: Babe, leave it blank for now.

| GAYA: You'll know when you know.

NOURA: And these profiles aren't helping with the
"no-bicurious," "no-bisexual" comments.

CLEO: [Sends meme: "YOU CAN BE BI EVEN IF
YOU'VE NEVER TRIED"]

NOURA: This was a bad idea.

It's been fifteen years since fate brought the four of us together. Fate and our master's of social work program. The first lecture of our first day of our two-year program.

"Good morning and welcome. Before you get too comfortable, I'm putting you in groups of four for the first term project, after which we'll go through the syllabus," Professor Sanam greeted the students as they hurried into the seminar room.

"When I call your name, please raise your hand so that your colleagues can identify you, and then sit in your foursome . . ."

They listed name after name—and then came to us. "Next . . . Cleo Aetós, Gaya Jeevanathan, Daniela Ibañez da Silva, and Noura Salah . . ."

And that's how it all started. We met. Clicked. And were inseparable. Every step of the way, from then on, a four-way conversation.

It was Daniela, Dani, who took the role of mother hen. It came to her naturally, bringing people together, taking care of them. She had a gravitational pull that made you want to be around her. She was from Maragogi, a resort town in eastern Brazil. Her parents owned and managed a boutique hotel until it was time for her to go to high school. Then they uprooted the whole family to Vancouver. She is the eldest of five, with three brothers and a baby sister.

She had filled the quasi-parent role for most of her life. With her parents always working, she was both loaded with responsibility and free to do as she wished. By the time her mother and father started to take notice, it was too late—Dani was already becoming who she was going to be. Social work was not what they had hoped for their eldest, and neither was marrying a woman. But Dani's attitude was *take it or leave it*, even with her parents. She knew her worth; it was innate. She moved to Toronto for the MSW program along with her sister (who had enrolled as an undergrad), and was still playing mother decades later. From her, I learn magnetism, by watching her be free and alive in her skin.

Dani and I both started working at RIGHTS ONE, a national children's rights nongovernmental organization, immediately after graduation and never left. We couldn't start working fast enough. We were itching to be out of the lecture halls and in the field.

Gaya was the only one of us who was married when we started the program. She and Jae met in high school in Scarborough, an immigrant-rich multicultural district of Toronto. By the time the program ended, she was pregnant with their first child, Adya, now thirteen. And soon after came their second daughter, Banhi, now ten. It was her choice to stay at home for the first couple of years and build a foundation for their daughters. Gaya was the middle child, between two brothers. Her amma—a single mother and refugee from Sri Lanka—had worked herself to the bone providing for them. When her mom passed months before Gaya's thirty-fifth birthday, I remember her telling me that her greatest regret was not knowing who her mother was outside of struggle. Gaya was determined to write a different story for her and her daughters.

Gaya and Jae budgeted for her to stay at home in the early years. But a year after her youngest, Banhi, started elementary school, Gaya gave birth to her private practice. A marriage of counseling and Ayurvedic practices. Her intuitive skills blended with her ancestral gifts and her education. Gaya was always going to pave her own way. She's the type who will look at a recipe and always see it as a suggestion. In the last three years, she has evolved her practice further into Vedic astrology. Her blooming business and devoted following created an abundant space to allow Jae to leave his corporate job. Her success inspired him to invest in his own dream project, AURORA, a camping app he founded with his sister.

Gaya is grounded to the core and wise beyond her years. She is the one who reconnected me to my own spiritual roots.

Cleo, on the other hand, never left school. They had a passion for learning and disrupting the status quo. They went directly into the doctorate program while working part-time for the administration. They made so much noise during our program years, fighting all the ways the school was blind to racism, xenophobia, sexism, homophobia, and transphobia, that the school thought instead of fighting with Cleo, they should get Cleo to fight for the school. Now Cleo is a professor in the social work department. Their courses include: "Gender and Sexual Diversity," "Seminar on Trauma and Resilience," and "Special Topics in Social Work, Social Welfare, and Social Policy." They are the kind of lecturer we all wish we had. Challenging yet supportive. Rule breaker and thought-leader.

Cleo is a second-generation Greek Canadian. Born and raised in Halifax. Youngest of four. You might underestimate them at first, with their eternally young face, bleached blonde pixie cut, and beanie that never leaves their head. But the moment they open their mouth, you are forever changed by their passion and heart. Cleo teaches me to be bold.

We all knew Cleo was in love with Dani—but honestly so was the whole school. It definitely caught us by surprise when we realized Dani was into Cleo. It was a full year after we graduated when the two admitted to Gaya and me that they were seeing each other. They had kept it from us, unsure how it would affect the friend group dynamic. Apparently, a drunken hookup turned into a real relationship.

Dani needed someone with Cleo's fire to make the world better. Cleo needed someone like Dani who would never back down from love. Their individual strengths made it safe to trust each other, let their walls down, and commit. Now they are married, ten years strong.

I am the woman I am because of them. They teach me by being themselves. They personify unconditional love. If it wasn't for them searching out lawyers, finding apartments, packing boxes, I would probably still be laying on the cold tiles of my bathroom in a puddle of tears after my own marriage ended. But they showed up, like they always do, and helped me rise.

For months, they had been trying to convince me to get on a dating app. It had been a year since my divorce, and they thought it would be good for me.

"I just want you to have fun! Remember fun?" Dani would plant seeds during our lunch breaks.

It was true. My divorce had burned me. *Buried* me. Dragged my soul through the depths of my shadows. I was just coming up for air, albeit slowly, remembering how to breathe on my own. It was my choice to leave, but it didn't make the process any easier. I was heartbroken, but free. Grieving, but relieved. A dichotomy of feelings on the blank canvas of my future self that I had yet to meet.

Everything was new. Daunting and exciting. I was ready to choose me, all of me. Parts of me that I had forgotten, and parts that I had yet to discover. And I was free to do so. It was a type of freedom that I didn't realize I'd been missing until I had it again. Like, *oh shit,* this was missing all along and I had no idea.

My ex-husband adored me. He adored me so much that he caught me and didn't let me go. I was everything until I wasn't. A butterfly he admired so much that he caught it and pinned it, and then resented it for not flying. Then I forgot how to fly, I forgot that I could, I forgot that I was even a butterfly.

At first it was all in slow motion. Apathy disguised as safety. So exhausted, with two young children, that any more change felt impossible. Then it started to get fast, too fast, like I was going to drown if I didn't get out. The air in every room dissipated, my chest always tight, holding my breath around him, walking on eggshells. No one saw it coming, not even me. One moment I felt like I could do this, and the next moment I knew if I didn't leave, I would be lost forever.

> CLEO: You need to shake off David's "bad dick energy" and get some pussy!

> NOURA: Well, that's a way to start a conversation. Good morning to you too, C.

> CLEO: You know I'm right.

> GAYA: What dick energy? That shit didn't work. Sorry not sorry.

> CLEO: And y'all think I'm bad! Yaaass G!!!

> NOURA: She's not wrong. I was married to an impotent workaholic.

| DANI: Foda-se!

| CLEO: Fuckkk! Is right!

Part of rediscovering myself also meant remembering desire. It had been years. I forgot what true desire was. I forgot what pleasure was. David had stopped looking at me, touching me, seeing me like that. I stopped seeing myself like that too. But ever since we separated, it's been making its way back. A whisper at first, now growing.

The curiosity about my sexuality took me by surprise. I was pregnant when I first noticed my fantasies shift to women. I thought it was hormonal, and I didn't overthink it. I was thirty-five at the time, which felt late for a sexual awakening. The more space I gave it, it grew. Moving from curiosity to desire. Now that I have the freedom, I want to explore. But I feel like an impostor. A tourist.

NOURA: I have a serious question . . . |
about dating women. |

| CLEO: Your Lesbian fairy godmother is here!

| DANI: Notice the capital on that L.

| CLEO: You know I got that gold star baby.

NOURA: What if I don't like it? What if I don't |
want to touch it or taste it or anything? |

| CLEO: So, you don't.

NOURA: Like, I hate blow jobs, so . . .

CLEO: Leeeesssbbbiiiaaannn!!!!!

NOURA: I'm serious! What if I hate . . . it too?

CLEO: Saying pussy is the first step.

NOURA: You're the worst!

DANI: If you don't like it, you don't do it.

CLEO: Good gays ask for consent at every step. And all boundaries are valid. So it's 100% your choice.

GAYA: My cousin Zoya went through something similar after her husband passed and she started dating women. If you want, I can connect you two.

NOURA: That would actually be super helpful, thanks G!

GAYA: Not to overstep, but I know you have a history of feeling like you "have to" do things when it comes to sex, even when you don't necessarily want to . . .

CLEO: That makes me so fucking mad!

DANI: Down, bebê!

CLEO: It's my Greek fire baby . . . and my hatred for misogyny and the patriarchy!

DANI: It's your Greek loud!

CLEO: Like Brazilians aren't loud!

DANI: Brazilians are a different loud than Greek loud!

GAYA: Can we wrap up the racial profiling for a second and get back to the issue at hand?

DANI: Right! Sorry!

CLEO: Take it step by step, see what you like. Ask, direct . . .

DANI: and if it's not for you then it's not for you.

GAYA: Or it might not be the right person. Just don't do anything with anyone unless you really want to. You need to feel something, want them. Desire is critical. Especially since it's your first.

CLEO: Noura needs someone with BDE!

DANI: Yes! Put that in your profile.

I stared at the app for weeks before I ever opened it. Terrified from the moment it downloaded.

How do people do this? Do they put their actual pictures? What if someone they know sees them? How are they not embarrassed? Embarrassed by what, Noura? Of dating? You're acting like you are committing a crime.

It was Gaya who opened the app for me the first time. Post-game night, we were laid out across the couch. Cleo and Dani were cleaning up in the kitchen.

"You tell me what to write, and I'll type," Gaya offered.

Deep in my carb coma, I submitted. "Fine." I passed her my phone.

"The app says 'Add a selfie,'" Gaya read.

We scrolled through my photos, and I tried to find one that I didn't hate. "Does everyone overthink this?"

"I'm sure they do."

I found one I had taken after a sunrise hike. The morning sun was shining on my face, I felt alive. Light brown skin glowing, honey almond eyes staring back at me, and my unruly black curls free. A woman in so many ways, and a child in others. Equal parts experienced and inexperienced.

"Yes, I love that one," Gaya agreed.

"Now it says, 'Add a full body shot,'" she read.

"Ugh!"

We started scrolling again. I found one from a work event, me posing with Dani. I'm wearing a fitted black boatneck midi dress and studded heels. I felt powerful in this look. I remember that night. It was the first night I went out post-David. I was returning to myself, and I can see it in the picture: confidence. It was a rarity most days, but when it happened, I relished it. Also, my curves were all snatched in that outfit.

"You two look great!" Gaya commented.

"Let's crop Dani out, no need for both of us to be exposed to the wild."

"It says 'Add another just for fun,'" Gaya read the next app cue.

"None of this is fun," I say, taking back my phone, "That's enough for now."

"We got two pictures up, I call that a success," Gaya cheered.

The next morning, alone in bed, I fill in the rest.

"Profile complete!" The app reads. *Here goes nothing.*

YOU THINK THE HARD PART is over after signing up. Nope. That was just the start to my anxiety. For weeks, I receive a series of matches. Each one I screenshot and send to the group. Some I get close to meeting, most I un-match, because I panic.

Nothing feels right. Even though I'm not sure what *right* feels like anymore, I know I'm not feeling it. I can discern when something is outside my comfort zone, and I need to stretch past my fears. And I know when something is wrong for me. It's subtle, but I've learned how to differentiate the two. More important, I've learned to not gaslight myself with the latter. Trusting myself is how I build back safety within my body, after the emotional avalanche that took over my life.

I also take seriously what Gaya noted. The part about desire. The part about not doing something because I "have to" but because I *want* to. Some matches feel good on the ego, get me feeling myself, but not necessarily feeling them. Some matches start off with a spark—until the person falls off the face of this earth, or sends me one too many photos of their cats.

NOURA: Why am I doing this again?

DANI: To have fun.

CLEO: To get laid.

Noura: This doesn't feel fun,
it feels like a lot of work.

CLEO: Your profile is too serious. Just write DTF and see what happens.

DANI: Don't listen to them.

NOURA: I think I'm going to delete it.

GAYA: You've gone into this whole thing with fear and that is what's coming out. Have you set an intention? Get clear on what you want. Shift the energy.

NOURA: You're right, like always.

GAYA: 🙄 . . . and if it still doesn't feel right, then you can delete it.

NOURA: Deal!

CLEO: Or like I said, write DTF and see what happens 😝

NOURA: This one 🙄

That night I set myself up at my altar. Daqqat al-oud incense burning, I do an automatic writing exercise. The warm, earthy, and sensual notes of the 'scent from heaven' fill the small space. After I come out of my writing meditation, I read the channeled message out loud to myself. The last lines stay with me:

"The Goddess in me sees the Goddess in you.
The Goddess in you sees the Goddess in me.
Enveloped in each other's light, we bloom, in tandem."

I gently fold the paper and lay it under my misbaha. *I'll give it one more week. Then I'm deleting this thing.*

I end up giving it two weeks, mostly because I'm so busy I forget. "You have a message from Luna," the app notification reads. I click.

> [4:13pm] LUNA: I can teach you how to play poker, also I love rummaniyya

Luna? I don't remember her. When did we match? I click on her profile and start swiping through her pictures. *How do I not remember her?* She's a whole vibe. I screenshot her profile in its entirety to send to the group.

NOURA:

Luna, 31

she/her, androgynous

1 km away 📍

Queer Latinx Afro-Caribbean

Blissed out on lavender kombucha

Sun chaser ☀

Moon watcher 🌙

Height: 5'11"

Sun Sign: Capricorn

Moon Sign: Scorpio

Rising Sign: Libra

[Screenshot Image:

Luna on a turquoise skateboard with an oversized denim jacket, ripped black skinny jeans, and cropped Sailor Moon T-shirt. Corkscrew curls.]

[Screenshot Image:
Luna in oversized tortoise sunglasses.
Full glossy lips. A tapered twist out.]

[Screenshot Image:
Luna in a black micro bikini showing
off her gazelle frame and endless tattoos.
Face hidden under a beige wide brim hat.]

This is the first match I'm actually excited about. Curious to learn more. This is the first match I want to meet. I feel . . . desire. *Finally!*

CLEO: Yes ma'am! She totally has BDE!

DANI: She's hot!

CLEO: She's into your witchy stuff too.

GAYA: "Witchy stuff" they say rolling their eyes.

CLEO: I mean, you know, I just don't get the whole sun moon stuff.

NOURA: I'm going to ignore all that.

DANI: You two would look good together. Just sayin'. 😏

NOURA: She's 31. Is that too young?
Is it creepy that I'm 41?

CLEO: Isn't David 10 years older than you?

NOURA: Touché . . . my heteronormative shit again?

CLEO: You said it, not me. 😔

I flip back to the app. I usually wait days to respond, or not at all. I'm usually filled with so much dread and uncertainty that doing nothing is the safest choice. But this time, I know what I want. *Her.*

[4:16pm] NOURA: You know what rummaniyya is?

[4:17pm] LUNA: My best friend is Palestinian. At this point I feel like I am too. And she's basically Dominican. We grew up together, since we were 8.

[4:17pm] NOURA: I get that.

[4:17pm] LUNA: I was hoping we'd match.

[4:18pm] NOURA: What made you swipe?

[4:18pm] LUNA: Your eyes. From only going off pictures. I did see that you're a social worker. I am an addiction counselor. So, similar.

My eyes. The comment makes my body react in a way I don't expect.

[4:19pm] LUNA: It's a full moon tonight. Doing anything special?

[4:19pm] NOURA: I have a little ritual I do. You?

[4:20pm] LUNA: I have a night shift at the center today. But I'll carve out some space to do some releasing.

[4:20pm] NOURA: Besides one of my best friends, I don't know many people who are into . . . the woo woo of it all.

[4:20pm] LUNA: I don't know about "woo woo," but spirituality and mysticism are essential elements to my life. Your culture is so rich.

[4:21pm] NOURA: I'm new to discovering it.

[4:21pm] LUNA: Your gifts are your power. I will probably pull some cards tonight. If you want, I can pull a card for you. No pressure of course.

[4:22pm] NOURA: Yes, please.

[4:22pm] LUNA: Tato', I'll message you tonight.

"You have a message from Luna," the app notification reads. I click, excited.

[10:10pm] LUNA: Your card:
"Loving yourself is the medicine you need."

> [10:10pm] LUNA: My card:
> "Embrace the softer sides of you."

I love this so much. I can't hide my smile. My excitement. I can't believe it but I am actually excited. Everything about this feels good. *God, feeling good. Imagine, what a thought.*

But there is something looming in my chest. I feel like I'm getting ahead of myself. We haven't met. We don't know each other. She doesn't know me. All that I come with. My divorce, my children. I don't want to go down this road only to be rejected for my truth. I don't know how to type all of this out. I don't know what to say. I see that there is a voice note option on the app. Here goes nothing. I press the microphone button and start recording.

[10:12pm] Noura: "Buenas noches Luna. Thank you for the card pull. It resonates deeply . . . I'm new to dating . . . so I don't know if this is an overshare . . . I feel connected to you, and want to get to know you more, but I feel like I should let you know . . . I'm recently divorced and I have two young children . . . It's just that, for me, it's better to be transparent so if we decide to meet, you know who you're getting involved with . . . I also understand if it's too much. God knows, if I was thirty-one, it wouldn't be what I would sign up for. Anyways . . . I'm rambling . . . thank you again, night."

Sent.

Wow, I just word vomited that whole thing, didn't I? Smooth Noura, super fucking smooth! Why did you mention her age? It's so patronizing.

I check my phone for the next hour. Nothing. I can't tell if she's listened to it or not. I don't have the paid version of the app. I can't delete it either. I feel rejected. Scared. Silly. All the things. I have to go to sleep. It's well past my bedtime at this point, and I have an early morning.

What was I thinking? I knew I shouldn't do this. My real life needs me with both feet planted on solid ground. My children need me. My career needs me. Not fantasizing about some girl I've never met.

I put my phone on airplane mode and try, really try, to fall asleep. The anxiety doesn't help. This is why I didn't want to date. This is why staying in a seemingly safe loveless marriage was easier in some ways than doing all this, out here in the wild. Out here, alone, and with scars.

I turn on some binaural beats, 432 Hz, to help me fall asleep. Eventually, at some point, I do.

It's 6:30 a.m. when my alarm rings. I feel tired. The spiraling last night didn't help. Nothing like tiny non-events reminding you of all your unhealed bits.

My morning routine is on autopilot. I cover my hair and jump into the shower. While the water massages my back, I do some breathwork. When I get out, I moisturize my body with my mom's infamous lotion, a mix of olive oil and beeswax. Today, less is more. I set my hair up in a topknot. I put on some tinted SPF, add some light mascara, and throw my cinnamon lip gloss into my purse.

In my bedroom, my beige wide-leg pants and white silk blouse are set out. During my mornings sans children, I indulge in silk and light colors. I go to the kitchen, start boiling water for my tea, and grab some labneh from the fridge. As I'm drizzling honey over my walnuts and labneh, I realize my phone is still on airplane mode. I go over to turn it on.

"You have a message from Luna," the app notification reads.

My stomach turns. I'm reminded of my rambling confessional from last night. I wonder if I should click, knowing the day I have in front of me. Then again if I don't click, my curiosity will get the better of me.

I open the app. There's a voice note.

| [12:12 am] LUNA: "My dear Noura," she starts.

I notice her use of "my" right away. It feels inviting in a way that surprises me. *This is how she will address me for the rest of our time together. "My Noura." Claiming me from the beginning, and not being ashamed that she wants me for herself. We will struggle with her possessiveness some days, but most days it will be a home we create together. I'm hers, and she's mine.*

"Thank you for your openness," she continues. "I'm sorry that I'm late in responding. You might already be asleep. There was an incident with one of the residents and I didn't want to rush my response to you. Especially when you were so vulnerable. You have nothing to explain. We all come with complicated, beautiful lives. But I appreciate the honesty. It's nice to connect with someone real. Dating apps can be superficial, to say the least. I hope you are sleeping well under this Full Pink Moon. If you are open to it, I would love to meet. Maybe a walk? Only if you are comfortable, of course."

I laugh. All the anxiety for nothing. *You didn't leave a marriage to continue to hide. If someone doesn't want to know you for you, then they're not the right person for you. Shape-shifting is not an option anymore.*

[7:16am] NOURA: I'm free Friday at 7:00 p.m. |

Later, she'll tell me that it was that voice note I sent that made her take notice of me. It made me interesting, complex, and real. She'll tell me that's when I started changing for her, from a woman with beautiful eyes to a woman with a beautiful soul.

MY PRE-DATE PREP LIST IS extensive. Bleaching, threading, waxing, hair conditioning, oh my. Thankfully, my nails are already done. Dani and I went during our lunch break today. Maybe I can get my legs and Brazilian wax done at lunch on Wednesday. Thursday night, when the kids go to bed, I can bleach my facial hair and condition my curls.

This might be completely unnecessary. Maybe dating women doesn't require all this. But I don't know another way to be beautiful. Since puberty, I learned to banish my dark body hair and perfectly groom my eyebrows (in all honesty, I over-plucked them in my twenties, then begged for them to grow back in my thirties). At least now I embrace my curls. After decades of straightening, my curl memory forgave me and returned.

Now, what to wear?

NOURA: Y'all, which outfit?
Black romper with spaghetti straps
and keyhole front tie? Relaxed fit.

Light blue mini knit bodycon?
Curves on full display.

CLEO: The blue one, easy access. 😶

NOURA: Access to what? We're not sleeping
together on the first date.

| DANI: You might.

                         NOURA: Do people do that? |

| CLEO: Yes, a lot has changed since the 1800s.

                         NOURA: I'm going to throw up. |

| GAYA: Just be comfortable.

| DANI: Comfortable is not a look. The blue
one shows off your ass. She's Latinx, we
need some fogo! 🔥

I don't listen to them and wear the black romper. It feels safer. I'm already waaay outside my comfort zone.

The blue knit dress will appear, however, on our second date. And it will in fact prove to provide easy access, which she'll use to her advantage under the table, during dinner.

We're supposed to meet at a park, the midpoint between our two apartments. On my way, I pick up some lavender kombucha for her. *Cute, right? Maybe it's cheesy? Regardless, it's definitely me.* I sit on a bench checking the time. I'm ten minutes early. I'm always early. *Should I text her that I'm here? Is that too eager?*

                NOURA: I'm on the bench by the purple slide. |

| LUNA: Be there in 10.

I see her walking up. She's wearing a mustard crop top, paper bag denim jeans, and platform Doc Martens. Her height is accented by her lean physique. She has a visible swagger even from afar.

"Noura," she says, giving me a double kiss.

"Luna," I return the greeting.

She sits, and we start exchanging pleasantries. Awkward small talk, trying to get a read on the other. She has a vibe that makes everything slow down. She talks slowly, stares slow, moves slow. I try to calm my nervous system to match hers, because I feel all over the place. Part of me wants to lean into the fact that I am a powerful woman in her forties. But I am also a woman coming off a self-worth-shattering divorce, feeling old and too straight. It doesn't help that I can't read her. Our short text exchange had more potential than this conversation. I feel like I'm at a job interview, a bad one. This seems like the last place she wants to be. I'm confused. *She's the one who asked me out!* This is going terribly.

"Is it just me or does this feel off?" I say, naming the awkward.

She starts to laugh, "You're right. This is awkward AF."

That seems to do it, shifting the energy.

"Oh, I almost forgot, I got this for you," I hand her the kraft bag with the lavender kombucha. She stares at it in disbelief and then into my eyes, like she's trying to figure me out.

"Gracias," she says, intense and intentional.

LATER, SHE'LL TELL ME THAT in these moments where she saw my heart, my thoughtfulness, is when she started to fall. The moments that connected us, past the surface swipes, into something more.

I offer that we could go to my place, have a drink, and change the stagnant vibe. She accepts, relieved. I already know I have no food in the house; I wasn't prepared for her to come over. But I feel safe with this person—safe enough to explore. Plus, the kids are at their father's for the weekend, and the house is clean enough.

When we arrive I see a ripe mango on my kitchen counter, I know I have limes and tequila in my freezer—this could be a winning combination.

"Mango, limón y sal?" I suggest, trying on my Spanish.

"My love language."

"Tell me about all these tattoos," I ask as I start cutting into the mango.

She settles onto one of the bar stools lining the island. She starts with her arms, then the one on her hip, neck, the little ones on her fingers, her ankle. Then she ever-so-nonchalantly lifts her crop top up, exposing her breasts to show the protection eye tattooed in the center of her chest. My body physically reacts to the sight of her naked body. The perky A-cups and dark nipples. It catches me off guard. *Am I blushing?* I feel self-conscious of my innocence.

I'm a girls' girl. I have deep friendships and expansive sisterhoods. Many nights in a setting just like this, lost in conversation and one another's company. But this is the first time it's a *date* date. The moment she flashes me and I feel my body react, I know viscerally, this isn't a *friend* date.

I pull up on the adjacent bar stool after plating the mango and pouring us some tequila.

"Sahtein," I say to her.

"Ala-albek," she responds with a wink, showing off her Arabic skills.

We graze each other's arms as our forks take turns. I am not sure how to engage romantically. I'm used to men coming in full force, and me either dodging or giving in. The nuance of the moment keeps me hesitant. I know I'm flirting with my eyes. I know I'm teasing with my words. But I'm unsure of where to go from here.

"You want to move to the couch?" she asks when we finish. "It seems more comfortable than these bar stools."

It all starts by her asking if she can hold my hand. This is how she feels energy, she explains. I offer my hand to her, and she massages it lightly. I stare at her as she does this. I remember an Argentinian girl, Alejandra, in my undergrad poli-sci class that used to do this to her boyfriend. Massage his hands attentively throughout class. It was hypnotizing to watch her. Her boyfriend was oblivious. I always wondered if he knew how lucky he was. This is what I remember as Luna massages my hands. I feel lucky at this moment.

Her hands are soft, and her grip is firm. We make eye contact as she squeezes the inside of my palm. I feel goosebumps race up my arm.

"You are golden on the inside," she comments as she reads me. The moment is tender and powerful.

"May I kiss you?" she asks.

I feel a rush of nerves sweep through me.

"Yes," I respond softly.

"You are sure?"

"Yes," I repeat with certainty.

She leans over and holds my face as her lips meet mine. We taste like mango and salt.

The initial shock—this is the first time I'm kissing a woman—wears off almost instantaneously, leaving only how good this feels. *I want more.*

I lean forward into the kiss. My weight makes her lean back on the couch as I take my place on top. I let my body press on hers, and she lets her hands move down to my waist. Our tongues play with each other, and our body heat rises.

"Do you want to go to your bedroom?"

For a moment, I think: *Should I?* And I realize the question isn't mine. It's society's noise making me wonder about the timeline of intimacy. Old, gendered cultural norms about chastity. None of this is mine. I gift myself by not overthinking it. I gift myself what I want.

I peel myself off her and take her by the hand. I walk her into my bedroom, and she stands face to face with me. Our height difference juxtaposes our age difference, as does her top energy.

"May I?" she asks, playing with my thin straps.

"Yes."

She drops them slowly and watches my romper fall to the ground as if it was designed for this moment. Beyond my black mesh underwear, I have nothing on.

She stares at me, enchanted. The look itself makes me wet.

"Tu si ere' linda," she comments with certainty. "You know that right?" she asks, holding my chin up, catching the hesitation in my eyes when she calls me beautiful.

The truth is, ten years ago I knew I was hot. Today, I'm not sure. "I'm finding my way back to myself," is the only way I know how to respond.

I take the next step and pull off her shirt, reuniting with her breasts. "Enty zay el amar," I comment. "It means 'you are like the moon.' It means you're beautiful."

"Enty zay el amar," she repeats back to me.

She takes my waist and playfully jousts me onto the bed. I laugh as I tumble down. This is going to be fun.

Her fingers meet the edges of my underwear and she pulls. "This okay?"

"Yes," I consent.

"You're sure?"

"Yes."

I am sure!

She's above me, staring. She's reading me, watching my body react to her gaze. With her eyes locked, she licks her fingers. The gesture makes my heart race. There is something about her certainty that makes me weak. She slides her wet fingers inside me. *She didn't need to lick them.*

The sensation of touch sends an electric current through my spine that makes me arch my back and moan. I don't hide the desperation in my voice. I want this. Maybe because it's been so long, maybe because this is new, maybe, maybe, maybe. All I know is I want more. I might be new to this, but I am a woman in her forties who knows her body. I direct her, telling her what I like and where to go. How to slow down, and when to go faster. She follows my guidance attentively, kissing my moans. I'm relishing in the touch, but it feels one-sided. I feel a frenzied need to discover her. I bite her neck. I take her breasts into my mouth. Lick her stomach. I squeeze her ass.

"Touch me," she requests, slowing me down.

I tense up. *What do I do?* I want to touch her. I don't know what I'm doing. *What if I don't know how?*

She's staring at me. I drag my hands down her body until I reach her lips. I slide through her slit. It's wet. I take some of her wetness on my fingers and lightly stroke her clit.

"Inside," she directs into my ear.

I slide in. The moment I do, I feel the warmth and wetness enveloping my fingers. The heat takes over my body in a way I've never experienced. Suddenly, all my worry dissipates and I fall into her. *Oh, right, I have one of these. I know what to do.* I listen to her noises and watch her rock on my finger, taking her cues.

"I want to taste you," I say, surprising myself. I spread her legs, my fingers still inside her, and find the spots that make her whimper. I use my tongue on her the way I like it on me, to see if it makes her body react. It does.

Everything is so soft. Our skin. Our lips. Soft. Softer than I ever imagined. Soft on the outside, soft on the inside. And wet. So wet. I can't stop touching her. Making her come is the greatest discovery. I've never had so much pleasure in pleasuring someone. Witnessing them in their desire. It's better than coming myself. I want to keep doing it.

"This doesn't seem like your first time," she jokes, as she lays back on the pillow recovering.

"Your first and your last," will be what she'll repeat to me for years to come, as we entangle ourselves in each other's flesh. She'll possess my body and she'll ask me: "¿de quién eres?" and I'll moan her name. This will be our sex game, how we play with power in between the sheets.

We take mini breaks that only last a minute before we start again.

At times, we are inside each other simultaneously and, at other times, we take turns discovering new places to pleasure. At one point, she holds my hand while she's inside me. The intimacy overtakes me.

"Come on top," she directs.

I straddle her and she enters me. I watch my body riding her fingers like waves, rhythmic and demanding, surrendering to the beauty of the fuck.

"Take what's yours," she whispers as she bites my ear, and I do.

Later I'll remember that the way she loved me made my inner Goddess come alive. She worshiped at the temple of my body, devouring me whole. Sex felt powerful and life-giving in a way I had never experienced. Our sacral connection fed and fueled the other.

"You know our names together make moonlight," I note, breaking the silence of our post-fuck haze. "Luna and Noura."

"Moonlight," she repeats to no one in particular.

From that day forward, whenever I call her, my name will appear as "Moonlight" on her screen.

She gets up and walks to the kitchen. Unselfconscious of her naked body. I watch this gazelle grace my home.

"Can I have some water?" she asks, already halfway to my kitchen.

"Of course," I respond, peeling myself off the bed and following her. I, however, am completely self-conscious of the fact that I am naked.

"It's late. If you want to stay over, you can," I offer.

She fills her cup with more ice than water and drinks it with urgency. "Okay."

Her hands are cold and make my body shiver when she places them around my waist.

"But who says we're done?" she teases.

WHEN WE FINALLY DECIDE TO sleep, I automatically roll over to my side of the bed, making myself as small as possible. I resolve not to move so as not to disturb her, knowing this will mean I don't sleep much tonight. I do this without thinking. My body is trained to do this. For twelve years I did this to not bother my partner, who never wanted to be touched when he slept.

"Why are you so far away?"

"What?" I respond, confused.

"Come here." She pulls me into her, wrapping her gorgeous limbs around me, and holds me tight.

"Oh, I just . . ."

"Shhh." She kisses me on the neck and holds me close.

In that moment, I realize how much I gave up for more than a decade. Always feeling like I was taking too much space, like I was too much. Now, I am held by someone wanting me to take more, to take what's mine. I mourn the years I kept myself trapped to one side of the bed. Silent tears fall down my face. I'm grieving the part of me that was lonely, that was hurting. For so long, longer than I realized. Longer than I admitted, even to myself. Even if this is only for this one night, I relish in the beauty of letting myself be held.

It isn't for one night. For years, we will sleep intertwined in each other's arms and legs. Like deep roots of an old tree. Even if we're too hot, too tired, too . . . we'll still choose each other's bodies to come home to. That night—and that now infamous question, "Why are you so far away?"—will be my very favorite memory.

The sunrise makes the room glow. Tones of brown skin, entwined. Shades of black curls, entangled. She squeezes my cheeks and kisses me good morning.

She'll always tell this story, of how I blushed when she kissed me that morning. How unexpected it was for an older woman. She was used to making younger girls turn red, but older women usually maintained an air of detachment. I was never good at hiding my feelings. And neither were my cheeks. When she repeats this story, I'll tell her to stop referring to me as an older woman, if she wants to continue to get laid.

We're standing in my hallway when it's time for her to go. She's leaning against my door with a smirk.

"You look cute," she comments, looking me up and down with her grin.

That grin.

I had thrown on an oversized sweatshirt when we finally got out of bed. My makeup was never washed off and my hair was tossed around all night. It's definitely a morning-after look. Of course, the post-orgasm glow helps. She is fully dressed in the same outfit that I met her in. Looking just as chic and effortless. *What do I do? Ask to see her again? Let this be a one-night thing? Take the lead? Let her take the lead?*

"I want to see you again." she states with certainty as if reading my mind.

"I'd like that."

"I'll text you," she says as she lifts my chin to kiss me good-bye. "Adio' habibti."

This will be our thing, mixing our languages and our lives. An ethnic mix of platano frito and za'atar. Learning each other's slang to create our own unique love language.

As soon as I close the door, I look for my phone. I find it abandoned in the kitchen from the night before. I jump into my bed and go to our group chat. This is not a texting situation. I press the group video-call button.

Cleo answers. Dani and Cleo are cuddled deep in their duvet with sleep in their eyes.

"Did you fuck?" is the first thing Cleo asks.

"We've been thinking about you all night," Dani adds in a drowsy voice.

"Look at her smile. You did!" Cleo cheers.

"Let's wait for Gaya," I say, trying to be patient.

Gaya doesn't answer. Instead she sends a text to the group.

> GAYA: At gymnastics with the girls.
> I'll call you later. xo

"Okay, spill, Miss," Cleo demands.

"It was amazing," I acquiesce.

"I knew it!" Cleo shouts, throwing her hands up in the air.

"Tell us every little detail," Dani pleads, now perking up in bed. So, I do.

. . .

NOURA: My sheets don't smell like you anymore. |

| LUNA: Is that an invitation to mess them up again?

I will later learn that touching her was a gift that she gave me.
A gift that she had never given anyone. Self-described as a "touch-me-not"—part trauma, part preference. Something I would have never guessed going off our first night together or our first months of endless fucking. But as we came out of our orgasmic honeymoon and started to peel back the layers of who we were outside of our sapphic desire, I learned that who I met was not who everyone else encountered.

She had slept with a lot of women. I mean, looking at her, it wasn't hard to believe. She was stunning, with a cool dominant air. It didn't matter what you identified as—if she was interested in you, you wanted to try. She would tell me stories of how she would rent a hotel room for the weekend, go out and pick up a girl, fuck them and then send them home. No sleepover, no contact information.

"You were clearly a fuckboi," I would tease.

"No!" she would protest.

"Everything you said is the definition of a fuckboi!" I would laugh.

It was a whole version of her I would never meet. With me, she was in love. Deeply devoted. She was so attentive to my needs, in and out of the bedroom. While ten years younger, she acted as if she were ten years older. Obsessed with the idea of making a home for us. Taking care of me and my, then our, children. There was a Luna before Noura, and the Luna after.

I wish I could be a time-traveling fly on the wall at those bars, to see what she looked like on the hunt. I wanted to see the fuckboi in action. But I never did. In our first year together her phone would blow up at all hours. After a year or so, it was dry. Her little black book finally closing, conceding that she was off the market.

I would ask her why. So many times. For years to come. *Why did she ask that I touch her? Why did she want me to? Why me, us, why?* And she would simply say, "the moment I touched your hand, I felt your energy. I knew you were special. And I was right. You were my wife."

I will learn how she reads energy. I will learn that she won't let people touch her so as not to absorb frequencies that she does not want. I will watch her in her rituals, clearing, manifesting, and healing. I will become more deeply dedicated to mine, knowing it is safe to explore and evolve. And like our languages and our foods, our spirituality will merge and expand in tandem.

But it will be in our touch that we heal the most. We will work back the layers for years to come, but on that first night together, we planted hope.

We will each become more of ourselves. Emotionally, physically, spiritually. And we will come to each other's bodies to pray.

She will later shave her curly top. This will release the hair that bound her to an identity that no longer fit, finding the sweet spot in her androgyny.

I, on the other hand, will grow my hair longer and longer. I will wear clothes and make art as the version of myself that I always desired to be, that I was destined to become. My divine feminine will bloom. She will call me Goddess, and I will believe her.

Luna met someone who let her heal, and I met someone who set me free.

Joy is how I took my power back.

☾ ● ☽

You are invited to the blessed union of

Noura Salah

&

Luna Isabel Rosário Reyes

Please join us as we celebrate our moonlight.

☾ ● ☽

Jess & Daya

PAMELA VACCARIELLO

JESS

A shock of pain wakes me.

I'm unable to stop the cry that breaks from my lips.

Next to me, Daya gasps, jolting awake. "What happened?" she asks, voice hoarse.

The light of early morning is dim, but I can see her eyes take in the scene, filling with fear.

"My shoulder," I croak. "It dislocated."

As I try to maneuver my upper arm back into its socket, a panicked whimper escapes my lips. Dislocations in my sleep have happened before, but waking to feel a limb slip from its rightful place is always an unwelcome surprise. After a couple of tries, I get my shoulder back in place. *Finally.*

Turning to face Daya, I can see she's trying to catch her breath. I feel awful for waking her like this.

"Are you okay?" I ask.

"*Me?*" She blinks, incredulous. "You're asking if *I'm* okay?"

"You've never seen one of my joints dislocate before," I say. "It must've been scary."

Daya shakes her head, as if to clear her mind of the image. "I'm fine," she says.

She doesn't look fine. Her brow is furrowed, a pinched look that briefly reminds me of my mother's face or the face of an ex-lover I'd rather forget. I'm briefly flooded with their reactions to my body—their disappointment, disdain, barely hidden disgust. Daya's never reminded me of those people before. Anxiety rises within me.

Then, in a tone of voice so soft and concerned, it surprises me, she asks, "Are *you* okay?"

"Yeah," I say. "I mean, it hurts. A lot. But, uh . . . it happens."

She bites her lip, stifling a laugh. "You're so nonchalant."

"I would shrug, if I wasn't so scared to move my shoulders right now."

Her burst of laughter makes me smile wide. My heart rate slows; I feel her here, present, with me.

"I mean, I put myself back together. No numbness or tingling or anything so far." I cross my fingers, keeping my hand safely in my lap. "We should be fine."

"You're sure?"

I nod.

After a second of consideration, she nods back, accepting my words, and I'm grateful. Someone else might have rushed me to the emergency room, or worse, disbelieved my pain, but Daya understands. Not only because she's an empathetic gem, but because she's also disabled. I have hEDS—hypermobile Ehlers-Danlos syndrome—which gives me joints held together by Silly Putty. Daya has cerebral palsy, which means she knows—among other things—that bodies can be *wonky*, to use a word she's fond of.

She leans over, giving me a careful kiss on the nose.

"Need anything?" she asks.

I hesitate for just a moment.

"Um . . . yeah, actually. I could use my shoulder brace."

"Where is it?"

I point to a shelf on the opposite wall, and she's already headed across the room, walking with her signature limp, which I've grown quite fond of. I'm surprised by how fast she's moving—adrenaline, I guess. Considering this, I feel a pang of guilt. *She shouldn't have to be nursing you; she has enough difficulties of her own.*

I sit up, and shooting pain breaks through my thought. The ache that is at a constant hum in my body intensifies, and I grit my teeth to keep from groaning.

Our dinner date last night flashes through my mind, and I grimace; we had fun, but I pushed myself too hard. The restaurant had steps—two to get in, and six more to go to the washroom, contrary to the assurance of the person who answered the phone when we called in advance to check ("It's totally accessible, hon!")—but we didn't feel like making a fuss, and the food was supposed to be really good, so we ate there anyway. I thought, *technically I can climb the steps, so I should*—a supposed marker of strength. I tried to use my cane as little as possible, and I tried to look as able-bodied as possible, and I tried to pretend I was normal for once, and now I am paying the price.

Now, Daya balances unsteadily on her knees, lifting the brace to me.

"How do you put it on?"

The question is so gentle and generous, my stomach does backflips.

I swallow.

"This goes here," I say, bringing my wrist through the sleeve.

Though the fingers on her left hand are quite stiff, Daya slowly brings the cuff up my arm. It tickles, as the fabric brushes against my skin.

Once it's in place, I grab the brace's strap. "And this," I say, "goes underneath my other arm."

I see her thinking over the movement that's required for this next step. As I gingerly raise my left arm above the strap, not wanting to hurt that shoulder, too, she quickly brings the strap underneath my arm.

Then it's in place. "There," she breathes, an adorable smile on her face.

I smile back and notice how close our faces have become in this little dance. My heart skips. I look down to adjust the strap so that it fits comfortably, and when I look back up, our lips almost brush.

She giggles, easing the tension. I cup her cheek in my left hand, and we kiss.

Just kiss, for a couple of minutes. At one point, she loses her balance and grips my shirt not to fall onto me. Seeing the fabric in her fist, I want the garment to come off. Badly. I want lots of things. But my brace is snugly on top of my shirt, and my body is in too much pain to take this further.

We pause so that Daya can grab a Magic Bag from the freezer. She snuggles next to me to ice my shoulder.

"Is that good?" she whispers.

"Yeah," I breathe, as the pain dulls slightly. "Thank you."

She smiles wide, looking at me with all the warmth of the morning sun, which eases the pain even more.

DAYA

My eyes slowly flutter open, as I stretch my arms above my head.

I blink, stare at the ceiling for a moment, rub sleep out of my eyes, then glance at the alarm clock on the bedside table. It's 10:00 a.m. *Not bad*, I think, happy we decided to go back to sleep

after our early morning medical emergency. Jess is still fast asleep,
tucked safely in her brace. She looks so serene, lips almost in a soft
smile. Freckles dot her entire face, concentrated on the bridge of
her nose. Her strawberry blonde eyelashes, only noticeable up
close, are so pretty. She's angelic, her shoulder-length waves
splayed out on her pillow, a ginger halo. I could stare at her for
hours.

Unfortunately, I have to pee.

I grab my phone from the nightstand and roll out of bed as
quietly as possible.

JESS

I wake slowly this time, eyelids heavy. Growing conscious of my
body, I notice that the pain in my right shoulder is still present,
though not as bad as it was a few hours ago. The rest of my body
pulsates with a familiar dull ache, ready to be ignited by any
movement.

I'm careful of my motions, as I bring my left arm to lift the
Magic Bag from my shoulder, where it still sits heavy, now room
temperature.

Then I open my eyes, and they go wide, as I take in the scene.
Daya isn't lying next to me anymore.

She left.

The thought makes me accidentally drop last night's ice bag on
my stomach, and the unexpected weight causes me to lurch forward, pain overcoming my body—the sharp pain on my abdo-
men, where the bag fell, radiates to my lower back and hips.
Goddamn it. I throw the Magic Bag to the floor, and my left
shoulder subluxates.

"Ow. Fuck!"

My breath comes heavy. As I run my hand through my hair, I hear my shoulder joint click, feel the pain growing. I want to cry. *Did she really leave?*

I strain my neck to try to look at the floor. I can't see her clothes or bag. I imagine her rushing to dress, sneaking out before I wake. I look at my nightstand. Her phone isn't there. My hand tightens into a fist on my hair. My eyes sting, vision blurring. Tears on the verge of spilling. *She left. She left, and she's not coming back. You scared her off; of course you did. Your stupid fucking body, repulsive, unlovable.*

Just as I'm about to really let the tears come, I hear a toilet flush. It takes a moment to register what this means. *Oh.* I wipe my face as quickly as possible, with the backs and palms of my hands, cringing at how quickly I jumped to such terrible conclusions.

Grateful that Daya is a slow mover like me, I take a few deep breaths. *She's here. She stayed.* I hear her unbalanced footsteps as she crosses the hallway from the washroom to my bedroom. The sound, her uneven gait, is a comfort.

DAYA

By the time I get back, Jess is awake. "Well, hello!" I smile.

"Good morning," she says, voice gravelly, a sleepy husk I find incredibly hot.

I bite my lip to keep myself from telling her how cute she looks with bedhead, strands of straw-colored hair pointing every which way.

As charmed as I am, I'm also concerned—getting out of bed proves to be difficult for Jess this morning. She winces while pushing herself to a sitting position, and curses as she tries to stand. She sits back down on the edge of the bed.

I hate that she's in so much pain. I try to imagine what it must feel like, and my stomach turns. I take her hand.

"Today is a bad pain day," she says. "I think I'm gonna need my chair."

We've only been dating a couple of months, but we've had enough slumber parties that I know the drill. Jess even taught me how to use her powerchair. I take a seat in it now and bring it to her bedside. Slowly and carefully, she transfers into it, then makes her way to the washroom.

WHEN SHE COMES BACK, SHE looks defeated.

"I think I just need to stay in bed today."

I start to tell her, *no problem,* but pause when I notice her eyes are watery.

"Daya, I'm really sorry," she says. "I know this isn't the hottest date."

"Oh, my God, don't apologize," I say, trying to reassure her. "I like staying in bed, especially if it's with you. We can just chill together."

I mean it. Jess's honesty is attractive; she's not trying to hide her pain from me. She knows what she needs.

"Even in acute pain, you manage to be good-looking," I tell her.

She blushes, pink moving from her neck up toward her ears, and I feel way happier than I should.

TOGETHER WE TRY TO EASE the pain using all the tools available: electric heating pad for her stiff back, fresh ice packs for her hips and shoulders, and braces for her knees. I hear her stomach growl and realize we haven't eaten.

"Breakfast in bed?"

I put on a pot of coffee, and while it's pouring, shake granola into two bowls and spoon vanilla yogurt into each. It takes some time—if I make a spoonful too big, my hand is likely to shake and drop the yogurt everywhere—but I've learned to be patient with myself. I'll finish eventually.

When I go to pour the coffee into a thermal bottle—a hack to help the two of us avoid spilling in bed—my hand spasms and I gasp, almost knocking the whole thing over. My heart races.

After catching my breath, I manage to add sugar, milk, and ice to the bottle, trembling a bit as I do. I grab a couple of plastic straws, rolling my eyes as I think of the last woman I dated, who gave me a lecture about my use of disposable kitchen items. The fact is, no one has the dexterity to clean reusable straws in this household. I grin, thinking how different things are with Jess, and how she'll understand the triumph of this whole endeavor. I didn't spill the coffee! And even if I had, it'd be okay. We'd make it funny. Or cry if necessary.

Jess lent me her powerchair to use while she's stuck in bed, making each task that much easier. I can walk without assistance, but the chair gives me speed and a feeling of freedom. I didn't have to balance on a stiff leg while making breakfast, and I don't have to take three trips to deliver the goods to Jess, all while worrying about tripping and dropping everything on the way. The seat is big enough for the bottle to lie beside my leg, and I hold one bowl with my right hand, while the other is balanced on my left thigh—which I have to be very careful not to bounce upward—as I slowly nudge the joystick forward with my left fist.

When I finally get back to her room, I find that Jess has closed her eyes again. She glows, a sheen of sweat gleaming on her forehead, the result of using a heating pad on a hot day. I feel unreasonably sad, my mood plummeting from high to low in seconds. Despite using the chair, I was so slow, she fell asleep. I imagine Jess waiting, hungry and in pain, wondering what could have possibly taken me this long. Hot shame creeps up the back of my neck.

As I get closer to Jess's bed, the hum of the powerchair wakes her. Her eyes flitter open.

"I'm so sorry," I say. "I took so long you fell asleep."

She shakes her head with a frown.

"I wasn't sleeping. Just resting my eyes. Was getting a bit of a headache. Better now."

Oh. So this wasn't about me being a slowpoke after all.

Or was it? Jess is giving me a look I can't read.

"Daya," she says warily, "Are you sure you want to stay? You're here as my date, and you're so fun, and I'm . . . making things so boring," she says.

"You're not!" I say.

My hand wants to reach out to comfort her, but it's holding a bowl of yogurt. Instead, I mean the words so strongly that my left leg kicks out, and I almost drop the other bowl. We both watch it wobble and settle on my thigh, before breaking into laughter.

"Close call," she says, breathy.

"Close calls are what I do best!" I say.

Then Jess gives me a sweet look and asks if I want to get back in bed with her (favorite question ever!), and I'm close to dropping everything again.

Quickly and carefully, she takes the bowls from me, saying, "Not again!" with a shake of her head. I check her face for any sort of judgment or criticism, but I am thankful that there's none. She has a huge smile on her face. There's only love.

JESS

The bottle of chilled coffee Daya brewed for us is perfectly centered on my lap tray, with a straw for each of us. It's like a milkshake shared on a 1950s diner date, except the shake is iced coffee and the booth is a soft, comfy bed. I tell Daya about my diner fantasy, and she asks me to pick out some music from the jukebox. I smile and put on a video I was randomly recommended on YouTube once, a woman playing Debussy's *Deux arabesques* on harp. With the beauty and lightness of the music, it feels like my pain momentarily melts away, and beside me, it seems as if Daya's body relaxes, too, swaying a bit with the music, as though her stiff limbs suddenly become fluid.

"Feels like we're in a movie," she says dreamily, smiling.

"Right?"

There's a stretch of silence between us, with just the music playing, and the smile on her face lingers like it often does—sometimes lasting long after a moment passes.

"Your joy is so beautiful," I say.

My words startle her. Her arm spasms, and instead of meeting her mouth, the spoon dabs her cheek, a glob of creamy white now smeared on her brown skin.

"Oh, no!" she mutters, giggling.

At the same time, I exclaim, "Sorry!"

"Don't apologize," she says, more serious now, eyes filling with emotion. "That was a really sweet thing to say."

She shakes her head, remembering the yogurt on her face. She moves to wipe it with the back of her hand, but I stop her.

"Wait—" I reach to grab a tissue from the box on my nightstand, then hold it up to her cheek. "Can I?"

"Yes."

I gently wipe away the mess, her breath stopping as I do.

"There," I say. "Perfect."

Before I move away, she angles her face so that our lips are aligned, hers hovering a centimeter from mine. Her eyes are the color of the iced coffee we've been sipping, a swirl of light inside each pool of dark brown.

"Thanks," she says, barely above a whisper.

And then our mouths collide, searching, desperate for a release from the tension, stress, and sweetness of the last twelve hours. I pour everything into this kiss, trying to tell her what I mean when I say "perfect." That's what this person is to me.

When we break apart, breathless, she says it again, grinning: "Thanks."

And when I finally respond, the simple words are a hopeless understatement for the way I feel: "No problem."

AFTER WE FINISH BREAKFAST, DAYA goes to grab water bottles for both of us because "it's important to stay hydrated." Thoughtful as she is adorable.

As she's settling back into bed, she says: "I like being with you. It lets me really rest without feeling guilty."

I feign offense, and she laughs.

"Okay, also because you're gorgeous and brilliant and fun to be around, obviously."

"I was gonna say!" I joke, smiling. "Are you just using me so you have an excuse to rest?"

"At least you know I'm not using you to skip the lines at amusement parks," she smirks. "Because I have that perk, too!" We both laugh. Still smiling, she says, "Wasn't it the worst, though? Everyone suddenly, eagerly, wanting to be your friend for a day in high school, just so they can skip the lines?"

"I didn't have that problem yet, not at that age. . . . I wasn't officially diagnosed until a few years ago." I was twenty-one when I finally learned the words for what I was experiencing.

"That must've been so scary to go through," Daya says, eyes filling with empathy. "Being a kid, not knowing what was going on with your body. . . ."

I nod heavily. Just remembering it makes my stomach churn. "Plus, no diagnosis meant no accommodations, no insurance for mobility aids or anything. . . ."

"Oof! Life is hard enough even with those things," she says. After a moment of thought, she adds, "Actually, people tried to make my life harder *because* I had accommodations. As a teenager, my so-called friends made me feel like shit for getting what they called 'special treatment.' Just constantly telling me *it's not fair* when I got extra time on a test or whatnot."

I scowl, hating that she went through that. But Daya waves off the memory as if it were a buzzing mosquito and leans toward me.

"Tell me what it was like for you? High school. Lots of girl-friends? Straight As? Smoking underneath the bleachers?"

"Believe it or not, it was . . . not the happiest time of my life. Junior year, just as things started getting more serious academically, my pain and symptoms started getting worse. . . . I was so desperate for help, I basically diagnosed myself. I googled my symptoms, and WebMD was like, *maybe you have EDS.* When I went to my sixth doctor, I was like, *I think I might have EDS, can you run some tests?* And he was like, *maybe you're a hypochondriac.* It was years later that I finally found a doctor who took me seriously. She did a physical examination, and I was right!"

"Seven doctors?! Are you serious? That's ridiculous."

I nod. "Thank God for the internet, though. It basically saved my life!"

"I feel that, too," Daya says. "Even though I was diagnosed as a baby, the actual words 'cerebral palsy' were rarely used, and I was taught to think that I could control it, that I wasn't trying hard enough, when really I just have brain damage!" she laughs, not because it's funny, but out of exasperation for the ridiculousness of it all. "And I never fully came to terms with that until I was, like, eighteen, when I randomly saw someone else with CP mention it online."

I sit with Daya's words. There are people in my life who *still* treat me like I choose this—like I want my body to be unwieldy and unpredictable, just to make their lives a living hell. My mother is eternally disappointed that I am not the perfect, ever presentable, always impressive daughter that she'd hoped for.

The silence between us grows. I stare at my hands in my lap, while Daya chews on a thumbnail.

Then she perks up. "Anyways," she says, "what we started this conversation with—you letting me rest without feeling guilty—I just meant that being with you makes me really happy, and that's partly because I get to rest without feeling bad about it. I'm realizing that a day spent lying in bed with you is better than most days spent pretty much anywhere else."

I open my mouth to speak, but find myself just gaping at this beautiful person saying all the right things.

"Now, please let yourself relax," Daya says, running her hand over my clavicle and down each arm, ever-so-gently pressing me into the mattress. "You deserve to rest. You *need* to rest, so your body can recover."

Is this person even real?

"You're incredible," I practically whisper.

I've never had anyone say those words to me before and really mean it. *I can relax; I should relax; we can relax together*—to hear that expressed so genuinely? It makes me want to weep.

Daya takes my hand, then turns her body toward me, curling into my side. Careful to avoid my knees, she cautiously lifts her right leg over my thigh, then places her arm over my torso, quietly asking, "Is this okay?" with so much attentiveness, I could kiss her.

All of it is much better than okay. Her thigh is an extremely pleasant form of compression; her arm is warm across my body, and her face nuzzling into my side is the best feeling ever. Even if it did hurt, though, I don't think I could bear to push her away or end this moment. I'm too happy for the company, for the touch that is so rare on painful days like this, and the intimacy that is so rare in general. I am so used to relying on blankets and heating pads for warmth, always the big spoon, wrapping my arms around my comforter. It's nice to have someone with me for once, especially someone as gentle and caring as Daya.

DAYA

It's a strange combination, feeling so pleased to be nestled into Jess like this, while still processing our conversation about growing up disabled. Even that word, "disabled," was once hard for me to learn to wear with pride. Lying here, I scan my inner landscape, and there it is—a smidgen of shame in me that still needs to be shed, a haunting at the center of my chest, my nervous system, my bones. Not a bellyful of butterflies, but a lone, black moth fly. Tiny, especially compared to the amount of shame I used to carry, but the fluttering of its wings is still enough to make me feel sick to my stomach.

The thought of that toxic feeling growing in Jess makes me want to yell.

So, I tell her what I wish someone had told me, all those years ago, when the shame first started to creep up:

"Hey," I say, pulling my face far enough away to bring her freckles into focus. "You're not a burden to me."

Jess looks surprised. "But I didn't say—"

"You didn't have to. The needless apologies—about being boring, being a downer. . . . I know the feeling all too well."

"But . . ." Her eyes brim with tears, and I take her hand, trying to comfort her. "You don't have chronic pain. You don't *have* to stay in bed all day," Jess continues. "I'm just holding you back from life out there." She gestures toward the window.

"That's not true. Jess, you're a light to everyone around you! And you're not holding me back from anything," I say softly. "This," I say, gesturing around us, patting a plush pillow beside me, "this day, spending time with you, relaxing in bed . . . this *is* truly living."

As I'm saying this, her eyes lift to meet mine, and I see them glimmer, recognizing what I'm saying, believing it. But it only lasts a second. Her face falls, bringing her gaze down to her lap. I can practically see her thoughts, clawing at her skull. She glances back up at me.

"But, your face. . . ." she says.

My face? Uh-oh. I bring my hand to my face, mortified, wondering if there's a bit of yogurt left from earlier.

"No, no, your face . . . this morning. When I woke you up, you looked so scared and disturbed. I don't wanna put you through that again."

"Oh! Well, of course I looked like that," I laugh. "I have CP! If you say my name when I'm daydreaming, I'll jump. So, obviously waking up in the wee hours, to you in distress, shocked me." I pause. "And my face . . . I can't always control what it does. But I'm happy, here, with you. And I don't know how many times I'll have to repeat that, but I will, until you believe it."

"Right," she breathes, nodding, shoulders dropping. "Okay." I watch her expression change, storm clouds moving aside to reveal a clear sky, and my own body finally relaxes.

This whole time, I have been tensing up, and tensing up, and tensing up, left hand balling up into a fist, left leg extending and foot twisting inward. And every single time my body made an involuntary movement, I felt a jolt of shame. But then I remembered who I'm with. I feel safe, comfortable here. I hope my presence can make Jess feel that way, too.

I wipe her tears with the back of my hand. "Your skin is so soft," I say.

"Thanks," she says, smiling. "It's the connective tissue disorder."

We both laugh, her freckled face exploding into bright constellations.

Then she entwines her fingers with mine and presses her lips to my cheek. "Truly, thank you," she says. "*So* much. For everything. I love you."

My heart blooms. "I love you, too."

Waves

ANIS GISELE

In the winter, she gifts you a trip to the sun. You are sun chasers,
both from islands where heat is a drenched outcry. She says you
haven't been sleeping. She has watched you make golden milk
with ashwagandha for calm, but you still stare at the ceiling, holding your breath.

You and your lover are on a hotel bed, watching cable together
for the very first time, and a series of trailers flashes onscreen. She
pulls back in alarm, asks of the white women, *Why do they all look
the same?*

You say, with a shrug, *Fillers?*

Your lover moved to America at twelve years old. She can smell
in the air the moment the seams of a season give way—when a
new sky is ready to undress the last one and begin. She is uninter-
ested in whiteness. She asks you what fillers are and how you
know.

You were raised to know. Your aunties gave you nose clips,
eyelid tape, bleaching cream. Your mother has been under the
knives.

YOUR LOVER SAYS TO YOU, again, again, that the first time she saw you, in that beige and rust locker room, the air stung through with disinfectant, the first time she saw you, she says, *time stopped.* All she saw was you.

This was eight years ago. You were young and held yourself behind glass. She approached you to introduce herself with a directness so unlike you. She has a face like the sun over the treetops at noon: She can look and see and see you. By the bank of lockers, her face fixed on yours, you hesitated before undressing. That day, you noticed her, enough, not at all like she noticed you. What you remember most is not her face but your grip on your towel and your damp, flushed body you were in the habit of being alone with.

IN THE HOTEL ROOM, SHE kisses you, her mouth a borderland of yes.

Yes, lantern skin, yes, party laugh, yes, collarbones exposed like ledges you could grip or dive from. You press your face, hard, against her throat.

The sex with her is so good you avoid remembering it in public because it knocks your head back to think of it. The newness in her stare every time she sees you naked, the way everything church vacates her face, and she looks at you, wild, like no one else gets to see her, and her mouth opens, wanting. You give her your favorite view of you, and there is your cum all over her belly. You drag two fingers through the slick and say, I've made a mess. She says, Good, without blinking.

SHE IS THE FIRST PERSON to eat you out on your period. When she does it for the first time, laying a towel underneath you, you say, in your straight girl voice, *You don't have to. I'm good.* Between your legs, she says, *It's not for you. It's for me.*

You watch her, her eyes closed, paying reverence, glory glory, to your cunt, for hours. On your period, your skin thins to charged translucence, every lick heightened. When she slips her tongue inside you and fills you with just the slightest vibration, you lose yourself and lose yourself until your inversion feels unbearable. You inch your hips back, and understanding, she stays still, her tongue out: invitation, request. Her eyes stay closed, and she is, since the morning you first saw her under your gym's wide sky-light, fuck-you-up beautiful, and you grind your clit against her wet tongue. Her lips are full and always melting-soft from almond oil, and when she senses your grinding quicken, she wraps her lips around your clit and begins to suck. You cum again and again and again and again. With sex, with her, somehow you are always first to say you're done. She lies down next to you.

You say, *Was that okay?*

She holds you to her, her torso a bolt of silk, says, *Your body's intoxicating.*

THIS HAPPENS MONTHLY. WHEN YOU are on your period and she wants you, she eats you out because she wants to: *Just let me have a little taste.*

When you tell a friend this, your friend yells, That's weird! She's so weird! And you cry so hard your friend cries too from realizing she hurt you.

You get it, why someone would think it was weird. On your period, your cunt has a different voltage, a box cutter to a tongue. In high school, girls made bets about you; you would pretend not to hear. Lovers in your twenties refused to touch you then, refused to be touched by you.

But isn't that the gods in this, gods of jasmine storms and thrashing wings. Isn't she what the skies surrendered.

Call this good.

No one has ever loved your body, like your body is complete. The tip of your tongue licks right where her mouth parts, the light divot of a summer plum. She kisses the dark briny patch on your armpit, braids her ankles with yours.

Desperate for a Good Time

CORINNE MANNING

❦

Clarice Manzella was handsome, clever, and exhausted. She more-or-less embodied the standard privileges and difficulties of a white-socialized queer; she had a comfortable home but was too often expected to shirk pay or accept less pay as a form of quasi-activism. In nearly thirty-two years of life, she had perfected her sense of what should distress and vex her and learned to express it in a way deemed correct by the internet. It was the fifth month of the plague's quarantine, and Clarice and her friends had arrived at a new understanding: *One cannot be expected to stay at home forever.*

First, she took a bike trip with her best friend, camping on another friend's farm on Vashon Island. This friend did not own the land but stewarded it for a local nonprofit. The wheat and rye fields were in full golden sway as the three sat together, each nibbling the end of a stalk.

"A lot of people here are secret libertarians," her farmer friend said. "They don't want any social programs. They want to get ahead and believe it's from their own sweat. At the board meeting, I stood up and said we should start taking down monuments to the pioneer families and replace them with markers of what really went down here. You know what they said to me? 'Those families are still on the island, and it would really hurt their feelings, because it's not their fault.'"

"Piss on that," Clarice's friend said.

"We built this city," Clarice began to sing. "We built this city without our boooooones."

The farmer continued.

"I know that actual stewardship means having a relationship to the land like my ancestors did, but working here? For what they pay me and how they treat me? I just feel the colonial knife of England and how none of us are meant to toil for potatoes. When did my ancestors last have an authentic relationship to the land? Do I even keep farming?"

Clarice knew this version of thinking through European colonization. Her family came from Italians, so far south that if the current was right, you could get your boat to Tunisia. The Italian Catholic family she came from didn't tolerate many things about her "lifestyle," so they were a far-off distance from her day-to-day. But she thought about her great-grandparents often, who died when she was seven. They were sharecroppers on an estate owned by a Northern Italian who always kept them in debt. "You can't eat the scenery," her great-grandfather said of where they came from, and was proud of saying that he spit on Italy.

"It sucked everything from me, like a vampire," he said. "I spit the poison out. I start fresh."

"Right," the farmer friend said. "I don't want to just be another vampire on this land."

THAT NIGHT, CAMPING ON THE farm, Clarice had a dream. It was the Washington Coast: evergreens and beach grass and a cloud hanging over everything like a specter. In the dream, a

beautiful woman with long black hair—resembling everyone in
Clarice's family, with the Juicy velour suit to match—climbed
into her tent and wrapped her arms around Clarice. Her eyes were
a brown so dark that their warmth suffused Clarice's whole body.
The velour was wildly soft and soon the mystery woman unzipped
her hoodie and said, "My tits are man-made, want to feel them?"
She brought Clarice's hand to the side of the tissue where she
could feel the implant's hard ridge. Clarice's clit swelled. She
grunted, reaching to pull the mystery woman's hair, and put her
lips to her neck, but the woman pulled Clarice's head away with
one firm nape tug.

The woman's nails were long and pointed with little jewels on
the tips of some of them, and they pierced into Clarice's skull. The
Misfits song "Skull" blared, *I want your skull, I need your skull,*
and she woke up screaming, her hands squeezing her head. A
truck playing the song pealed down the road at the edge of the
farm, but the pain in her head continued. She turned on her lamp,
ran her hands over her head, and felt something squiggling and
alive. She pulled: a flat brown tick, its little wiggly parts kicking
at the air.

"FUCK YOU!" she shouted as she smashed it with a book, and
then burst into tears. Lyme disease. Was her life over? Her friend
in the other tent woke up wondering what the noise was about.
They googled pictures of ticks until they found a website that said
this one wouldn't give her Lyme disease, because it was a female.
A female tick is less likely to carry Lyme than a male.

"A lesbian tick," her friend said, trying to make her feel better.

The dream stayed with Clarice in the way sex dreams and
nightmares tend to, with no relief. All she could think for days
after that was *go to Long Beach, Washington.* The Pacific coast with
its evergreens; the waves crashing at Cape Disappointment. She
closed her eyes and heard the Misfits' riff as she looked at the

Pacific Ocean extending out forever. Her fingertips felt the edge of the implants.

A WEEK LATER, SHE WENT for it. Clarice packed up the car and drove to the coast. She played the song on repeat and really listened to the lyrics, which were gross: young men getting off on the death of little girls. The turn to the hipster trailer park appeared, and in the distance, she could see the foggy roll of the Pacific Ocean.

Clarice parked the car and looked in the rearview mirror, pulling on her cloth face mask. She saw the familiar profiles of queers: one Black with her long dreads in a ponytail, the other white-appearing with straight sandy hair loose except where the mask tightened it to her head. They both wore all black washed to a faded gray: jean shorts that cuffed tight just above the knee, and tight muscle tanks that hugged their rolls and bloomed desire in Clarice. She got out, hoping they might see her too, but they were already climbing into an attractively beat-up purple Saturn.

"Protect me from what I want," she muttered to herself and started to make her way to her trailer.

Just as she grabbed her suitcase from the car, she saw someone. No, she didn't just see someone; she *saw* this person in that special way that a dyke *sees someone*. Long dark hair divided in two braids. Lashes curled on a round face—potentially round, from what Clarice could imagine under the mask, which had neon geometric designs. And then the person *saw* Clarice: A glance of acknowledgment followed by a purposeful, slow gaze. Clarice was suffused with the glow of recognition and a jolt of something like fear. In the Before Times, Clarice might have been able to smell the woman as she walked by: sunblock, shampoo, animal. But at six feet apart and through her own mask, Clarice just smelled the carbon filter, clean and reassuring.

. . .

AFTER A DREAMLESS NIGHT OF sleep, Clarice woke and rode her bike along the Discovery path, a memorial to Lewis and Clark's trail. She didn't even know whose land she was on, she realized. She pedaled between the Pacific, which crashed in riptide zigzags just to the west, and a line of some kind of evergreen trees—all the same height, planted after what must have been devastating logging—to the east. The path broke across the road, then began again in the woods as she climbed up the hill that would become the cliff of Cape Disappointment. Just another instance, she thought, where settlers named a beautiful thing in relation to how the land resisted them.

She pulled up her mask whenever she saw someone approaching, but no one else wore a mask. Some glared at her in a way that she could only interpret as being related to guilt and shame. She pedaled harder and wound her way up the spiraling tar path: an old wooden water tower, a concrete foundation with a window buried partially in the ground like a hobbit hole. She'd seen this before at Port Townsend—typical sign of an abandoned military fort in the Pacific Northwest. There was a sheen of sweat and sunscreen on her skin. Her arm hair, bleached from the sun, glinted. She got off her bike and rolled it over to a historical marker. The bunker was intended as a strategic outpost during World War II, but the soldiers stationed there experienced weeks of nonstop gales and other fearsome weather.

"What could be fearsome about the weather of the Northwest?" Clarice muttered sarcastically into her mask and imagined soldiers shivering against slanted rain, or dodging branches from giant cedar trees, broken by the wind. The bunker in front of her looked like the condominiums people were building in Seattle, square and a confusing number of levels, no color.

A crunching sound on the gravel path startled her.

A family of blonds approached, red-faced, maskless except for the father who wore a mask pulled down below his drooping nose. They looked at her with angry impatience, their eyes darting to the bunker. *It's our turn*, their gaze seemed to say. The Aryan mass crowded closer and watched her. She reached for her bike and tightened her shoulders to push past the bodies, these maskless faces—the cloth on her nose and mouth protecting them from her. She would have pedaled away and left them in the dust if she hadn't heard a collective gasp.

When she looked back, she wasn't sure what she was seeing. Down on the lowest level of the bunker, there was a body crawling impossibly flat to the ground, black hair spreading like a lake. Was this just someone slipping out of the underground window after exploring the bunker? A trick of the eye: a body looking flat and then refilling. But then there was that woman with the braids, suddenly emerging from below and walking toward the crowd, body full and upright. A shadow trick.

Perhaps the family isn't gasping at a ghostly spectacle after all, Clarice thought, *but at the sight of another dyke.* The father and his lookalike son practically jumped to clear the way for the woman as she stepped between them. Her eyes, endless in depth, met Clarice's.

"I know you," Clarice blurted behind her mask. She hoped the mask made what she said inaudible, made it sound like a cough.

"I know you too," the stranger said. Clarice bit her tongue to keep herself from clarifying that she knew this woman from a dream. That would sound thirsty, and the truth was they probably had seen each other before—at some Portland dance party in her years of heavy drinking, or in pictures from some mutual's Instagram account—thus the woman's uncannily accurate appearance in Clarice's dream.

"Oh, community," Clarice said clear enough for anyone to hear. But both sets of eyes stayed steadied on the other.

Clarice had been alive and gay long enough to know the consequences of this kind of look. She was hit with conflicting thoughts: *We're gonna fall in love, it's gonna be a whole thing,* mixed with the fear of *if I don't move fast enough, we won't fall in love, we won't have a whole thing.* There was also something else creeping up inside of her, something like hunger that would be pleasurable if it weren't for the cold cramping of her guts. Fear of the inevitable ending? Desire to prolong the good part? The stranger looked away and walked to the lookout. Clarice watched her body in motion for a moment, and then followed to the top.

A LARGE WOODEN DECK LOOKED out over the ocean. On a marker, there was an old picture of the coastline, the way it looked before the jetty was put in. It was difficult to compare the picture and the actual view. Whatever was once there had been eaten up. She focused on the map for Dead Man's Cove and leaned a little to look at the real thing below. The woman from her dream mirrored her, leaning on the post six feet away.

"Do you know that's called Dead Man's Cove?" Clarice asked.

"Isn't that great and creepy?" There were lines that indicated decades of smiles around the woman's eyes, hinting at her age, though there were no streaks of silver in her hair yet. "If you read that whole sign it talks about how bodies of sailors used to just wash ashore. You couldn't see every ship that crashed, so body after body would appear after a storm like dead fish."

Clarice wanted to ask who was finding these bodies back then, and whether finding them was a relief or foreboding, but she hesitated—this person didn't know her or trust her, and it was possible that what she was thinking was highly colonial. Clarice paused so long considering this, tense and motionless, that the stranger cleared her throat. As Clarice met her gaze, the woman tightened her braid, her fingers moving fast like scurrying tick legs.

"See you around," she said, appearing to float down the hill.

It was disappointing, Clarice thought, but this stranger whom she may or may not have dreamed up was just a person. And would fade fast enough. She once had a crush on someone who worked at the organic market—loved to ask him for help in the produce aisle. Then, when presented with the perfect moment to ask for his number, she didn't; quickly the sparkle and opportunity were gone. Fantasies dissolve. Clarice wasn't here to have sex anyway. She was here for solitude. She was here for the beach. This is what this land and its visit could provide for her, she reminded herself. But all the rational thinking in the world couldn't stop her from getting back on her bike to see if she could find the stranger on the trail. Like most things that Clarice wanted, the woman had vanished.

CLARICE WOKE THE NEXT DAY tired and disturbed. A dream had rolled endlessly through her mind all night long, as she woke briefly then slipped back into the same world over and over, like a TV marathon. Her ex told her about a channel that started playing *Beverly Hills, 90210* from midnight to 7:00 a.m., when the pandemic began, and she had been watching all night recently, sleeping during the day and getting her work done in a frantic rush in the last few hours before the show started. But this dream was a series of senseless images: bodies washing ashore, fake breasts, a pulse to cum, the rain. A figure huddled against a tree by a bunker, damp to the bone and unfolding like an accordion, coming toward her. Again and again, until she finally got up, too haunted to sleep.

The sun came out at 11:00 a.m. with a glare, and Clarice made her way to the beach. The sand burned her feet; she liked this.

Since living in the Northwest, her feet had become too tender and vulnerable. She dug them into the sand, the top of her feet burning as she read. When it became too much, she cursed, pulled them out for a moment, and then buried them again.

She'd left her phone at the trailer, so whenever she got bored of reading, she people watched instead. A dad slept while a mom and son kicked a soccer ball back and forth. A straight couple and their two children came running from the water with surfboards. They all stripped from their wet suits. Clarice accidentally saw the kids' small hairless scrotums before the family climbed naked into their Jeep.

Then—as in a dream, when you think of something and it appears—there was the stranger. She wore a turquoise bathing suit that zipped in the front, and her black hair was long and loose behind her. She didn't appear to see Clarice, turning her back to the beach and stomping her way into the ocean. There was a long shelf, so the few people willing to deal with the cold summer Washington ocean were able to go out far, the water still at their knees despite signs that warned about riptides. The stranger eventually dove in, probably skirting the sea floor with her belly and thighs, and swam parallel to the shore. Clarice had to pee, but she didn't want to just head to the water because the stranger was right there. She waited until the stranger was down the shore a bit before she stepped onto the cool, wet sand. Once the water reached her calves, she looked to the horizon and released her bladder. Her suit crotch filled with fluid, warm and sexual, before it began to drip down her leg as clear as the Pacific. The water reflected light like paparazzi bulbs, and the waves hit crooked against her leg.

As a child listening to *Love Line* on Z100, Clarice heard a teenage boy call in because he was worried about his crooked penis. How would he have sex? "It's fine," the host said. "You might just have to lift your leg a little." The ocean didn't have to do that, Clarice mused. It could slap her at whatever angle it wanted.

There was a brief sound before she saw the physical flailing: A scream gulped up by the wind, then drowned by crying seagulls. Clarice scanned the water to find movement and was certain: there was a person out there in need of help. She saw a few onlookers stand up from their blankets, but they did not move any closer to the ocean.

As Clarice approached, she realized with a shock that the flailing person was the stranger. She was lifting her arms in the air and then getting swallowed by the water, repeatedly. It was almost sexual, the waves spasming around her body. *The ocean's so wet.* Clarice shook off the thought and charged toward her.

The stranger had gotten tired. It's what riptides do. As a child Clarice had learned that you swim parallel to the shore during a riptide. Sometimes people get so exhausted, they can't find their feet under them again. The stranger popped up enough to swing her arms and legs around before sinking, and Clarice caught her by the back of her bathing suit just as she was about to be drawn out. It all moved slowly for Clarice, despite the urgency, her eyes focused on the stranger: The water in her hair that was now tangled over the front of the face, a triad of cherry angiomas on her clavicle, the strong fighting arms, her torso's rolls and ripples, the crease where the thighs met the pelvis. The woman was delirious and couldn't hear Clarice telling her to stand.

Clarice rotated the stranger onto her back and held her firmly, one hand on her midback and the other hand on her diaphragm.

"I've got you," Clarice said. The stranger's mouth dropped open and Clarice could see the gaps between her teeth—she hadn't had braces. One of her incisors was slightly twisted, and one tooth had come in through the top of the gums and not at the gum line. The woman who had been playing soccer with her son came out with a blue foam boogie board. The stranger was able to put her hands on the board and feel her feet under her. They all made their way to shore.

WHEN YOU'RE ON VACATION, SO much can happen in a day. Saving a stranger, sitting with her while the water evaporates off her skin. Giving her your water bottle during a pandemic. Sharing your lunch. Seeing her for the first time without her mask.

"I don't know your name," Clarice said, even though they were now in a pod due to the stranger's mouth on her water bottle and their hands in the same bag of chips. The new U-Haul.

"Angela," she said. Her eyes weren't as bright when her mask was off, but her cheekbones were broader than Clarice had imagined, her cheeks rounder. Clarice watched Angela drink from her bottle and wondered if she still needed to listen to the panic and urgency running through her body. Maybe she's already mine, she thought, breathing deeply to calm her nervous system. Yes, they already belonged to each other. She could feel it. On the other hand, Clarice had been disappointed before.

TIME CAN STOP FOR WOULD-BE lovers but continue moving for the rest of the world. Angela and Clarice locked into the thrumming stillness of their vortex, and soon the sky was pink.

"Damn, girl, time just flies with you." Angela said. She bit her own lip gently as if she was posing for a thirst trap, but there was no phone screen anywhere near them. The only lens was Clarice's own eyes. *Remember this*, she thought.

"Is it okay to call you girl?" Angela asked.

"Yes," Clarice said, her heart swooping like a bat. "Thank you. What about you?"

"Call me whatever you want." Angela's chilled fingers touched Clarice's shoulder for effect. "You must be hungry."

"You must be cold," Clarice said.

"I'm always cold." Then she smiled a little. "And I'm always hungry."

"Want to come back to my trailer for tea?" Clarice pictured them with incredible clarity, sitting closer than they were now, the sunset melting around them.

"I have things to do tonight," Angela said. "But can I see you again tomorrow?"

THAT DELICIOUS FEELING IN THE stomach and chest, that mix of joy and dread! The rush for something to happen, and the terror that once it happens, we will be so much closer to the end. Clarice felt all of it in her tiny trailer, and then in her tiny shower with the slow stream of scalding water rinsing sand from her body. She cut vegetables and imagined cutting them for Angela. The knife slicing down down down down on the carrot. Disc, disc, disc, disc. She found herself narrating in her mind for Angela. *The shower stream is thin but scalding. Don't you love the rhythm of the knife into the vegetables?* She even wanted to tell her, as the knife pierced her finger, about the bloom of blood that rushed from the wound. The image of the sink as the faucet spiraled blood down the drain. The metallic taste of her blood mixed with the sulphureous well water as she searched for a Band-Aid in her toiletry case, her left finger clamped tightly between her lips. Outside, the sunset was a lozenge dissolving in a mouth.

CLARICE TUSSLED ALL NIGHT. SHE dreamed of pulling back sheets to find ticks crawling all over the bed. Then Angela's breast in her mouth, the other pushing against her cheek as she pulled the nipple. Long sharp nails drumming on her skull, but the sound like them clicking over a phone screen, like syncopated tapping on a door. *Tip, tip, tip.* The dream dissolved *tip, tip, tip.*

The wind rushed against the trailer. The ocean, just a little closer, crashed. *Tip, tip, tip.* A clicking at the door. It was a clicking at the door. Clarice's clit pulsed with the rhythm, and she felt terrified about opening the door and finding Angela there, getting to fold that soft body into her own sleepy warmth. *Tip, tip, tip.*

Clarice pulled herself from sleep. She stumbled as she walked to the door and caught herself against the trailer's fake wood paneling. She opened the door and only the night waited for her. The main lodge's porch light. A smattering of stars. It was a new moon night, a bit too cloudy. Another clatter against the door as she held it open and then she saw: Her own keys left in the lock.

WHEN CLARICE STEPPED OUT OF her trailer that next morning, feeling a bit tortured, she saw someone beautiful sitting at the picnic table outside her trailer.

"Good morning," Angela said, dragging the tip of a nail file under her nails—black polish—and wiping the gunk off on her thigh. She wore all black again, and everything hugged her a little tighter. She wore smoky eye makeup like it was the early aughts, and her hair was loose and thick around her body.

"Don't worry, I'm really good at fucking with these."

"What?" Clarice said.

"I'm joking," she said and tucked the nail file into her bra.

"That looks dangerous."

"Hmm . . ." Angela's brown eyes looked like they could swallow Clarice. "Might be dangerous that I'm in a pandemic pod with someone I don't know."

"Not really that dangerous."

"You thinking it could be more dangerous?" And here Angela's smile returned. They both waited a few moments for Clarice to say more. Finally, Angela climbed out from behind the picnic table.

"Can I show you something?"

They walked to the edge of the property, past the collection of rusty bikes. Clarice's heart beat like she'd had too much caffeine. A force pumped through her, life-giving and so painful. She walked next to Angela trying not to seem drunk, trying to seem like she didn't care if their skin touched. But not only did Clarice need their skin to touch, she needed some sort of release. She wondered earnestly if her head would explode when they finally kissed. That's when she saw where Angela was bringing her: a rusty car parked in the woods just before the edge of the beach.

It was probably from the fifties—it had those wide headlights and sleek curves and frame, but the texture was rough. Just from a glance, Clarice could tell how the car would feel. She rubbed her fingers together imagining the sensation on her hands. How easily the rust would cut. The windows and windshield were all blown out. The leather seats were flaked like old bound books. Angela, apparently unafraid of what her hands touched, opened a creaking car door. Clarice took this opportunity to cruise the woman's hands; they were veiny and strong and tan. The fingers were short, and she could see how this hand could slip inside her, even with the nails. She could feel this wrist at the opening of her. Angela snapped her head toward her the way a crow might. This time Clarice did not shy away from Angela but looked into her eyes the way she did in the dream, her own gaze soft. She was able to feel into her whole body. Angela could see in if she wanted.

There was that delicious stillness, a moment of relief, until Angela turned her head and the tension resumed again. Angela sat down in the driver's seat and leaned over to open the side door.

"Get in."

Clarice slipped in next to her, feeling familiarity, like they had driven this car together, like she was always meant to be sitting next to Angela in a car. Like she could lean her head against the doorframe and just fall asleep while Angela drove, waking to Angela's lips on her cheek when they arrived home.

The doors stayed open. Clarice stared out the windshield at the trees in front of them, the rest of the junk and trash on the ground. Angela leaned over her and snapped open the glove box. Snakes spilled out.

"The fuck!" Clarice leaped from the car, snakes still slipping over her wrists. They writhed in a pile, rolling like the sea on the rusty car floor. She was shaking, her own skin crawling. The wet sensation of those snakes on her skin, the unusual way they moved, unusual to feel on her own body. They were so cold, and she was so warm, and the contrast made her feel like they wanted something from her.

"Or do you want something from them?" Angela asked. Her eyes, Clarice swore, were completely black. But then she blinked a few times, laughed, and the bright dark brown reappeared.

"Girl," Angela said. "Honey, come here. They are rubber. See?" She picked one up and held it out and Clarice took a step away. It dangled limp and heavy between Angela's long sharp nails. She somehow had missed a detail about those hands: Each pinkie nail had a single white gem. Clarice stepped on a snake, and it squeaked.

"I'm not into that kind of shit," Clarice said.

"I'm sorry," Angela said, still smiling but remorse true in her voice. "I grew up with brothers. I'm kind of a practical joker."

Was this actually kind of romantic, though? A hint of a smile tugged at Clarice's mouth, and Angela looked at her hopefully. Clarice uncrossed her arms.

"So you came out to this car—last night? This morning?— filled the glove box with snakes, and then brought me here."

Angela thought about it and tentatively nodded her head.

"And the whole time you were setting this up, what did you—I mean, were you feeling, like, excited or something?"

"Well, yeah. Excited and something else."

And now, somehow, Angela was out of the car. There had been no perceivable movement between her sitting there seconds ago, and now standing in front of Clarice. She stepped even closer, the front of their shirts at the brink of touching, the fibers twisting toward each other. They were sharing molecules, droplets. Clarice could feel the air pressure change with Angela so close. She could see a small clump of mascara in her eyelashes, a wayward eyebrow hair. Clarice lifted her hand, which was not sanitized, and used the pinky to fix the hair that was curling down toward Angela's right eye, gently brushing it in line with the others. She rested her hand on Angela's cheek. They pressed together in this way, Clarice increasing the pressure against Angela's face and Angela pressing her face into Clarice's hand. Angela's face was cool, and it felt good, and Clarice absorbed her energy until they were the same temperature and there was no difference between where Angela's skin and Clarice's own palm began.

Clarice clutched Angela's hand as she led her back to the trailer. Angela's pace was slower, lagging a step or two behind, but Clarice didn't look back. She felt assured by the eagerness of the hand she felt in hers. Still, Clarice was surprised when Angela squeezed her hand a few times, rapidly, creating a vibration like the quick movements of a cat tail. Clarice squeezed a steady pulse back. They were getting away from something—or away with something—she could feel it. As if that old car was some gateway from the underworld. Clarice didn't quite have the language yet to say that they were rescuing each other, but climactic scenes from various horror movies flickered through her mind. This was the moment; to hesitate now would be too much like splitting up when a killer with a chainsaw was on the loose, or going down the dark cellar steps while the audience screams *no*.

Clarice only let go of Angela's hand when they arrived at the trailer. She bumbled inside, pulled her shirt over her head, reached impatiently for Angela. When her shirt hit the floor and she opened her eyes, she was surprised to see Angela standing outside. There was heat somehow, in the trailer, as if they were standing right next to each other. As if Angela's skin was there. But her skin wasn't there, and Clarice was done with the theoretical.

"I need your skin right here."

"Ask nicely," Angela said.

"Please bring your skin here."

"You're being rude."

"I said please."

"You missed a step," Angela said, sitting casually at the picnic table now, as if the situation wasn't urgent. Despite the teasing, her gaze on Clarice's body was much warmer than her cheek had felt in Clarice's palm.

"You need an invitation? Please come in," Clarice said. "My home is your home. Entrez-vous?"

And Angela's lips were on hers again. Clarice's hand crawled under Angela's shirt, palming the ribs and then dragging her blunt nails along them.

"Your skin is so cold," Clarice whispered.

"It's too much, isn't it?" Angela twitched and took a small step backward, away from Clarice. "We can keep my clothes on if it's too weird for you."

"Are you kidding me?" Clarice pulled Angela close again, over-come with the desire to fold her into her own body, to envelope her. She wanted to share every bit of her heat with Angela.

And then, it was on—firm touch, light touch. Hands clawed the scruff at the back of the neck. Hips bucked. A smell like cake rose around them.

They spent at least one fevered hour with the top half of the body, before one brave hand pulled a zipper down. Urgency. Shorts kicking off. Thigh to thigh. One temperature.

"Your smell is everywhere," Clarice moaned. Knees wet. Tops of the thighs wet. Hands sunk in.

"Fuck," Angela said. Her whole body moved with her arm. When it's new, how do you choose just one thing to do?

"I want," Clarice said, flipping Angela over. Mouth at the crease of the underwear and the thigh. A tongue can move the elastic to the side, but she just drank from the fibers, sucked in anything of Angela she could taste. She pushed her face deeper, gripped the top of Angela's thighs with her hand. Then a new sensation, like a latch and sucking, sucking, sucking on her own clit. Even though Angela's mouth was nowhere near that part of her body.

Clarice wondered if she was just being empathetic—there had been times when she was going down on someone and felt like she could come from it. She stilled her mouth for a moment. The latch and sucking sensation continued, though with less intensity.

"Do you like it?" Angela asked. "Is it too weird?"

"Who are you," Clarice murmured, then pressed her face back in, dug her nails back into Angela's thighs. Angela was in her nose, in her mouth, so salty that she was salivating and somehow the latch grew stronger on her own body, the sucking more insistent. And soon Clarice was the one coming and writhing, her mouth on Angela as she bucked and was swiftly released.

CLARICE LOVED WHEN THIS HAPPENED after: the stunned silence. Their bodies were close, their breathing even, bodies resting in the silent agreement of completion. Clarice was starting to doze when Angela's voice, soft and golden, roused her.

"You liked it?" Angela asked.

Clarice laughed aloud. "Are you serious right now?" She propped herself on an elbow to look at Angela's face; tears shimmered in her eyes.

"Oh, you're very serious," Clarice said. She pulled Angela against her, as tight as possible, so that her face rested in her neck. "It was like nothing I've ever felt. It's so hard for me to really be there, but that wasn't the case with you. You're stunning."

Angela laughed at this. "Sorry for the tears. I think I'm just feeling self-conscious after the whole snake thing. I don't want to keep getting the vibe wrong. And in bed, I can be kind of . . . I can be kind of a monster."

Clarice touched her lips gently to Angela's then said. "I wish all of it could happen again."

WHAT IS THE SLEEP THAT comes at dawn? Heavy like an end, then a shock: awake. Clarice gasped and sat up much faster than her own body was ready for. She saw little worm shapes in her vision. The sun was bright, and it was midafternoon. Angela was gone. Her shape still in the sheets. Ocean sounds.

She was so thirsty, her throat burned like there was smoke in the air. *Wait, was there smoke?* She gulped a glass of water and looked out the window. There was a haze in the air. She drank another glass, then put her mouth to the faucet. Her belly bloated with fluid.

She didn't have Angela's number and didn't know what trailer she was in. *I guess I'll find her?* They were in a pod now, after all.

She put her mask on to go outside, and it felt efficient to have this double use—against a virus and against smoke. Her eyes burned, the air was textured on her skin. *Where was the wind? Where was Angela?*

Her walk to the ocean was labored, and she felt nauseous. There was no horizon, or somehow the horizon had come closer. She didn't see any cars or people. It was hot and sticky, so she walked to the water and stripped off her clothes. There were a few purple marks on her skin from the night before. She felt hung over, like all the moisture had been leached from her. The air sat on top of the salt water like smoke blown into a wine glass. She trudged in and bellied down. The tide was out so she rolled in the weak surf; the ocean's energy drawing away from her. Her stomach turned. She rested on her hands and knees, gagged and gagged, and finally her throat opened and out with the water she drank came a small ball of wet sand. She shivered. Spit more bile. Her throat burned where the sand had scraped out, and there was more in her teeth that crunched when she clenched her jaw. There was something shiny poking out from the clump of sand, the stuff that'd come from her throat—a shell, a bit of bone? She was already revolted, so there was no new revulsion as she pressed her fingers into it. It was round and iridescent . . . and bloody? No, purple. In her hand was a dark pearl.

SHE WAS SICK. BACK IN her trailer she sipped water, then just spit it up again. She tried a tiny bite of cracker, but that was wrong too. She dozed in and out of sleep, clutching the pearl in her hand, waking with a start thinking she'd dropped it. She felt a fever behind her eyes, while the pearl stayed cool. She rolled it over her forehead.

Angela, Angela, she thought. *Angela, Angela.* And then a quiet tapping on the door.

Clarice fell into Angela's arms.

"Oh, honey," Angela said. "Oh darlin', you're like a thousand degrees."

How cool and soft and endless Angela's body felt.

"Baby girl, come on, let's get you back to bed."

All these pet names, Clarice thought. Angela wrapped around her, their legs tangled, and despite the illness, desire rose in Clarice. Her hips thrusted forward and back gently. Angela held her tighter.

"I found this," Clarice said, and she put the pearl into Angela's hand. She didn't want to say that she spit it up. That felt way too vulnerable, and she wasn't ready to be a body that did body things around Angela, fucking aside.

What was this look on Angela's face—worry, fear? She wasn't trying to hide it the way Clarice did: a flash of emotion and then a straight face, an empty face. Was this disgust, the way that line between her brows creased, the way her bottom jaw shifted briefly in an underbite? Clarice hated it when someone asked what her own facial expressions were about—hence the skill at hiding them—so she wouldn't do this to Angela.

"I was mad at my mom this one time," Angela said. "Well, not the only time, but this time in particular. And she used to collect all these pearls. She had someone who would dive for her and she would pry the shells open herself and collect the pearls in a box that she kept next to her in bed. At night sometimes I'd go into the room, and I would see her running her hands through the pearls. I was so mad at her this one day that I swallowed them all. First one by one, and then I wanted to feel five, six at a time rolling down my throat. She searched my shit for a week but she never found them."

She took the pearl and rolled it back and forth across Clarice's forehead. Then she brought it to the sternum and rolled it down the bone, around Clarice's tits.

"Why were you mad at her?" Clarice asked.

"She made me get on a ship again."

"What kind of ship?"

"A kind that does bad things. Open your mouth." She put her hand around Clarice's throat, and Clarice obeyed. Angela dropped the pearl in and held Clarice's jaw shut like she was a cat.

"Fucking swallow," Angela said. And Clarice, rocked by terror and pleasure, did as she was told. The sea gathered between her legs.

"That's my baby," Angela said. "That's my baby girl."

One finger, two, skip to four, yes the thumb.

"You're gonna open for me, baby," she said. "Show mommy how good you are."

"Fuck," Clarice growled as Angela's hand slipped in, the fingers finding their place in a closed fist. Suction on either side. *Who was drinking who?* Clarice felt like she could swallow Angela's arm, her muscles pulsing and clenching like a giant snake and its slow swallow. And yet there was this opposite feeling, as Angela gently tracked the muscles in her arm back and then forward like she was drawing everything out of Clarice, including an orgasm that felt like an emptying, a spilling, a loss of form, a terror, a hole full of pearls and then done and then a limp fist and then an unraveling and her body was her own again. Angela's hand rested on Clarice's thigh, fingers curled together, stiff and tired. Angela's mouth rested on Clarice's hip. She tongued the skin. Clarice thought, *I'm in love.* Angela looked up at her and smiled. Slipped up her body and kissed Clarice like she loved her too.

"Did something bad happen to you on the bad ship?" Clarice asked, but all she was really thinking was *love you, love you, love you.* They were getting away with something. They were surviving together. Angela curled into her neck, brought the sheet up around them.

"Something bad happened to all of us, which was good."

CLARICE WOKE AGAIN TO ANGELA gone. The smoke so thick in the sky, the light was purple, and she couldn't tell whether the sun was rising or setting. Her throat hurt. Water from the tap tasted gross. She was tired. Her bones hurt. She opened the trailer door and the air smelled like burn. Ash dusted the picnic tables. She closed herself back inside, woozy, turned to the bed, and pulled the sheet back.

A legion of small ticks spilled onto the floor, writhed on the bed like it was their own sea.

Her brain flashed a series of strangely familiar images before she could process what was happening in front of her. Snakes. Gems on black nails, blood in the sink. Latch and suck. Dark cellar stairs. Angela flailing in the ocean. And now—a bed full of ticks. Clarice screamed, but there was no one to come running in response. She'd only ever screamed like that once, at a haunted house when an animatronic person getting electrocuted turned out to be a real person, who jumped forward and stopped just short of touching her. These ticks had no such restraint.

She ran from the trailer, shaking and crying, energy suddenly a force through her body. She pounded on the glass door to the front desk. She didn't have a mask. Someone came out of the back and mouthed to her: *Put on your mask.*

Help, Clarice mouthed, no sound coming from her mouth.

Mask, the person mouthed back. They looked at each other.

"My bed is full of bugs," Clarice said in as loud a voice as she could. The person on the other side of the glass tilted their head.

"Stand back," they finally said. And Clarice stepped far away, more than six feet. The person emerged with a vacuum and a fabric mask. They put it on the end of the vacuum's attachment and extended it to Clarice.

"The fires are so bad, Portland is evacuating," the attendant said, as they rolled the vacuum behind them. "We're letting people come camp here for free."

"Is it better here?" Clarice asked.

"Wait outside," the attendant said. Clarice waited for the scream but there was none, just the sucking sound of the vacuum and then a sickly pallor as the attendant emerged.

"That was fucking crazy," the attendant said. "Could probably get you a 10 percent discount or something."

"Can you put me in another trailer?"

"We're all booked, otherwise I totally would. Also it's like such a process to clean things right now, so it would be a help to us if you either stayed here or went home. Like I said, I could get some money knocked off."

"There are so many bugs on that bed, it was roiling."

"Not anymore," the attendant said and tapped the vacuum. Clarice studied this person's eyes, but didn't see smile lines or brightness or any glee. What was happening under that mask?

"Considering what's going on," they motioned to the masks between them and then pointed above to the smoky air, "it's really not a big deal."

CLARICE WANDERED, COUGHING, ACHING, IN search of Angela. She thought about all the things she didn't know about this person she was probably falling in love with: What trailer she was in, what her last name was, her birth date, if she had any siblings, was she an aunt? A parent? How many cats? Was she from Alaska? Who else had experience being on ships, let alone "bad ones"? Had she ever seen a wolf?

The smoke was getting worse, and even clogged the air of the trailer despite its closed everything. Giving up on her search for the moment, Clarice made a meal of whatever was left in the fridge—rice noodles and vegetables, clippings of smoked salmon. There was one night left in her stay here, and she and Angela hadn't even eaten together. Then it hit her: It was about to be over. And the awareness rocked her like a legion of bugs were under her feet, a riptide carrying her out and away from the meal she was cooking. Her panic was a sweat that started in her lower back and dripped down her legs. What if she didn't come back tonight? Oh God, she hadn't thought of that. No, no, that's nuts, because she swallowed a pearl for her, and Clarice remembered how Angela looked at her when that happened. Wasn't there security in that primal look of wanting?

Clarice sighed. People had disappeared after greater things.

Was there anything greater anymore? She wanted Angela to be her Alaskan girlfriend, her pandemic love, her pod. She'd swallow anything to make that happen.

She swallowed the salmon, the vegetables, the noodles, the broth. Something wasn't right. The texture of the food was too sharp, and with every swallow it became more and more difficult. She kept adding salt, and then hot sauce, but there was no flavor, everything tasting like some kind of sodium-free Play-Doh. She dropped her spoon.

"Do I have it?" she said out loud. She tried to eat again. This time she thought she might vomit.

"Did she give it to me?" she said to no one. She began to shiver, even though it was not ten minutes ago that she was sweating through her shorts. Was this the lesbian tick, maybe? Her body ached. Where was Angela? Did this stranger just give her the virus and bolt? Clarice wanted to feel something, hear something.

A knock. There it was. And her own hand pulling the door back.

"I feel so bad about the bugs," the front desk attendant said. They held up a black machine that was half the length of their body. "We have an extra air filter, and I wanted to offer it to you." They had on a new mask—orange with pink unicorn heads all over it.

"Oh," Clarice said. She didn't get out of the doorway and stood there looking at this person with a unicorn mask, who she now understood as queer, offering her something for her lungs.

"Can you put a mask on?"

"Oh, I'm sorry. Sure."

"And can I come in?"

"Oh, yeah, of course, except . . . wait." Clarice's lips rubbed on the fabric of her mask.

"I'm not sure if I . . . like, it could just be the ticks—Here, I'm gonna come out."

She stepped down. It was late. The sun had set.

"My name's Cam," they said and pointed to the pronoun badge on their shirt.

"Oh, okay, hi. Um, Clarice. She/her."

"Cool, nice to meet you." She watched Cam step inside with the filter and adjust some settings. They were one of those queers with meaty arms and a lot of tattoos—some done by friends that were faded to smudge, and more professional ones layered over the old work. The air from the filter briefly blew their scent outside, and it was stronger than Clarice expected: Old Spice deodorant and garlic.

"I like your mask," Clarice said.

"Thanks, I change it every hour. I go through a lot of them in this job."

"Wow, that's a lot of laundry."

"There tends to be a lot of laundry in this business."

They stood looking at each other, both simultaneously blaming themselves and the other for the lack of momentum in the conversation.

"Look, I want to know if you would like to get coffee with me tomorrow before you head home? It's policy that I can't engage with anyone in that way until after they've checked out as a guest. So, like 11:00 a.m.?"

Clarice was relieved that Cam couldn't see her face under her mask, and wondered what kind of fear her eyes were revealing.

She suddenly felt like Angela was watching them, and wondered if Angela would blame her for this exchange. *Wow, that's super unhealthy*, Clarice thought. *I could blame her for getting me sick.*

"We could also just go for a walk up the trail. Look down at Kah'eese. That's the Chinookan name for Cape Disappointment."

"Are you Chinookan?" Clarice asked.

Cam blinked slow like a cat. "No. I grew up here, but I'm not Native."

"What's the name mean?"

"I don't know—it's not on the sign up there, and I never was able to find anything online. It might not translate."

"You must have a lot of good stories, having grown up here."

"I do." Cam's eyes came to life. "Actually, my favorite is this ghost story that happens this time of year, about this settler girl who washed ashore alive one summer. The only surviving member of her ship. When their bodies washed up, they looked like they'd been eaten. She drowned a few weeks later—in a confusing way. The story goes that she still washes ashore and drowns every summer."

"What do you mean in a confusing way?"

Cam smiled, and it was charming. They leaned against the doorway with a kind of ease like they were winning something.

"I always wondered what that part of the story meant; I think like the weather was stormy, but the water wasn't deep? I mean it is confusing that a ship had that kind of trouble during the summer. That's what I love about it."

Silence stretched between the two of them as Clarice remembered what it felt like to be on her knees, retching until she produced a pearl.

"I can't answer right now," Clarice said. "I sort of have something going on with someone here right now."

"What? Okay. I didn't realize." Cam's neck flushed red.

"No, I'm sorry. You seem nice. And it's not like an official, monogamous kind of thing. I mean, I mean it's super new. We haven't even talked about it, but we're . . . Can I check in with you tomorrow?"

"Totally. Yeah, it's no big deal."

They awkwardly traded places, Clarice holding her breath as an extra precaution. She didn't even want to sit down, just wrapped her arms around herself and made a horrified face for no one to see. She was cold, and she could feel poison moving in her veins, something frigid. The smoke poured in. The air purifier clicked itself on to the highest level.

WHEN DID ANGELA START DOING the dishes?

She wore black latex gloves, the kind Clarice often used for fisting strangers—the gloves she would have used if she'd hooked up real quick with Cam, because who knows what a queer like that working at a place like this had going on under their nails.

"I haven't been here long," Angela said without looking away from the sink. Clarice shook herself out of her fog and felt embarrassed—she hadn't done any dishes during the trip, and the pile had gotten sticky and gnarly.

"I said hi, but you didn't respond," Angela added. She rinsed the last dish and took her gloves off the safe way, never letting the outside of a glove touch her skin.

Clarice covered her mouth with her arm and spoke in a muffled panic. "Angela, wait—did you bring a mask? I think I might have—"

"You'll feel better soon. It's not the virus, it's—" Angela guided Clarice to sit on the couch. "It's happening faster than I expected."

Angela's craggy incisor caught on her lip briefly as she gave a timid smile. She brushed these lips on Clarice's neck and sat down next to her. "You're becoming something else."

Clarice was having a difficult time tracking the meaning of Angela's words. Was she a doctor? What could make her so sure she wasn't sick, dying, contagious?

"There were ticks in my bed," Clarice said, suddenly eager to change the subject, state the facts. It was hard to feel Angela's touch. Even with her chest pressed against her arm, flesh spilling over flesh.

"Weird, there was a mouse in my place late last night. Had to call the attendant over to help with that."

"Cam?"

Angela frowned. "Didn't catch their name. A queer though."

"They didn't mention anything to me. About the mouse."

"Should they have?" Angela asked.

"Did they ask you out too?"

"No," Angela said, and moved her body away. She pulled at the hem of her dress and Clarice finally took it in: maroon and skin-tight, hugging all of her thickest parts. Heels with straps that went up the ankle.

A rush filled Clarice's body, a hunger that pounded. Also the feeling like drinking liquid antibiotics as a kid: cold ooze down her center. She could smell Angela, but also could still smell Cam's Old Spice—could feel the potential of their service top hook up.

"Where do you live, anyway?" she finally asked Angela.

There was a flinch. Angela moved to a chair across from the couch. Crossed her arms.

"Alaska?" Clarice asked.

Angela shrugged. "You're acting weird," she said.

"How am I acting?" Clarice asked.

"I don't know. I can't read your face. You seem cold."

"I don't think I'm acting weird," Clarice said. They were both quiet for a full minute. Clarice shivered. "I don't like people saying how I seem."

Angela opened her eyes wide and shook her head a little. "Got it."

"It's really not cool."

"Heard."

Then Clarice spoke before she thought about it. "I mean, I guess if I'm feeling weird about anything, it's that I don't really know you or what we're doing. I don't do long-distance relationships. They aren't good for me."

"Did I ask for that?"

"I just want to be clear." Clarice salivated, not quite recognizing her own voice but feeling powerful. She felt energy moving through her in a cleaner way than it had in days, despite the illness or whatever this was. It was like she could breathe despite the smoke.

"This has been really hot and fun, and I would love for it to happen again someday, but I need it to be cleaner. A clean break, I mean. Goodbyes are good. We can let ourselves feel things acutely, rather than staving it off with long distance calls and yearning."

The vibrancy in Angela's eyes dimmed. "Again, did I ask for any of that?"

The rush of ending, the rush of desire and hope draining from lust-swollen veins. The relief of no longer waiting to be left, forgotten, never friended on social media, never blocked. Clarice's body drank it up.

Stand up. Clarice thought. *Walk out.*

And Angela stood. Walked toward the door.

"You suck," Angela said. She was going to cry. Or retaliate.

Clarice fed her a concerned look, which she definitely meant. She felt concerned, but she also knew that the moment Angela walked out the door, this thrill would be greater. The relief of extraction. Caught with tweezers, little legs squirming in the air.

Monster, she thought, unclear whether the insult was meant for herself or for Angela. But instead of calling names, she said, "Thank you for making my vacation so special."

Angela shook her head. Bit her lip. Walked out. Obeyed.

A ripple of regret, and then euphoria, spread through Clarice. She leaned back on the couch and her eyes rolled back.

No one was there to witness what happened next, but it would have frightened almost anyone. To walk into Clarice's trailer—as seconds of stillness ticked into minutes, then a full hour—would mean to see a body still as in death, the eyes showing just the whites, the skin taking on a scaly shimmer. To be in Clarice's body for this hour would be to feel an astounding peace.

Then, the anxiety returned as a trickle. Clarice needed to feed. Her eyes rotated out of her skull and took in the room with a bee's perspective—*when did it get all these shades of ultraviolet?*

SHE PACKED HER BAG QUICKLY, Angela's smell rising around her as she folded her clothes. She wanted to kiss Angela again and she couldn't. She shivered. A tick crawled across her arm and she smashed it. The first dream she had with Angela came back to her in a rush. And that first truly magical moment when their skin became the same temperature for the first time. She lowered her lips to her own shoulder, and it was frigid, just like having her lips on Angela. She'd made a mistake. *The fuck is wrong with me,* she wondered. *Am I avoidant or am I anxious?*

Her hunger grew. *I'm not sick,* she realized. *I'm just in love.* She could run through the park and find Angela. The sooner she acted, the sooner she could hold Angela to her. The longer she waited, the colder Angela would become.

Clarice put her bag in the car and wandered. She breathed in smoke and exhaled filtered air. Her senses focused, the night glittered. She heard a sound like weeping and followed it to the car in the woods. Angela. Then a flash of movement in the back seat, and another body was there. Cam.

Clarice froze, jealousy and nausea tumbling through her. Angela looked up, birdlike, just as she had when Clarice first thought the words *I love you*. Tears streaked Angela's face, and blood covered her mouth. Cam's eyes were wide open, as if staring at some invisible screen, as if watching a horror film. *Don't go down the stairs*. Their lips moved slowly—who were they speaking to?

Come here, she heard Angela say.

Clarice slipped into the passenger seat, her body instantly gripping Angela's. Both of them wept. And there were those lips on her lips, and those tits in her hands, and her own hard nipples, and their mouths full of each other. Then their mouths full of Cam. How easily her teeth sank in, like she had always done this, how joyfully she gulped, how she'd never tasted anything so sweet. And when Cam was gone, they were consumed in each other.

"I could do this forever," Clarice whispered to Angela.

"Return the land by becoming the night," Angela responded.

They depleted each other. Clarice understood now, what Angela meant—*you are becoming something else*. This was the good time Clarice was desperate for after months of careful isolation, and a life of perfect retweets.

THANK GOD FOR GOODBYES, THIS gift of death, and how we drain one another of our failings when we part. They came wildly, screaming into the dark.

Unstoppable

RONNI TARTLET

This morning in temple, yellow sun streamed in through the eastern stained-glass window and made everybody drowsy. Rabbi Nussbaum gave his usual inflated bar mitzvah speech, *mazel tov*'ing Evan on achieving the milestone of manhood, the victory of virility, the pinnacley peak of penistude. Well, practically, the way he went on. You know he doesn't have hardly anything to say to the girls. Anyway, Evan was standing next to him, rolling his eyes so intensely he had to be getting a headache. All this was punctuated by the uneven snores of Dara Bloom's grampa, dozing in the front row as usual with his mouth hanging open.

Evan was just launching into his haftarah portion when somebody opened the door to the sanctuary and a crow flew in. Its shimmering wings brushed the air, *whhshh*, as it swooped above the bima and over Evan's head. The whole congregation murmured in awe and consternation, while Evan kept singing, higher, louder, not breaking cadence except for one exuberant cackle that melded right into his next phrase. A single perfect black feather whispered free, drifting back and forth in the humid air, finally settling in the aisle. I longed to touch it but sat still. Cantor Peres marched right over it and held the door open until the bird decided to leave, kerfuffling its wings in his face. He spat out the door after it. And Evan kept singing.

The video guy, who'd been grazed by a flapping wingtip, sat clutching his camera to his heart and repeating the story to David Mizrahi's stepmom, who nodded vigorously, declaring: "They need to call pest control. They really do."

Some adults noisily shushed the others, adding to the disruption. I tried to take advantage of the minor chaos to sidle into the aisle and pick up the feather. As I reached out for it, my Grema Charna locked eyes with me. She touched the gold hamsa around her neck and shook her head at me. I froze and slowly withdrew my hand. My mother looked over at us, noticed the feather, and cried out, "Feh! Somebody get a plastic bag!"

Eventually we were released into the steaming outdoors, with many sunny hours to kill until we had to report back in fancy outfits for the evening party. Evan was being kept at home all afternoon to be kissed and pinched by visiting aunts and uncles. On an ordinary Saturday afternoon, the two of us would be climbing the stout mango tree up onto the roof of Martinez Grocery, chewing on grass and pretending to smoke cigarettes. We'd take turns wilding out, yelling and spitting, inventing tumbling tricks and courting gruesome accidents. Our recklessness made us breathe hard and grin till our faces hurt.

But this was no ordinary Saturday. Today, Evan was becoming a man. And I had nothing to do. I snorted derisively as jealousy wafted up into my throat. *Yeah, that sissy's going to make a really impressive man all right. I'd make a much better man than him, and I'm a girl. Jesus.*

I laughed. Saying "Jesus" always made me laugh, I don't know why. *Not much of a man either, that Jesus,* I thought. My stride lengthened and slowed to a swagger as I crossed the crowded parking lot to my mom's minivan.

She and Grema Charna were nearby, arguing with Raoul Feinstein about whether our synagogue membership was paid up. I took off my stupid flat shoes and leaned back against the minivan, pressing hard to get my dress dirty. Sari Katz went by with the whole huge Behar family, and I caught her eye and winked. She looked at me and then looked away. I crossed my arms and kicked the tire behind me. The black smear it left on my tights made me feel mean and glad.

"He's such a nudnik," my mother was saying as she approached the driver's door. "Get in already, let's go." She made annoyed, sighing noises all the way to Grema Charna's apartment building. I gave my Grema a hug and kiss as she got out of the car, her soft cheek fragrant against my lips. "Okay, so get some rest," yelled my mom at her mom, the way countless generations of Seidman women must have yelled at their mothers back through time. My head swam with the inevitability of it. "I'll come get you for the early bird."

The two of us zoomed down Biscayne Boulevard toward Book of Life Cards, Gifts, and Judaica. Operated by my mom, Grema, and Aunt Ruthie, Book of Life was barely sustained by the small purchases of the elderly Holocaust survivors who populated the apartment building above it. There was always a palpable, dusty odor in the narrow shop, no matter how many surfaces we sprayed with lemon Pledge.

I worked there most days after school and on Sundays. But today, knowing I was available, my mom gave Grema Charna the day off and dragged me in instead. She set up at the desk in back to pore over bills, while I leaned on the counter, remembering the crow. "We'll go dancing in the dark, walking through the park and reminiscing," sang the radio softly. Old people music.

A lady with orange hair poufed into a cloud stepped gingerly around the greeting card display, squinting. Her polyester pantsuit almost matched her hair. "Yoo-hoo!" she cried at me. "Yoooohoo!" I exhaled loudly and walked over to her. She gripped my arm, chipped manicure digging into my skin. "Yes," I said evenly, breaking her grip with my other hand and depositing her arm at her side. "You're looking for a card?"

She looked confused, but then her face cleared. "For my grandson. He's graduating now." She reached for my arm again, but I blocked her. "Got into a very good college."

"Great," I said. "Here's cards for that, right here. Look."

She wouldn't look. "I want you to find me something nice."

I felt irritated, swamped by the smell of beauty parlor chemicals. I wanted to be outside, tumbling dangerously toward a precipice under the brilliant sun. I turned to the Graduates area of the greeting card rack and with exaggerated care rifled through the Boys section. Then I jumped to the Girls section. Feeling vindicated, I pulled out a rosy soft-focus tableau with a kitten on it. In swirling script, it declared: To a Lovely Granddaughter on Her Graduation Day.

"Oh, this is nice. He's going to like it." I fished out the matching pink envelope and pushed the set into her bent fingers.

She nodded at me, pleased. "Give me two. His brother graduates next year."

After she left, my mood was brighter. I hummed along to the radio as I unpacked a box of yarmulkes and arranged them by color. One of them was very sleek and black like the crow in the synagogue. I put it on, pinning it in place with a sparkly purple barrette from the hair care bin. *Evan would love this barrette*, I thought. *I'll give it to him tonight.*

I wondered how he was doing on his big man-day. Ptah. As I broke down the box and took it out through the humidity to the dumpster, I smiled in spite of myself, remembering his gleeful laugh about the crow while his voice soared in song. Evan really liked to sing. He could hit most notes in every Whitney Houston song. Chava Alberstein, too. He really wanted to do a singing number tonight at the party, but his mom said absolutely not.

When I came back into the store, there were customers. An old lady, a middle-aged lady, and a teenage boy huddled around the challah knife display under glass at the counter. I strolled up to the register and greeted them. Only the middle-aged lady glanced up, peering at me through low-slung glasses. "Gut Shabbes," she said. "Show us this one."

I pulled out the knife she'd indicated, a solid silver piece that sat heavy in my hand. Its handle was woven around with a tight coil of silver wire. The fine serrations of the blade caught the fluorescent lights. I set it gently on the counter and the boy picked it up, passing it from hand to hand. The old woman watched the boy with skepticism. "Since when do you even bake challah?" she demanded. "You're going to want to keep kosher now, too?"

I looked at the boy, whose gaze stayed down beneath lush dark eyebrows. There was something about his hands I liked, the way they were finding a good seat for the weighted handle, measuring its heft and gleam. Small, capable hands. I felt a pleasant warmth brewing between my legs, then a sudden slickness in my underwear.

The middle-aged lady said, "You like it?"

I dropped my eyes in a rush. Saw the boy nod out of the corner of my eye.

"Well, it's your birthday."

And I wrapped up the knife. Made sure to brush the boy's hand with mine as I slid the tissue-papered steel across the counter.

He looked up. "Thanks," he said quietly, and smiled at my yarmulke. I touched it fast as they walked out.

For the next hour, I paced the store.

My mom looked up once. "Do your homework," she ordered distractedly.

Instead, I strode up and down the two aisles, pushing everything on the shelves out of order on one pass and then straightening it all on the next. I tried to see if I could manage this without breaking my stride. Only then did I allow myself to go back behind the counter and reorganize the knives. The knives, the knives! So cool and serious. How had I never noticed before?

I took up the heaviest one, handle inset with blue glass beads. I walked to a corner of the store where no one could see me and pressed the handle between my legs as hard as I could stand. Stuffed my fingers into my mouth to keep from screaming. Took three deep breaths and walked slowly back behind the counter, put the knife away, took out my math book and drew hummingbirds in the margins until 5:00 p.m., when we locked up.

Clicking off the radio, I kept the song going in a squeaky falsetto: "Everybody's talking 'bout the new kid in town . . ." Sorting her papers, my mom looked at me strangely as I switched off the lights. Then it was dark.

I got dropped off at home to get ready for the party, while my mom took Grema Charna out to dinner at Chen's. Resignedly, I got into the silky blue dress I had to wear on all these occasions. Sometimes I argued for the purple corduroys but I never ever won.

I pulled off the cotton underwear I'd been wearing all day and examined the milky streak centered in the crotch. Its smell, enticing, was not unlike the aroma coming off a steaming pot of Grema Charna's matzo ball soup. I scratched at it with a fingernail, decided not to taste it.

I had a secret for tonight, something that made the girly dress almost bearable. Rummaging around the back of my sock drawer, I pulled out the pair of tighty-whitey boy briefs that Evan had brought over last week, in trade for my pink cotton underwear with little yellow flowers. Tugging them up around my narrow hips, I turned both ways in front of the mirror, holding my dress up. The briefs sagged only slightly in the ass, and the wide swatch of fabric hugged my front close. I pushed my hand into the slit and pressed down on my pubic bone. I felt like a rock star.

I was sashaying around the house, enjoying the unfamiliar feel of the stiff briefs scraping the blue satin, when my mom arrived to pick me up for the party. Grema Charna was in the car too, wearing black slacks and a heavy sequined shirt with an orange butterfly across the chest. "We're going to go too," said my mom. "Your Grema's feeling better."

"I'm ready to party," said Grema. "You ready to party with me?"

I giggled. "How come you get to wear pants and I don't?"

My mom snorted. "When you're an old lady, then you can dress like a boy."

The car smelled salty-greasy from the takeout container half full of leftover garlic eggplant. I dug out a glossy, purple-skinned chunk with my fingers and ate it. Then Grema and I held hands across the cassette storage bin all the way to the synagogue.

Once we went inside, the three generations separated. I was assigned to table 17, which was the table for kids that Evan actually liked. Table 18 was for kids that his parents invited, like the spawn of his dad's business partners and his grandparents' friends' grandkids. Stopping off at the snack table, I ate three knishes and savored the oily sensation that lingered on my lips. Reaching up under my dress, I wiped my hand clean on the rough white fabric of my briefs. With my eyes closed, it felt like no one could see me.

"Kasha!" cried Mrs. Dennis, marching my way in a long skirt and serious heels. My English teacher and Evan's auntie. She married a ba'al t'shuva and had four kids so far, even though she was young still. She always looked tired, but pretty too. She swept me up in a hug. I liked how sometimes she got all exuberant, so you knew she really liked you. "Could you believe that bird this morning?"

I giggled. She leaned down. "Hey, have you seen Malka? The rebbetzin says she's here but I can't find her."

"Yeah, I think I saw her over by the bar maybe," I whispered. We both knew Malka was not supposed to be drinking. Mrs. Dennis gave me a serious look. "Okay, well, don't tell anyone else that. I'll see you later. You look great!" She beelined for the bar, waving at me over her shoulder.

Malka, the rabbi's daughter, was like six feet tall and made me kind of nervous. She used to go to Yeshiva University in New York but now she was home again. Mrs. Dennis and Malka were good friends, I guessed. I could see them talking, their heads bent close together, Malka's thick, red-dyed hair curtaining off her face.

I felt a tap on my shoulder. Sari Katz stood behind me in a yellow dress with a ruffle across the chest. She had lipstick on and pouted at me with it. "Isn't this dress so dorky?" she demanded.

I frowned, looked her up and down a few times, shook my head. "You look pretty good," I ventured. "But it's too long to really dance in."

She flounced the front of her skirt up at me. I caught a flash of tights-encased thighs. "You're supposed to go to your table already. You're at 17, right? The centerpieces are really cool. Like fake peacocks." Sari strutted off toward the bathroom.

Just then the lights dimmed portentously, and Mrs. Dennis started herding everyone into the party room. A few other kids already sat expectantly at table 17, gaping at the band, a bunch of white guys in dark sunglasses tuning up. I waved at everybody and sat down at the back. Scanning the perfumed crowd, I saw my Grema's orange sequins flash beguilingly across the room. She was sitting at one of the old-people tables holding a drink, probably a vodka cranberry like she likes.

I leaned across the table to fiddle with the elaborate peacock centerpiece, trying to break off a feather to tickle Sari Katz with later. Pink strobe lights began to flash and jump. The band kicked into "Celebration" by Kool and the Gang as the double doors at the back of the all-purpose room flew open wide, and the Kaufman family danced awkwardly into the room. It was Evan Kaufman's bar mitzvah party, and I was ready to start something.

Did you ever get that feeling where your heart gets bigger and thuddier than usual? And it sits higher up, almost in your throat? And so many different things could happen, it makes you practically dizzy? Even the silver glitter on the ceiling drapes was reflecting back at me, encouraging, instigating. And then the slender, sharp-tipped peacock feather came loose from its foam-core mooring, and I was unstoppable.

The procession steamrolled past: Evan's mom, makeup shellacked on, determined smile locked and loaded, radiating anxious joy. Evan's dad, already sheened with liquor, spinning the third-grader twins around by their puffed shoulders. And Evan, looking insane as usual, overlong hair flapping free of the mousse prison constructed by his mom, slapping out a wild hand toward mine as he shimmies by.

I let Evan jerk me up and we danced wildly across the floor. There was nowhere to put my contraband feather so I shoved it down the front of my dress, its iridescent tip tickling my neck. I hate not having pockets.

Evan and I swung each other around and around, as the band sped up and the crowd clapped out the beat. Lights pulsed and glitter swirled as we spun faster. Suddenly, giddily, Evan flung me into the twins, and we three became a tangled mass of taffeta and sprayed-sharp hair, sprawled across the dance floor. Upended, I caught a glimpse of Evan bowing elaborately and running off the dance floor. Then my view was eclipsed by the grasping arms of a dozen concerned yanker-uppers.

Out of breath, I stumbled to my seat. Sari Katz was sitting in it, chewing gum and shaking her head at me. "You guys," she said. Then she laughed. Feeling bold, I sat down on her lap. She let me, for a minute, and then toppled me back onto the floor.

"Maybe I should just stay down here," I said, rubbing my twice-banged elbow. "I'm not going to bother getting up."

Sari ignored me. We both watched the band two-step in unison. Then she leaned down and announced, "I bet you can totally see up my dress."

I had already thought of that. I tried to look nonchalant. "I don't know. A little."

She glanced away, and spread her legs a bit. "Can you see my underwear?"

"Um," I said. Holy shit. Be cool. I shifted partway under the table and craned my head. She had taken her tights off. I saw bony knees, smooth thighs, and then darkness. I held still and willed my eyes to adjust, make out details.

"Oh, hey, Gabi," I heard Sari yell cheerily over the bad Pointer Sisters cover. "Yeah, cool, huh?"

Without thinking, I slid the rest of the way under the table so the tablecloth hid me. Then I sat there breathing nervously. *Dang it, Kasha, now you're stuck under here!* I cursed my bad judgment. Then, movement in the shadows caught my eye. Sari Katz, spreading her legs open wider and letting her black shoes drop to the ground. Maybe this was a good idea after all. I felt a foolish grin wash over my face as I moved in closer.

For a minute I just looked, and inhaled. The air was old-carpet stale, but there was something else: warm, rich, and appealing. I breathed it in as the dimness resolved itself into shadowed thighs and a pale patch beyond. Sari Katz had on white underwear.

With a vigorous scrape, she pulled her chair closer to the table. She opened her legs all the way wide—wide enough that there was no way this was an accident, a coincidence—her knees almost touching the chairs on either side, thankfully empty. She continued her cross-table conversation with Gabi. She was sending me a message. She had my undying love.

I moved in slowly, and her slight scent got stronger. Finally, I decided to dare a touch. I brushed her thigh with my fingers, asking permission. She didn't kick me, didn't close her legs. Not even a little.

So I let my other hand rise too, and stroke her other knee. I slid my fingertips back along her thighs. Back into the radiant shadows, back toward the white patch of Sari Katz's underwear. I stopped, suddenly, just before I got there, dropping my hands to my lap. What the hell was I doing? Does she really want my hands on her like this? And what was I supposed to do when I got where I was going?

She shifted her butt forward to the edge of the seat, squirmed a little, wrapped her ankle around the chair leg. Her conversation with Gabi had ended. I could hear murmuring voices, rustling fabric, pulsing blood. Her right hand moved under the tablecloth. She beckoned, silver nail polish sparkling in the darkness. I sat and stared. My hands were rising again, reaching. I leaned in.

Something That Only Shines in the Dark

BRITT ASHLEY

Standing next to Helen Rainey past midnight in the liquor
aisle of Schnucks grocery, Angie becomes an actual criminal
for the first time. Despite her desire not to be; for most of her
eighteen years, Angie has been basically a good girl, her Southern
manners slipping out along with the Texas accent she keeps trying
to hide.

Angie has only known Helen for a couple months, but already
she has thrown herself into the task of impressing her like it was a
full-time job and she was desperate for a promotion. Where Angie
was quiet, content to sprawl out on the porch at house parties or
slouch against the back wall of basement punk shows, Helen demanded attention. She was pharmaceutically tense, beautiful, and
incredibly foul-mouthed. Angie loved her mangled bottle-black
hair and the way she had walked up to her and introduced herself
simply by saying her name. *Helen*. Like she was such a fucking
fact.

Helen says sometimes you need things that aren't yours. She
says it casually and often while opening Angie's coat, snaking one
skinny arm past her ribs to liberate a single cigarette from the

battered pack Angie keeps in the inside pocket. Angie holds still, looking off to the side like none of it matters, the delicious rustle of the exchange and then the sharp smell of fire scattered across her skin.

Even when there's no question asked, Angie knows the only answer she has for Helen is *yes*. Sometimes you need things that aren't yours.

This is how Angie finds herself in Helen's oceanic, two-tone Chevy Malibu, both of them wine-drunk on a cheap bottle of Ernest and Julio Gallo. The car is ridiculous, simultaneously muscular and frivolous, like riding in a roaring slice of coconut cream pie. Helen drives through the snow, blasting a chaotic mix of the Pixies, Nina Simone, and Iggy Pop.

"Get educated, bitch!" she yells at Angie, who is laughing, cheeks flushed from the full blast of the car heater, windows open wide on her first real winter.

They coast safely into a snow-banked parking spot and stumble out into the lot. The pneumatic doors of the store hiss open and the girls barrel in. Helen is whooping and shouting, grabbing things from every aisle. Angie knows for a fact they only have enough change between them for more cigarettes but she follows anyway. At that moment, she can't think of a single thing that doesn't belong to Helen.

The girls cut through aisle five, stretched out long and empty, bottles twinkling like an open jewelry box. Helen leans into Angie, lips grazing her neck, and says, slurring just slightly, "I wish we had more wine."

Angie presses back against her, gently tugging the hair at the nape of Helen's neck, pulling her gaze up. "I wish. . . ." She trails off and looks away, unable to name what she really wants.

That's when she sees it, high on the shelf, the beautiful drink with an ugly name. Goldschläger. Cinnamon schnapps with flakes of real 24 karat gold floating in it. Tacky for sure, but right now it looks like the most gorgeous thing in the store.

Before she really knows what she's doing, Angie palms the bottle in her hand and then safely tucks it under her jacket, pressed tight to her side like a love note. Helen raises one eyebrow and smirks, impressed. Angie slips her arm down to Helen's waist, gripping the sharp cliff of her hip bone.

She steers them quickly, but not too quickly, to the checkout line, smiles at the checkout boy, and buys them a pack of the cheapest cigarettes and single can of coke. Everything sweet, everything burning.

Standing in the parking lot, the girls stare at each other, the air around them heavy with want. Angie thinks about the liquor, exquisite and vulgar; Helen's upturned face, her lips and throat tender and beautiful even in the harsh street light. Sometimes you need things that aren't yours. Sometimes what belongs to you is right in front of you, saying take me, name me, treat me as treasure.

Heart of Stone

SOPHIA BAHAR VACCARO

Skba rushed through the forest, the tender thorns of August blackberries slicing at her arms and the tops of her hands.

But even as she bled, even as the dogs lost pace and fell behind, distracted by rabbits or water or rot, Skba ran and ran, sweat streaming down her face. Her feet were getting tired, but she could not stop. Her mouth was getting dry, but she could not drink. And her hands were getting clammy, but she could not wipe them, as not for a second could she risk putting down her cargo: a large, dark rock, scrubbed clean, worn smooth, approximately the size of a human heart.

THEY SAY THAT DOGS CAN sense ill intent; that's probably why every single dog for miles around howled and brayed at the sky at the moment of Skba's birth.

As for *whose* ill intent—well, that was a long-held point of contention.

Some said Skba was just as beastlike as the dogs, dirty and angry and hopping about from leg to leg, slinking around corners, always on the hunt for her next meal.

Others said the village itself was the problem; these were the villagers that fed her, clothed her, shoved her through the back door of the schoolhouse even as her parents complained that such nonsense only kept her from the farm.

The farm. The blasted farm. It never grew much, just handfuls of withered greens and measly potatoes, barely enough to get them by. Barely enough to last through the winters, which Skba always spent cold and shivering in whatever hidey-hole she could find. Her parents and brother stayed warm by making gallons of sour scrap wine and drinking it in large quantities, but Skba never liked the way the stuff made her feel, her stomach turning over each time she moved.

But one year, winter came early, and spring, even earlier. With that came a change: Suddenly, Skba and her family weren't the only ones hungry. The off rhythm of the seasons had decimated the crops that the village relied on: corn, large green peppers, and the small sour melons called *pirrus*. When summer arrived, it was so very hot. And everyone was so very hungry.

But not Skba. As the villagers starved, she only seemed to grow stronger, her belly rounder, her eyes clearer. She skipped through the village, radiating with energy, smiling so big and wide with all her yellow teeth that the old men glared and hissed.

Don't tempt a starving man.

IN TRUTH, SKBA WAS HUNGRY as ever, but she was fast as ever too, faster than the dogs who ran behind her. She was so fast that she almost ran smack-bang into a pair of strangers on the dusty road that edged the forest. The taller of the two was a middle-aged man, hair and beard flecked with gray; the smaller, a figure cloaked in fraying robes of ocher. The figure was hooded, gloved, and booted, even in the summer heat, and the larger man was holding them up with one burly arm.

"Sorry," Skba mumbled, wiping her nose with a dusty forearm. The dogs wended around her feet, hoping for scraps. She was about to slip around the travelers when the man reached out with his free arm.

"Please," he said. "Can you help us?"

Skba eyed him warily. "What do you need help with?"

The man chewed on his lip. Skba found herself wondering what it would be like to have a beard; something that never stopped growing, even if you wanted it to.

"We need supplies," he said.

Skba frowned. "What sort of supplies?" she thought of her meager tools, wrapped up in leather and stashed in one of her hiding places: a rusty hammer; a half-rotten turnscrew.

The man didn't answer right away, and the two of them stood, staring at one another, until Skba had half a mind to continue on her way. She took a step. The dogs huffed.

"Wait, please! I need a—a heart," the man said.

"A heart?" Skba repeated, nonplussed. "Like a pig's heart?"

"No," the man said, with a nod toward his companion. "I need a new heart for my son. They stole his heart, the people from my village. They ripped it right out." He shivered.

Skba eyed the figure. They were slumped to the side, barely standing, but certainly breathing, not a speck of blood on them. They definitely did not look like someone who just had their heart ripped out.

"*Please*," the man said again. "It's not difficult, to make a new heart. It won't take more than a day."

"That's what they all say," Skba said, backing away slowly, so slowly even the dogs had yet to notice. They were too busy sniffing the hooded figure, nosing its gloved hands and tight-laced ankles.

With a sigh, the man reached under the figure's hood and pulled a cord. The cloak fell away, landing on the road in a cloud of dust. Underneath was a young man, his head tipped back, arms limp at his sides. As Skba watched, his head lolled forward, his eyes fluttering open and shut.

Skba normally made judgments on people based on how they moved: fast, slow, nervous, jerky, frantic. But he was so still, besides those eyes, so she catalogued him the only other way she could: she looked, long and hard.

His hair was dark and curly, his skin light brown. His fingers were banded with pale stripes where rings had once sat, and his left ear had a notch that could have been from birth or bite. On high, broad bones, his lashes lay long and thick, just like moth wings, sputtering and desperate on their way toward the light.

Skba's skin itched as she watched the older man reach toward his son's shirt and lift it. He was wincing all the while, though the boy made no move to stop him.

Skba had seen plenty of men working shirtless on the farms. What she saw now was a body like any other, except for one thing—right where the boy's heart should have been was a little copper door hanging loose on two hinges: one intact, the other snapped in half. Behind the door, Skba could see a mess of wires and cogs crowded in a small chamber. A few of the wires had been cut or ripped. And some had been burned.

Skba stilled. The dogs did the same, eyeing her from the side, as if waiting for an order.

"What is he?" she breathed.

"My *son*," the man said, his face twisting in anger or sadness, Skba couldn't be sure. She wished she could ask the dogs. She was sure they could smell it. "He is my son, and without a heart, he will die."

Skba hopped forward once, twice. She reached out a hand to the little door, then pulled away, eyeing the smooth brown skin under the wide white shirt. Skba knew that skin would be soft, unlike her dry, blistered self. Besides the door, he seemed so—real. Whatever he was, his construction was seamless. Artisan. Such a thing should not be destroyed.

She looked at the man. "What do you need?"

Relief flooded the man's face.

"It's not so much *what* I need as *who*—the more people, the better. It doesn't matter what the heart is made of; it matters that people *believe* it's a heart. Everyone just needs to agree that it is such."

Skba let out a bark of laughter. "Everyone needs to agree?" She thought of the hard-faced men and the scheming women of the village. The trickster children, the vicious roosters, the ragged cats who kept their claws sharper than needed to catch the bony mice. The people of her village couldn't agree on the color of the sky, much less the constitution of a heart. Even more so when there was nothing in it for them.

In fact, in all her twenty-one years, Skba had only ever seen them agree on one thing:

They were *hungry*.

Skba shot another glance at the boy. Perhaps, just this once, everyone could get what they needed.

She turned on her heel and headed across the path. Behind her, the older man made a sound of distress, but she ignored him until she found what she was looking for. She wiped off some clumps of dry dirt, some strips of bleached grass, and walked back to the pair.

"Do you have a pot?" she asked. The older man nodded, and into his free hand she shoved her prize. "Wash this in the well and put it in a pot of water on boil in the village square. The villagers will try to start a fight with you, but don't listen to a word they say."

She made to leave, turning on her heel, but the man stopped her with a raised palm, his fingers splayed like the rays of the sun.

"And what about you? What will you do?"

Skba blinked. She was so used to the dogs, who could smell her plans before she made them.

"They will come with complaints, but I will come with questions. And when I do, you have only one task: Say yes to everything I ask."

SKBA KNEW THE PEOPLE OF the village would do their best to scare the travelers away. She had seen them run out a tinkerer family with tales of bears; chase a fortune teller halfway to the next village with talismans raised high. Once they even scared off a flock of wild sheep by throwing stones and banging drums late into the night, as they feared the sheep would plant seeds of liberation into the other animals' heads.

But still she waited, slotted between the smithy's workshop and his ill-fitting backhouse. In the coldest months, she would often come here to warm her hands and feet against the adobe. Sometimes trash would fall into the tight little space—or was dumped there—but Skba didn't mind. Once, she had found half a loaf of bread amongst the debris, which she shoved deep into her jacket as she leaned against the backhouse, waiting for it to be softened by her skin.

The dogs were rather cross with her for that.

She cocked her head like one now as she listened to the villagers, who had already started their campaign:

"This is the village square, this is. This is no place for pots and pans."

"Beggars! More and more every year. What do you have to say for yourself? What do you have to offer more than the dirt on your face?"

"You know, those that sleep outside tend to go missin' round these parts. The bears, you know."

Skba suppressed a snort. That last speaker was a drunk and a gambler with a pretty wife and three doe-eyed children, yet he made it his mission to never sleep a wink in his own bed.

"We don't like strangers here, mister. We don't like them one bit."

Skba strode from her hiding place round to the front of the smithy's. She was relieved to see the older man had not moved, despite the heckling. Even better, he already had a large pot of water set to a merry, rolling boil. At his feet was the boy, his eyes still fluttering, one hand splayed against his chest. She watched as his fingers curled around the place where his heart should be.

She swallowed something down, a strange feeling. It was from all the looking, she knew. This was why she never did it.

She huffed silently to herself. Enough of that.

"My goodness, what's that smell?" she said loudly. The villagers nearest her jumped. They always complained how she came and went from nowhere. You would think the dogs that followed her would be a good tell, but no one paid any attention to them.

She walked closer to the pot and arched over the steam, taking a long, audible whiff. "Heart soup. Don't tell me it's heart soup!"

The older man looked up at her, confused. She widened her eyes.

"I—yes," he replied haltingly.

"To think you brought such a delicacy into our humble village!" she went on. She suspected she was laying it on a little thick, but she was enjoying herself. She had so few opportunities to put on a show.

"May I?" she asked, reaching toward the man.

Still blinking in bafflement, the man handed her a long wooden ladle. It was made of a beautiful, smooth, two-tone wood, oiled and perfect.

She dipped it into the bubbling pot. Sniffed. Blew. Sipped.

It tasted vaguely earthy.

She gasped. "It's just as delicious as I've been told!" she turned to the others. "You see that heart in there? That dark, round thing? It's the heart of a Yubiba. You can only get such a thing in the North. I've heard all about it from my father."

Skba's father used to be a traveling salesman, so this was a fine excuse. No one would dare bother to ask him unless they planned on buying scrap wine. And there was never any left to buy.

Parle the baker cut in. "I'm from the North, and I've never heard of a Yubiba—"

"*Far* in the north. So very far," Skba continued. "Up in the mountains where few ever venture. Except for the mountain people. Are you mountain people?" She turned back to the man.

"Yes," he said. "It's very . . . cold there."

"Hah! I bet. But . . . *hmm*." She took another sip. "It needs something. Something hearty. It wouldn't be true heart soup without . . . potatoes." She stared at the man hard.

"It—no, it would not!" he said, getting louder with each word.

Skba sighed wistfully. "And what a waste that would be. I would give you potatoes, if I had any. I would give you *bushels* of potatoes, if I could share a bowl."

"And I would happily give you a bowl, if you were to be so generous."

"I—I have potatoes!" came a cry. Skba whipped around, feigning surprise.

It was Parle. "Now that you mention it, I do remember the Yubiba. Yes, the big . . . scaly thing. With the fur. And the—claws. I can complete your soup, for a taste."

With a wave, Parle sent his wife to the shop to fetch the potatoes. She looked at him sideways, but did as she was told, mumbling all the while.

A few minutes later she emerged.

"This is all we have," she said, holding up a small cloth bag. "I don't know if it will be enough." She handed the bag to the older man. With a surreptitious glance at Skba, he took the potatoes out one by one, making a show of inspecting them before dropping them into the pot alongside the stone.

There's hope for you yet, Skba thought.

The water kept on boiling; the villagers waited with bated breath. The children raised on tiptoes to sniff the air, clutching their mothers' skirts for balance; the men shot jealous glances at Parle; the women watched Skba, their hands crossed tight over their chests.

Skba, for her part, still held the ladle. Before anyone could stop her, she dipped it in the water again, blew the liquid cool, and took a taste.

"Oh, wow. It's even better than I could have imagined. I already feel full—it's so rich, that heart. So flavorful. But—"

She held out a hand. Around her, the chatter ceased immediately. "It's not quite right. Wouldn't you say so?" she said, handing the ladle to the man. He took it from her gingerly. After a quick sniff, he too tried a taste. Skba saw him hold back a grimace.

"You are right," he said. "It needs . . ." he waved his hands about, gesturing vaguely to the land past the square.

"Peppers," she said gravely. "We don't have those spicy ones, like in the mountain farms, but we do have—"

"The big green ones!" came a voice from the back of the crowd. A large-boned woman pushed through to the front, clutching a woven bag to her sizable bosom. "I was going to trade these for cold beer, but—"

"Hey!" shouted the innkeeper. "We had a deal!"

The woman clutched the peppers closer. Skba could no longer discern which lumps were crop and which were chest.

"Would you deny me a taste, when the baker gets a bowl? I deserve this just as much as him. And these are fresh from my garden!"

"*Your* garden, girl? You mean the one I tilled and watered after you killed half the seedlings?" cried another voice.

The woman flushed. "That's neither here nor there, Hangi—"

And so the villagers began to yell and scuffle and argue, and send their littlest back to the house to grab whatever they had left: withered parsnips, garlic ends, cracked peppercorns red as rubies, corn squirreled away and frozen in the cellar since the summer previous.

The heart soup was stirred, cooed over, glared at, transferred to a larger pot courtesy of the innkeeper. Children reached sticky hands toward the flames before their mothers swatted them away; elderly men tried to steal the ladle from Skba, but she danced away as the dogs snapped at their heels.

Dreaded beasts, grumbled the men. *Dreaded girl.*

To deny an old man his last taste of Yubiba!

All the while, the older man sat back on his heels and watched, occasionally granting a nod or a smile as more and more lined up to deposit their offering.

"A cup for little Jakib," said the seamstress, offering a pinch of pinkish salt. "He so dreams of the cold mountains."

The man nodded mutely.

"A bowl for me and my wife to share," said the shoemaker, dumping in four fistfuls of cowpeas. "Don't forget the name *Jida*, and we'll fix those for you before you take your leave." The shoemaker nodded toward the worn soles of the boy's high boots, which were peeling and thin. The older man whispered a weak *thank you*, but the shoemaker and his wife were already on their way.

Skba watched as the man patted his son's leg, as if to convey the good news, though even the yelling and arguing hadn't inspired him to wake. She had only seen him stir once, blinking owlishly at the crowd before he curled into a ball, warming himself with his back to the fire.

Midwife Cece offered to take a look at the boy, a single green onion clutched in her sunburnt brown hand, but the older man turned her away, pulling the cloak over his son's body protectively. Skba felt a blaze of envy, but she couldn't put a finger on why.

At the end of it all, a mammoth pot simmered, the older man sweated, and the entire village drooled.

Skba had retreated to a corner, where she played tug of war with the dogs and picked ticks off their bellies as they wriggled away. But now, as the villagers began to reassemble, she couldn't help but join them, a thin tin bowl from the inn clutched in her hands. It was undeniable: the air smelled incredible.

In the light from the giant soup pot fire, with the dogs at her feet, and the promise of that smell—oh, that *smell*—Skba could barely feel the cold stone floor she would sleep on tonight.

When she got her bowl, she nearly forgot what she had to do next, for it was so very good; the best meal she had had in weeks. Months. Years? Not since the family soup pot had been repurposed for scrap wine. Not since her grandmother died, the only one who knew how to make their paltry crop into something worth savoring.

As her spoon scraped the bottom of the tin, she shook herself head to toe. One of the dogs at her feet mirrored her movement, as if it had been instructive. She let that dog lick out the last scrap of potato. The other dogs moaned.

"Don't be so dramatic," Skba said absently. Then she got to her feet and headed to the new center of the village: the pot, still massive, still hot as the disappearing sun, and still bubbling. Skba wondered if there would be enough for seconds. Then she dug her nails into her palms. She had a job to do.

"Was that not the most delicious heart soup you have ever tasted?" she called out. "I told you it was a rare treat!"

The villagers closest to her nodded in agreement, scraping the bottom of their own bowls.

"You tasted the heart, didn't you, Parle? Hangi? Midwife Cece? *Didn't you?*"

Parle waved a hand in her direction. "Yes, we did, girl. What's gotten in your bonnet?"

But the older man was nodding, his eyes bright in the light from the fire. Skba caught his gaze, and he waved her on with an almost-grin.

"Wasn't the heart so tender?" she asked, clutching her hands together at her chest.

The shoemaker and his wife nodded.

"Wasn't the heart so sweet?"

Jakib licked the inside of his cup, gave her a thumbs up.

"Won't you remember this heart for the rest of your days?"

The innkeeper shook off her hands from where she clutched him at the wrist. "Yes, yes, now get off me, little beast!"

She bared her teeth at him, but sat back on her heels. She spared a glance at the pot.

The older man had the ladle again, and he had lifted it to the lip of the pot. Peeking out over the edge was a smooth, round dome, dark as the fields around them.

Skba watched as he stared at it, rotated it slowly. Touched it ever so gently.

Tear tracks shone bright from his grimy cheeks. As if he knew she watched, he looked up and caught her gaze again.

Thank you, he mouthed, and she knew then the source of her envy.

She wanted to pull a cloak over someone, gather it around their feet, as the older man did; she wanted to smooth hair from a sleeping face. She had learned well and good how to tuck herself in each night, but it had ceased to be enough. What an awful surprise to realize your heart was overfull, with nowhere for its excesses to go.

She knew she couldn't take the older man's place, but perhaps more watching, more of that awful looking, would sate her.

So she took her fill, of the soup and of the watching, until the fire was dead and there could be no more of either.

The whole village slept well that night. Even Skba. Even the dogs.

THE NEXT MORNING, SKBA WOKE feeling better than she had in ages.

She flexed and stretched her fingers, which were not stiff from the cold, but prickly from how she had laid heavy upon them, so deep in slumber that the morning sounds of the village had not woken her.

She rolled out from the spot behind the smithy's, moving the dogs out of her way, placing them gently back into a pile to sleep.

She felt ready for a bath—a rare occurrence for Skba. Why be clean when grime set so easily into her floating black hair and the cracks of her dry skin? Why wash her clothes when soot would smear them black in moments?

But she felt renewed, somehow. And she wanted the feeling to continue.

She headed to the river. It was drier than it should have been this time of year, but there was still enough for a bath, so she slid off her shoes, stripped off her overskirt. She was about to remove her grimy top when she heard a sound, and she stilled. The sound came again, and she swiped her clothes from the ground and scrabbled behind the nearest bush.

She didn't mind if people saw her bathe; it was more that she minded if people saw her at all.

To her surprise, it was the two travelers, spiffy in clean hand-me-downs that had been traded for bowls of soup. The boy stumbled along while the older man guided him to the riverbank, where he set to lay him down gently at the river's edge.

Skba stepped out from her hiding place.

"Hello," she said.

The older man jumped. "Oh, it's you. Where did you go last night?"

Skba shrugged. "To sleep."

He stared. "I wanted to thank you. Repay you, somehow—" he stumbled as the weight of the boy dragged him toward the river.

"Here," Skba said, skipping to their side. She took her overskirt and set it in the dust below the boy.

Together, they stretched him out onto the ground.

"What are you doing to him?" Skba asked.

The older man glanced at her briefly. "I am going to restore his heart."

Skba's eyebrows raised. "Can I watch?"

"Yes," the older man laughed, "to anything you ask."

Skba sat back on her heels as the man prepared. He talked as he worked, taking the soup-stone from a pocket within his new-old pants and rinsing it in what was left of the stream; drying it with a soft cloth from his bag; setting it on another spotless silver cloth he kept in a tiny pocket in his vest.

He told her his name was Vin, his son was Marqo, and his wife, who was missing, was named Guadalupe.

He and Guadalupe had tried for many years to have a child, to no avail. But Vin was good with tools and making things—he had made the ladle—and so one day he decided to make a son. His wife had been overjoyed, but when she learned her son had no heart, she could only cry. For four long nights, she wailed, and each night the people of the village gathered around her, and sang, and cried with her, and helped create the heart that would be Marqo's for nineteen of his years. Each night Vin made a chamber, soldered from old clocks and watches and melted coins and jewelry gifted by his brothers-in-law, his friends, the priest, and his niece, who had provided the final piece, a rosary she had been gifted as a baby.

The heart, Vin told Skba, had been his most brilliant creation: shining with jewels, clicking with gears, its polished copper surface smooth and clear as a mirror.

The people of his village had loved Marqo at first, Vin told Skba, for he was handsome and kind. But most important, Marqo reflected back to the villagers their own noble sacrifice.

But when the crops went sour, the hunger came too hard and fast for people unaccustomed to want. Vin, it turned out, was not of some fantastical mountain people, but from a village far south of Skba's, where suffering was measured in degrees. And with each tick upward of the mercury, sacrifice started to look more like subjugation.

It started with small requests here and there—*where's my watch, do you have my necklace, please return to me my silver coins*—but Vin refused each one, reminding the villagers why they had gifted those things in the first place.

You gave me your watch so Marqo could be strong.

You handed me your necklace so Marqo could be wise.

You slipped me your coin so Marqo could be good.

But eventually, the people of Vin's village had had enough; they didn't want Marqo to be strong or wise or good. They wanted their gifts back so they could eat.

One night, they came for him.

Vin stopped talking now. Skba saw his hands shake, and she did not know what to do. Even though she wished to be like Vin, she didn't know how. Her overfull heart was spilling over its edges, gathering at her feet, halfway a flood.

She drew her hands back and curled them into hard fists. The skin on one of her knuckles cracked. "How do you fix him?" she asked.

Vin cleared his throat. "It's very simple," he said. "But the change is rather abrupt."

Carefully, he removed his son's cloak, unbuttoned his new shirt. Pulled the cloth to the sides like the wings of a beetle.

Curses all along the river and back. She thought last night had been enough, but she couldn't help but look again now. She liked to pretend she had a nose like the dogs, and her eyes could see no colors. But colors her eyes did see, and they drank Marqo's up like the water from the very bottom of the well.

His hair was dark chestnut, his lips the orange-red of the flowers that grew when spring came at its rightful time. Sprays of dull red and brown lived in the old scars that pitted his cheeks, and his hands twitched this way and that, even as the rest of him remained still as the stone at his side.

It was strange to see someone alive, and not. Awake, and not.

Vin took the stone from its resting place on the silver cloth and cradled it in his large, weatherworn hands.

He glanced at Skba.

"I think it may be better, this heart. Stronger. No jewels or gold. Precious only to the body that will hold it."

Skba shrugged. Until she met Vin and Marqo, she had never really thought of hearts or bodies—hers or those of others—as precious or not. They were vessels for food and cold and sun and waste and a pillow for dogs' heads. Nothing more.

Slowly, Vin placed the stone into the little cabinet. He poked around at the sides, tucking away this and that wire. The hinge had already been fixed.

And then he closed the door.

The change was instant.

Marqo sat up, eyes wide, mouth open in a half-formed gasp.

His eyes were brown as rye. His final color.

"Papa!" he cried, lunging toward Vin. The two men embraced, and Skba sat back, startled. No one had ever hugged her like that.

Her bare feet slipped on the mud, and Marqo looked about at the noise. When he saw her, his eyes widened farther, and he pressed himself to his father's side with a yelp.

Skba looked at him, agape. She had never seen someone so afraid. She had never seen someone shake so much, every inch of them from tip to tail like a leaf in the breeze.

Vin wrapped an arm around his son.

"Marqo, do not worry. She will not hurt you."

I will not hurt you.

Skba had been wrong. She *had* seen someone so afraid: every poor, injured, scarred and slapped dog she had ever met. She had tempted countless from behind outhouses and under porches; had splinted legs, bathed sickly little puppies in the river when it was full and ice-cold, to sooth their blistered skin.

I wouldn't dare.

"Your name—what's your name?"

Skba realized Vin was speaking to her.

"Skba," she told him, unable to take her eyes off Marqo. Now that the hinged door in his chest was closed, it had smoothed away into his skin, as though it had never been there in the first place. Her fingers twitched. For some reason, she wanted to find the seams.

Marqo buried his face in his father's side. "No! They—they are too close!"

They?

Skba whipped around. A rustle in the bushes, a face between the blackberries.

"Hey!" she flung herself around the bush, lashing out with fast fingers. The tips of her nails caught at the thin tunic of a boy about eight—the baker's son, Simbl, dust ground into his knees and the palms of his hands. He had been spying.

"How long have you been watching?" she hissed. But Simbl just stared. He was scared, like Marqo—scared of the beast girl and her outsider friends.

She shoved him down the river.

"Go home, Simbl."

So, he did, stumbling along, glancing over his shoulder every few steps. Vin and Marqo stared at Skba in astonishment.

She flushed. "I'm sorry. I'll go," she said, and started toward the path.

"You have nothing to be sorry for, Skba," Vin called after her. "But please, let me repay you. If you do me one more favor, I will have the means."

She turned back to the pair, eyebrows raised.

"I promised to help some of the villagers in exchange for food and goods for the road. I can't turn them down, but Marqo is not ready to assist me. Can you stay with him, watch him for a few days, in exchange for meals and a place to sleep? Marqo does not want to be around people, and I suspect you feel the same."

Skba blinked. Marqo was no puppy, and she did not know how to fix a boy. But she could still help.

"If the dogs can come, you've got a deal."

VIN REJOICED, FOR HE NEEDED the ground corn and the winter clothes and whatever else the villagers had promised him. He made them a lean-to, near enough to the river to drink and wash but far enough so they would be neither seen nor heard by anyone except the dogs.

He left them most of his things, citing books (Skba could not read), tools (Skba did not want to make any more hearts), and a wooden game with smooth glass rounds for playing pieces (Skba did not know the rules).

The first few days passed in silence, Skba at one end of the lean-to and Marqo at the other, sleeping or pretending to, emerging from his cocoon only when his father returned with bread and cheese or dried meats that he shared with them while the dogs complained.

"Don't be so dramatic," Vin said to them one day. Skba smiled into her jerky.

It was horrible in some ways, the silence, for Skba was not used to the quiet of another pressing so loudly upon her own. It felt like a bell ringing incessantly in her ear, louder each time Marqo inched away from her in the lean-to or flinched when she pushed a cup of water toward him across the ground. The dogs, for their part, had come in droves, napping during the day and huffing and stalking about during the night. Marqo did not seem bothered by them, at least.

Vin offered to expand the lean-to so she could more easily sleep under its roof, but she turned him down. She preferred the warmth of the dogs, the open sky. And she knew that Marqo didn't want her there. Even so, she felt more comfortable pacing about their little camp—collecting berries and bits, catching rabbits for them to eat—than she had in years.

After about a week and a half of near-silent days, Skba was bored enough that she started fiddling with the wood-and-glass game, dropping the rounds into the carved cups on the board indiscriminately, if only to hear the sound.

Thunk thunk clink clink clink.

She had reached some kind of meditative state, no thoughts between *thunks* and *clinks*, when Marqo spoke.

"That's not how you play."

Skba looked at him, startled.

Marqo looked itchy. Not literally—the fever had left him long ago, and he was no longer blotchy and swollen—but his fingers were dancing an odd little rhythm. He looked like he was wont to step out of himself at any moment and flit away a wraith.

Vin was right when he said his son was handsome—but it was in a strange, alien way, his skin pulled so tight it was like he was wearing a mask of his own face. Skba rather liked it.

"I—will you teach me?" she asked.

Marqo opened his mouth, closed it. He looked pained.

Skba sighed. She pushed the game board closer to him, and then scrambled back on the balls of her feet.

"I'll stay right here," she said.

Marqo looked grateful for this assertion, rather than offended. He gathered the glass rounds in little piles in each cup on the board.

"I won't just teach you how to play," he said softly, his eyes still on the board. He glanced up at her briefly, so very briefly, but long enough for her to note that his eyes were darker than she thought. Toasted rye.

He made his first move. *Plink.* "I'll teach you how to win."

AND SO SKBA AND MARQO became friends, or something like it. She did not come close to him, and he did not approach her, even to gloat when he won at the wooden game (almost every time), even when one of his favorite dogs needed a new splint (Skba showed him from afar how to make one). He did not even move an inch as he told her what had happened to his mother, Guadalupe.

The day the villagers came for him was the day Guadalupe was nowhere to be found.

"My father," he whispered, ready to make his next move, his hand hovering over one of the tallest piles of rounds on his side of the board, "thinks she may have known what they were planning to do. He thinks she left so she didn't have to watch."

He frowned and picked up his pile, distributed them across the board. Then he stood and walked away so Skba could take her turn.

Skba approached the board with some trepidation. This conversation felt like napping at the base of a tree only to look up and find a half-cracked branch dangling overhead.

"Do you agree with him?" she asked. She distributed her rounds and went back to her seat.

"No," said Marqo. "My mother would never abandon me. I'll find her again one day. And then my father will know he was wrong."

Skba frowned. She didn't know one way or the other, of course. But she did know that sometimes it was more important for someone to believe something than it was for it to be true.

They played without speaking for a few rounds, walking back and forth to the game like a dance to the music of that loud silence.

The more they had played over the past week, the more certain Skba had become: Marqo was the reason she loved their camp by the river. At first, she'd convinced herself that it was the sound of the water, the fresh rabbit, the sour bite of berries always at her fingertips. But no—it was the way he slept like the dead, the sun kissing his face and those strange moth-eyes. It was the way he fed the dogs his own jerky and bread more than he fed himself. And it was the way he watched her when he thought she didn't notice.

She wondered if he was watching her now, as she dropped her final piece. "You are probably right," she said at last. "I don't think anyone could abandon you."

Marqo looked at her sharply, but Skba cried out before he had a chance to reply.

"Hah! I won!"

So she danced, and gloated, and the dogs pranced at both their heels.

He rolled his eyes and laughed, teased her, reminded her of her many losses. Still, he did not come any closer. And it would have been fine, if Skba hadn't realized she wanted him to.

Skba agonized over this for days. She was a fool for thinking the loud silence was enough. Things were too comfortable now, too slow. There was only one thing—one person—who sent her blood ricocheting, who widened her eyes like the moon. And he was so very far away.

One morning she went to the river for water and returned to a sleeping Marqo. He was pressed against the wall of the lean-to, which was closer to a hut, now; Vin had filled out the sides with old scrap lumber, insisting on protecting them from nonexistent wind.

Haltingly, she stepped over to Marqo and crouched down to place a cup of water on the ground near his head—not too close, just within reach.

But he was awake; with his face beneath his cloak, she had not been able to see his eyes, which were wide as saucers when he rolled over to take the cup from her, extending one long tan arm across the space between them.

His hand wrapped around hers and she stilled, not knowing whether to draw back, to place her free hand upon his, or to drop the cup and run.

The dogs laughed.

"I . . . I—" Marqo stuttered, a high flush rising on his cheeks.

"Sorry," Skba said, mortified. She *had* been getting too comfortable. Marqo was not the villagers. He wasn't used to the way she showed up in places she wasn't before.

"No, no, it's not your fault," Marqo said, sitting up fully. Even as she lowered herself all the way to the ground, trying to steady the cup, Marqo did not remove his hand, which was getting warmer and warmer on Skba's, as if he was made not of skin but sheets of hot metal.

And maybe he was.

"It's all right," Marqo said. "It's all right."

Marqo's cloak had fallen from his shoulders, and Skba found herself fixating once more on the place on his chest where she knew the door to be. Now, she didn't just want to find the seams. She wanted to dig her fingers deep inside them.

A singular, rational thought managed to claw its way to the surface: Marqo breathed, but his heart did not beat. She could hear her own, pounding against her rib cage, but it was the only noise she heard in that endless, silent space between them.

She caught herself and sat back, knees at her ears, like a dog waiting for a signal, but Marqo did nothing, only turned progressively redder.

Gently, she slid her hand out from beneath his. The second they were no longer touching, Marqo rolled back around to face the wall, wrapping his hands around the back of his neck.

Skba considered him for a moment.

"Marqo," she said softly. "Are you okay?"

"No," he replied. "I can't do anything. I can't help my father, and I can't leave this hut. If I see anyone besides you or the dogs, I start to shake and I want to hide."

Skba sat cross-legged in the dirt. "You want to fix it," she said. Marqo nodded into his knees.

Skba considered, chewing on her lip. "When the villagers hurt you, it was very fast. I don't think you can fix it the same way."

Marqo twisted back around. "What do you mean?"

She thought back on all those big little scared dogs, eyes wide as Marqo's had been.

"I have an idea," she said haltingly. "But only if you want to. We can start tomorrow?" Her voice rose, stuttered.

Marqo stared at her for a moment. "Yes. We can start tomorrow."

Skba smiled brightly. Then she stopped. She didn't want Marqo to see all her yellow teeth. Instead she nodded, jumped to her feet, and marched away.

Marqo watched her go. His favorite of the dogs sauntered up, showing off her new splint. She nosed at his hand until he scratched her chin.

"Do you think she knows," Marqo said to the dog, who was definitely not listening, "that I would say yes to anything she asked?"

Every morning, right after breakfast, Skba would sit across from Marqo and ask him to do one thing. Nothing more, nothing less.

The first day, she pulled a moldering glove from the belt of her dress and tossed it at Marqo's feet.

"Put this on," she said.

He did so, puzzled. Then she placed her hand, palm up, on the ground between them. Now he was no longer puzzled, but nervous, itchy, redder by the second.

"Put one finger to the tip of my own," Skba said softly. "For as long as you can."

That first day, Marqo was hesitant. But he did it, pressing the pad of his pointer finger to her middle finger, gulping in air all the while.

"You can stop at any time," she reminded him. "We can start again tomorrow."

"No," Marqo replied, and pressed his finger down harder.

They did this again and again, for almost a week. It started to feel conspiratorial; they leaned toward each other, closer and closer each day, though they never touched beyond that one point, sharp as the tip of a pin. Something radiated outward from that point—something like pain, but not. Instead of talking about it, instead of giving the feeling a name, they leaned in just a little bit closer.

They talked of other things, instead: town gossip, Vin's time as a dollmaker, Guadalupe's prize-winning recipes. They even gave the dogs names.

"I don't think she looks like a Belinda."

Skba turned to Marqo, retort at the ready, when she realized their faces were inches apart.

Her eyes widened. Marqo's did the same.

"I . . . I—" Skba had forgotten how to speak.

A crash came from the path that had formed from their comings and goings. Panicked, Skba and Marqo flung themselves away from each other.

It was Vin. He had come home early, face flushed with effort, more lumber strapped upon his back. "I fixed the rotted porch at the inn," he explained. "And they let me keep the extra."

"Wonderful!" Skba said.

"Great!" Marqo exclaimed.

Skba was not sure who wanted to explain what they were doing less. Mercifully, Vin only grinned and set to work on the side of the hut.

The next day, Skba asked Marqo to place the length of his finger upon hers. He did so without hesitation, and they smiled at each other a little too long. A few days later, she had a new request.

"Place your hand upon mine," she said. "Keep the glove on."

Haltingly, Marqo complied, covering Skba's hand with his. Her hand twitched beneath his wide palm. She told herself it was only a reaction to the sticky surface of the old glove. It was not.

That night, Vin brought them a piece of roast chicken and a sleeping pallet for Skba. She refused it, and Marqo slept on two pallets like a king.

After another week, Skba took the glove from Marqo and placed it on her own hand.

"Go on," she prompted. "Just like before."

Marqo set his hand down on hers, and this time, his fingers curled around her own. Just like a handshake, but not quite. Just like an embrace, but not at all.

Every day Vin came back with more good news. More work, more food. Some of the crops had recovered, and people were feeling generous. Or at least in a bargaining mood.

Vin returned with tiles, linens, real bowls and cups. He made a fire pit, a rack for drying clothes. The hut had a floor, a door, a mud-and-grass roof.

Still, Skba slept outside with the dogs.

"There's plenty of room inside," Marqo reminded her.

Skba chose to ignore this. "We don't need the glove anymore," she said, her voice determinedly even.

"We don't?"

Skba shifted on her tailbone. This whole week, Marqo had reached out to take her hand without thinking. She couldn't delay the next step to save herself.

"My . . . my shoulder," she stuttered. "Place your hand on my shoulder."

Thank god her dress had big puffy brown sleeves. Or at least they had once been puffy.

Marqo set his hand on her shoulder, his eyes dancing from tree to bush to ground to the far-off river. He placed no pressure, but Skba wondered if she was going to sink into the earth, as if she had been planted.

Another week went by this way. The door had a window, now. To see who might come.

"They still ask me about the soup," Vin said. "I tell them it's a secret family recipe."

Skba laughed, but really, she was thinking about Marqo's hand on her shoulder. That's how it had been all week. She was dropping buckets, slipping on stones, a jester for the dogs' court. And it was not the hand itself that was the problem: It was the question of where it would go next.

At the end of the week, she decided to torture herself further: "Today," she said, "you choose where to put it."

Skba could see him hesitate, could see the gears turn—perhaps literally—in his head. Skba could only assume he would place his hand on her other shoulder, or perhaps her ankle, where her skirts were dyed with years of dirt.

But some treacherous part of her hoped that he would press his large hand fully onto her stomach, right below her belly button, and stretch his fingers as far apart as they could go. Some scheming bit of her hoped he would place his hand on her chest, and feel her heartbeat, and she would ask him how it felt different than the stone. Some cackling witch inside her hoped he would then slide that hand up to the back of her neck, and he would kiss her and never stop.

He surprised her. "Turn around," he said. Eyebrows raised, she did so, spinning in the dirt, little rocks grinding into her knees.

He placed both of his hands on her back, wrists together, fingers arched to either side, like wings. Skba realized her mouth was open, and she snapped it shut. It was a small mercy he could not see her face. She was strangely relaxed, and it took everything she had to keep her eyes from closing and her head from lolling. All she wanted to do was lean back into Marqo and sleep.

Skba had wanted to escape this village for so long. But even if she had been gifted real wings, she would not have left this moment for anything.

"Marqo! Skba!"

Vin's voice, ragged and frightened.

They flew apart.

Vin burst out from the trees, leaves and dry branches falling around him in a rain. "The villagers . . . they're coming." His hands were clenched in fists. "The crops are sick—some fungus upon them. The people are hungry again, and they have nothing left to give me. I've taken the lumber, the tiles, the hand-me-down beds . . . but they don't want anything else to be fixed. They want the heart."

A wave of horror suffused Skba. Somewhere nearby, a dog let out a mournful howl.

"Do . . . do they know where it is?"

Vin shook his head. "No, but they think I have the means to feed a village. They think I can solve their problems, not with my tools, but with the magic of the creature from the mountains. I told them it wasn't me who fed them—it was their own stores, of which I have none. But they didn't believe me. They think the heart is here, and they are coming to find it."

Skba felt cold, remembering the small face in the bushes from the day Marqo's heart was restored. Simbl, the baker's son, running off along the river.

"Vin . . . I think they *do* know."

She locked eyes with the older man, and recognition fell upon him. He gasped.

Skba shrunk back, at a loss for what to do. Marqo retreated against the wall of the hut, his hands wrapped over his knees.

"No," he said. "Not again."

With each passing day, Skba had the seeds of calm plant themselves in Marqo, and it only made him more strange and more beautiful. Now, there was only fear. The villagers had ruined everything. Just like they always did.

So, she, too, would do what she always did.

What does a dog do when it finds a prize?

She strode forward, placed a hand upon Marqo's clothed shoulder. From the corner of her eye, she saw Vin's eyebrows raise.

"You must give the heart to me," she said.

Vin gaped at her. Marqo lifted his head from his knees, his eyes wide.

"You two go one way, I'll go another. If they come upon you, show them the empty space. Say someone beat them to it."

Vin and Marqo were silent.

Skba almost jumped to her feat. She didn't know who she was trying to convince, now. "I won't let them touch you again!" she cried. "They can touch me, they can scratch at me, I don't care. They will have to find me first." Her eyes narrowed. "And they never can."

Vin's mouth opened, closed. He squeezed his eyes shut.

"It is up to you, Marqo," he said at last. "It is your heart, after all."

Marqo's expression was unreadable. Skba wished she could embrace him, for what a terrible price he was about to pay.

He placed his hand over her own, and she nearly jumped out of her skin. "Yes," he said. "You can take it. Take my heart and run."

SO SHE DID. AND IT was awful beyond measure, those minutes and then hours after she left them. Every time she closed her eyes, she saw Marqo writhing on the ground, feverish once more, his father standing over him, face shattered.

Marqo had not wanted to give her the heart, she knew. But Marqo also did not want to be at the mercy of another mob.

Skba gritted her teeth and shoved herself farther into the rocks.

She had hidden herself the best she could: Far from the village was a cave in a tumble of rocks and bramble, at the base of a broad hill that eventually became a higher pile of rocks and bramble, which eventually became the base of a cliff, then the cliff-dwellers' villages, and then—beyond.

She followed the river to get there; there were other, better ways, but it had been many years since she had made this trip, running from her parents and brother after she realized that the best medicine for drink was to be unseen and unheard entirely. Return for clothes, shoes, a cup of grain; spend the rest of your days with the dogs and your skin peeling from sunburn.

The thin little cave had been refuge, once—why not again?

The problem was, at the time of her last, self-imposed exile, she had been younger, shorter, and thinner. She ran a hand over her stomach, filled out from her nights feasting—relatively—on Vin's wages. And she felt weak, so used to the consistent meals, the fire and the warm dog-bed.

I'm getting soft, Skba thought. Then she smiled. Not the worst fate. God knows there were worse—

Crash! Bang!

Startled, Skba swung her head around, nearly cracking her skull on the rock wall inches from her temple.

A rush of sound, just like that herd of wild, free sheep, made its way into her cave.

"Skba! We know you're in there!"

Skba clutched the heart to her chest. They had found her, or tracked her somehow. She thought no one knew of this place. She thought they never noticed where she went.

She stared into the shadowed rocks around her. Nowhere to go. What was she to do, melt away down the river?

She closed her eyes. No more running. She was no dog, no beast. She stood on her own two feet, and it was time they saw it.

She slipped from the crevasse and faced the crowd.

"The heart is not yours to take," she said, her own beating frantically. More of them had come than she anticipated. They all looked dusty, tired, and thin.

To think, this is what they became after a few weeks without decent food. To think of what she had become in the same stead; a woman who held hearts in the palm of her hand.

"It's not yours, either!" came a voice from the back. "Just hand it over, and we can be done with this!"

She clutched the heart tighter, as if she could slip it in alongside her own.

"You can't eat stone!" she cried. "Why try?"

"You little beast," said another, "You don't get to punish us for everything you didn't have. You're used to starving, and that is your place. You say we can't eat stone, but neither can you!"

Skba's face fell like a crumbling wall, all broken planes of mortar and ragged bits set to slice your palms.

But then it rebuilt, brick by brick, until her face was as smooth and hard as the rock in her hands. She stared, even and cold, at the villagers, as many as she could. Parle the Baker, Mr. and Mrs. Jida, Midwife Cece—they all looked away. She took a breath.

"Watch me."

And she raised the stone to her mouth and took a bite.

"No!"

The villagers at the front surged forward, but it was too late.

Don't offer food to a girl raised by dogs.

She ate the heart so fast, it was like it had never been there. She ate the heart so fast, it was like she was hungrier than all of them put together.

She ate the heart so fast, she didn't see Vin and Marqo emerge from the river path, shoving the villagers away from her just in time to see her take the last delicious bite.

And she had been right; this heart was the most tender, the sweetest thing she had ever eaten. And she would never, ever forget it for the rest of her days.

"Skba!" Marqo cried. He was weak, shaking, still burning up from the inside out, but he had managed to run all the way here at his father's side, a long flat board in hand, ready to fight. He flung it aside when he reached her, grabbing both of her hands.

"I can't believe you did that," he said. Skba felt herself freeze, blood cold in her veins. But when she raised her eyes to Marqo's face, she saw he wasn't angry. He was happier than she had ever seen him.

"Don't you understand, Skba, what you have done for me? Don't you see?"

He smiled, with all his yellow teeth. And then he kissed her.

It was bliss, even with the villagers shouting around them, Vin holding them back. It was bliss, even though Skba was scraped up and hot against the hard edge of the crevasse. Perhaps Marqo was made of hot metal after all.

Or maybe it was her. Skba's eyes widened as something burning like the white rind of the mountain peppers traveled from her belly to her chest to her throat to the edge of her lips. She pressed them again, hard, against Marqo's own, which had no business being that soft, after all this endless heat.

Marqo pulled away and gasped, pressing his hands to his chest. Worried, Skba did the same, slipping her hands beneath his.

Thump-thump

Thump-thump

Thump-thump

Skba raised her eyes to Marqo's, and he laughed and laughed, and pulled her close as Vin yelled, and the dogs scampered up the rocks to herd the villagers away with snapping jaws and nips never quite deep enough to leave a mark.

A good dog never does.

But a girl like Skba always will. And that's why, when Skba raised up on her toes to whisper her final question, there was only one answer he could possibly give.

Marqo, do you love me?

And in between the beats of that newly minted heart, she could just hear his reply:

Yes.

Runner

RACHEL MCKIBBENS

The summer I decided to love someone, I wanted to mean it. Watching the news before bed each night had driven me to a near catatonic state. Within a six-week period, eleven girls and women had been murdered. By Girl Six, the deaths could predict my weather. I became obsessed, scrolling through lunch breaks, flooding my brain with every monstrous detail I could siphon from news stories. I'd stare into the victims' eyes in photographs, as if I might concentrate each ghost back to life. The woman in the elevator. In the suitcase. In the pond. By the highway. The shallow grave. The parking lot. The girl, the girls, the woman, the women.

It wasn't some macabre goth fascination. I wasn't being a tourist, I was getting prepared. Felt my murder inevitable. I lived alone, three thousand miles away from family. My chronic depression made it difficult to go out and meet people. I didn't drink, didn't party, didn't do anything that allowed me to make small talk with strangers. By Girl Eleven, I realized I hadn't been touched in fourteen months. My skin ached like a forgotten tooth.

Every night before bed, I'd daydream of being needed by some-one. Not just by a lover, but by my Dead Summer Girls. Imagined them reaching out for me, screaming my name in a final effort to be saved. I was losing my shit. I knew it. Insomnia had become my loyal wife. As darkness cradled me, I'd stack each loveless hour in my head, a deranged hoarder of broken time.

By the end of July, the news moved on to its usual stories. Pol-iticians' dick pics. Ten-car pileups. Bombed villagers seeking re-venge. With no girls left to fixate on, an emptiness settled in me. I'd come home from work and sit in my car for hours. Sometimes I'd wake up still there, watching the day's early light thorn the wall of the carport.

Five months later, I awaken to an unimagined life. The man lying next to me breathing steadily to the whir of his C-PAP, his chest rising slowly, as though lifted by a careful wind, wedding ring waiting atop a novel on the nightstand. I spend hours watch-ing him sleep, sometimes practice being his widow, crying as his side of the bed becomes a casket, whispering his name as I kiss his face or cradle his leg.

WE MET WHILE I WAS on one of my night walks. Late August, back when I started leaving my bedroom window open, quit lock-ing my door. I had moved too far from all who loved me, wanting to drop the world. My loneliness demanded I do something reck-less. Blood-filled.

For weeks I wandered Brooklyn's streets at night. The dark, my cold accomplice. Lingered out front of bodegas, making eye con-tact with men, telepathically challenging them to duels I intended to lose. I was raised Catholic, its residual fangs burrowed deep in me. Killing myself was not an option. So, I decided suicide-by-man was the answer.

There were only a handful of creeps who took the bait but, ultimately, I'd end up in my own bed, staring at the fractured paint on the ceiling.

"You need something, friend? You okay?" A voice stood beside me as I leaned against the brick wall.

"I'm fine," I said, blowing smoke without a cigarette.

So fine, never finer. Why don't you quit the polite shit and bash my goddamn head against the pavement? Chop me up and throw me into the Hudson. Light my sad little face on fire. "Thanks."

The voice stepped beneath the flickering streetlight in front of me. Lean dude. Clean. Thin mustache. He carried himself like my Uncle Juan. Chin up, shoulders back. He was three or four inches taller than me. I assessed his lack of danger and figured I'd be better off not putting up much of a fight.

"Can I go home with you?" I asked.

He gave me a confused look and chuckled. "What's that?" Then repeated my question back to me, as if weighing its truth in his mouth.

We stood there, watching each other. He leaned to the side to look into the store.

"You in trouble? Someone in there following you?"

I stared into him, wordless.

"Need me to be your boyfriend or something?"

I was getting visibly irritated by his helpfulness. "I'm not in trouble," I lied, "I just want to be touched. Hard."

He eyed me like a ticking suitcase, glancing at my empty hands, a year's worth of static needling the air.

Maybe he sensed the hunger lodged in my throat like a dead girl's name. Or maybe, like me, he suffered from a devotion to impermanence. Whatever it was, he needed more time to figure me out.

He motioned to his car and said, "Let's go." I wasn't scared. Wasn't excited. I was numb. Still. So, I went.

As he drove, I became curious about the aftermath of my potential death. How long would I be missing? How many novena candles would be lit as offerings for my return? Who would find me and where? Would my mother have to identify me? Would she even recognize me? Which of my exes would mourn me, gaze at my missing poster with longing? What would my obituary leave out?

"Mind if I connect to your Bluetooth?" I asked.

"Go ahead," he said. "Curious to hear what you're into."

His interest in my music taste made me anxious, I didn't understand why. I suddenly felt under pressure, which pissed me off. I nearly puked from the stress. Fuck. I put on Radiohead and gritted my teeth.

"Ohhhh," he said, "moody."

I suppressed my rage at his flippant assessment, felt my blood zap the tips of my fingers and toes.

"*Moody*," I repeated, with a brick behind it.

Three songs later, we were heading to the lobby of his apartment building. He punched a code, the door made a loud metal click. I followed closely behind as he checked his mailbox: Zielinski. A murderer's name for sure.

It was a three-story walk-up. He headed toward the elevator.

"Can we take the stairs?" I asked, already three steps into my climb.

"I have a bad knee," he replied. "I'll meet you up there. 313."

Once the elevator doors closed, I raced up the stairs. It was important to me, I needed a win, wanted him to resent me. I regretted how hard it left me panting, made me look desperate.

When he stepped off the elevator, he grinned. "Built up a little sweat there, huh?" He chuckled to himself.

I wiped my brow with the back of my hand. I hated it.

. . .

HIS APARTMENT WAS SURPRISINGLY COZY. Woven tapestries on the living room walls, an ornate lamp with a fringed velvet lampshade. The living room was dim and smelled faintly of church. Frankincense.

"So *Bohemian*," I said, like a bitch.

"Moody," he said, then winked, dropping the stack of mail on his dining table. I took a seat on his fancy blue couch.

"So what are you, a fortune teller?" Snarky, but I truly believed he might be one.

He sat across from me in a luscious red armchair and shook his head no. "I wish I was. Probably a lot less stressful."

This made me sit up straight. "So, what *do* you actually do?"

I gauged from his deep sigh he didn't want to talk about it.

He responded to our awkward silence by lifting the right leg of his cargo pants just above the knee, then pushing a button on his inner thigh. It let out a *pssssh* sound. He carefully pulled his leg away and leaned it against his chair.

"More comfortable to sit without it," he said, then rolled down what looked like a thick sock, used to protect his skin from the prosthetic, revealing the remaining portion of his hairy leg.

"Shark attack?" I asked.

"Hopscotch accident," he said, fast, answering my brat with his brat.

"You thirsty? I don't really drink but I have seltzer and plenty of cold pressed juices that might interest you."

He stood up and hopped to the dining table, using its edge to steady himself before hopping to the doorway and swinging himself by a bar I hadn't noticed before. He swung across the hall, gripping another bar until he was in his kitchen.

"So, you just sorta Tarzan your way around the apartment, huh?"

He laughed as he opened his fridge. "Apple, beet, and lemon juice. Or I have a pretty tasty pomegranate blueberry one. Doesn't taste as earthy."

I'd come there to die, but the options made me freeze up. I wanted to seem like I knew which juice was healthier. I needed to seem cultured. Something. I don't know. Panic nipped at the edges of my chest. This was the most I'd spoken to anyone in more than a year.

"I'll take the apple beet shit," I said, so he wouldn't judge.

He tucked a bottle in each pocket of his pants, then swung back to me.

"Maybe try a little of this one first, then if you don't like it, the pomegranate will save the day."

I hated how he knew I secretly wanted the pomegranate. He sat beside me as I removed the cap and gulped down the disgusting beet apple lemon juice. Before I had time to gag, he asked, "So, what are you? A sex worker?"

The juice landed in my gut, but I played it off.

"What, do I look like a sex worker?"

He shrugged. "Everybody does to me."

Funny. "And why is that?"

He smiled. "I'm a forensic photographer so, take a guess."

Oh. A brief sadness shot across his face.

I wondered if he'd taken photos of any of the girls I'd been fixated on. Two had been local. Did he ever fall in love with a subject? Did he do like in movies, closing dead eyes with the swipe of his hand? Did he hold his breath as he leaned in? Did he wear a mask or maybe a clothespin over his nose to avoid breathing in the air of death? What if there were no eyes to close, what happens if there is no head? Did he follow blood trails like a grisly Hansel and Gretel? So many questions rung in my brain.

"Do you believe in God?" I asked.

He shook his head no.

"Do dead women turn you on?"

He shook his head no, again. "Never."

I looked down at the residual leg peeking from beneath the folded cloth of his pants.

"Do you ever feel it, still?"

He smiled. "All the time. You wanna know what it's like?"

I nodded yes.

"It's this excruciating current of pain. Electric jolts, shooting up and down the missing limb. Sometimes I hammer at it with my fists. Strike at the absence until the leg is bruised back into existence. The worst part is I miss that leg more than I love the one I still have. It has become my body's most perfect memory."

Then he asked, "What's your death wish all about?"

I narrowed my eyes. "What do you mean?"

"I mean, why are you standing around dimly lit streets, climbing into strangers' cars?"

I resented his accuracy. Again. But then it softened inside me, his knowing. As if all those nights, alone in my room, I'd been waiting for someone to ask me that question.

"I just . . . don't think I belong here," I said, no longer interested in being interesting. I wanted only to hear myself be honest.

"Yeah," he said, then took a sip of his juice. "I feel you. I don't really think any of us belong here. It's just where we've ended up."

"I didn't come here to have sex with you."

He shrugged. "That's good, because I don't have sex. I fuck."

The words opened inside me. The truth of himself, spiking the air. Zero shame. My Dead Summer Girls sat beside me, their hands on my back as if to push me forward. We trusted him. We needed to. I heard myself admit everything.

"I haven't been touched in a long time. I don't really get along with any of my family. I don't have any friends. I just . . . want someone to touch me so hard that I die."

He stared just beyond me, calculating his own needs. "How 'bout I touch you until the day you die?"

Panic turned its head toward me. I waved it off. An ambulance siren outside the building tore into the room, its slow red pulse caressing our faces.

Forest Bae

AMBER PATTON

THWACK!
THWACK!
THWACK!

Each time his ax makes contact with the large, dense piece of oak, she flinches. Not because it scares her, but because it reminds her of what his hand can do when he is doling out a well-deserved punishment.

THWACK!
THWACK!

She bites her bottom lip, feeling her body yearn to be touched, to be placed in position before she receives a steady, firm . . .

THWACK!

Her pussy clenches as the wood finally begins to submit to his will. That subtle crackle of the splintering of the wood before he brings the axe down for another blow makes her toes curl.

Her knees nearly buckle underneath her as he adjusts his stance. She grips the ledge of the window. He takes a step back and pulls his shirt off, exposing his taught, muscular, dark brown skin and sinewy muscle. He curls his thick fingers on the axe handle before coming down with one more strong swing.

THWACK!

The log bursts open, and she feels herself on the verge of her own breaking point. With her eyes closed, she imagines one of his large hands coming into contact with her backside, causing her to audibly moan.

"You all right?" His voice, low and steady, washes over her, snapping her back to the present. Her lower stomach tightens.

She stops herself from answering him.

A sly smile appears on his face. He takes off his thick gloves and places them on the table.

"The silent treatment? Again? I thought we learned our lesson from the last time."

She bites her lip and rubs her legs together, knowing what's coming. His steps are sure as he comes up behind her, getting a clear view of his chopping stump. One of his hands caresses the side of her face and gives her tight coils a gentle tug.

"Last chance, baby girl. You want to tell me what's got you all . . . tense?"

She swallows in defiance.

He sucks his teeth. She can feel him eyeing her hungrily.

"Okay." He lets out a sigh. "Have it your way." His voice becomes a low growl.

She immediately bends at the waist—expecting to feel him behind her—but is only met with the cool air. She doesn't dare look behind her. If she's caught looking, he won't give her the thing she wants more than anything: a real punishment.

Finally, she feels him step closer. With just his index fingers, he pulls her booty shorts down to her ankles. Her breathing speeds up, lungs tight with anticipation.

"You ready, my love?"

"Yes Sir." Her voice like gravel in her throat, desperate for what is coming.

A nice . . . hard . . . solid—

THWACK.

The Camping Date

SABRINA STUART SMITH

He caught me wrestling with black flies and wincing at the sight of the ants trekking in figure eights around our belongings. He smirked at my reaction to every light brush against my neck; the wind was driving my flyaways to tickle my skin, forcing me into a frantic dance, slapping my neck and shrieking.

"You are definitely not an outdoorsy person," he said.

I smiled, trying to conceal my embarrassment. "Truthfully, I'm not."

"You could have just told me. We could have gone to a movie."

But that would have been too easy. Plus, I abhorred being stereotyped. I wanted to be the Black girl who enjoyed a good hike through the woods, spending the night in a sleeping bag, getting eaten by bugs. I wanted him to think I was that girl. And since I was aware of his thirst for all things outdoorsy—an affinity he, to stereotype *him*, must have gotten from his mom's side—I wanted to mirror his enthusiasm on our first date. I wanted him to enjoy being in seclusion with me. I knew the charade wouldn't have lasted long; I would have had to be real at some point. But I was hoping that before my revelation, I would have gotten to sleep with him, at least. I hated myself for making it obvious to him at that point, only twenty minutes since our arrival at the campground, that I was not that girl.

He was toffee or burnt latte. Wore his hair in a coily manbun, and his beard was that coarse, mountain-man type of beard that I desired to twist with my fingertips, to make tiny ice-cream swirls along his chin. He smelled like sour onions and sage. His teeth were perfect to me, because they were slightly coffee stained. I had never dated a man who oozed the sexual magnetism that he did. I was used to men who looked like him passing me by without giving me the double glance they—without fail—gave my sister.

I asked him for some insect repellent. He tossed me his travel kit. I unzipped it and sifted through the contents, pushing left and right. I took visual inventory:

- one half-smoked joint in a translucent container.
- natural deodorant, sage and milkweed fragrance. I knew the brand well. It didn't work.
- three Trojan Magnums, XL.
- a few black elastics, thin black curls tightly trapped around them.
- a nail file. Seemed odd to me, because his nails were not very well kept.
- a frayed toothbrush with missing bristles and food particles stuck within; and water visible inside the plastic sleeve that encased it. *Yuck!*
- a tube of mineral oil-free sunscreen.
- insect repellent.

I retrieved the tiny bottle, removed the cap and, in a frenzy, sprayed myself everywhere, almost like I was applying body mist after a warm shower. He laughed at me.

"What's so funny?" I said, mid-spray.

Repellent landed on my tongue. I spit unattractively. He laughed harder.

"Don't spray it so close to your face," he instructed.

I immediately felt silly. Of course, repellent application is something I would have learned if I had ever gone camping before that date. He tossed me a canteen of water from his backpack. I guzzled it, mainly to cool my embarrassment and to avoid having to address my naiveté.

"When you're done," he said, "you can help me build a fire if you want."

Great, I thought, *yet another display of my ineptitude for outdoorsy things*. I had wondered what would be next. Perhaps he would ask me to splay a rabbit on a spit. In my mind, I rolled my eyes, but outwardly I beamed. Inwardly, I agreed with his previous statement—*we should have just gone to a movie*. But aloud, I said, "Sure, I can help."

We searched for twigs in the brush. I lagged several paces behind him and picked up things I thought would be useful to build a fire, then hurled them miserably into the dirt when he informed me otherwise.

"You sure you're okay?"

"I'll be fine, really. Just show me what I can do."

He commenced a tutorial on the appropriate ways to gather kindling. "Anything dry," he said. "But not green. We'll make a pile. Twigs, dead leaves . . ." He was gracious when answering my obtuse questions. We laughed. We flirted. We felt raindrops hit our foreheads. He seemed unconcerned by the change in weather. I yearned for the umbrella I had left at home. We journeyed back to our campsite. He decided a few speckles of rain weren't going to thwart his attempts at building a fire. I watched him fail at his first attempt, then his second. I played with two twigs, wrote my

name in the dirt. He seemed to have had a solid spark going when
I felt three decent raindrops land on my nose in quick succession.
I'm sure I grimaced at that point, and he saw me.

"What's up?" he asked.

"I'm not much of a fan of drizzle."

"Ah."

He was unsympathetic. And continued his business with the
flint.

"I just like to get wet in other ways," I said.

He paused mid-kindle. I caught the formation of a smirk before
he wiped it away with his soiled hands, pretending to smooth
down his beard.

"Let's get in the tent, out of the rain," he said.

I dropped the twigs without hesitation. Dusted off my hands
on my jeggings, and crawled through the entrance of the tent. I
felt his eyes watching my behind as I wiggled past him. He
smoothed his beard again, then crab-walked in behind me and
sealed up the tent.

"How about some coffee?" he said.

"Would love some."

He retrieved two enamel mugs from his backpack, placed them
in front of me. I made myself comfortable on the high-end sleeping bag I had purchased solely for this date. He poured us steaming coffee from a metal Thermos. I sat cross-legged on the puffy
nylon. He got comfortable next to me. We clanked our mugs
together.

"Cheers to our official first date," he said.

We had attempted to meet up on a few occasions prior to that
day and were successful just once. A nonsuccess, in my mind. An
afternoon date, during lunch hour, to which I had arrived late and
had to rush back to work. And much of the moment was shared
with a random lady who sat next to us on the park bench and

rambled on about the history of the monument that was to be removed from that very park. So, this camping date was our first time alone.

"It's been a long time coming," I replied.

He took a cautious sip of the steaming coffee, then, stretching across to the far corner of the tent, placed down his cup.

"Too hot to drink that now," he said.

I blew into my mug, drew some coffee onto my tongue.

"Yep! Too hot."

He reached over and seized my mug, placed it beside his. He moved beside me, crossed his legs and let his knee fall atop mine. He slung his arm around me, softly rubbed my waist.

"It's raining harder out there," he said.

I listened. Sure enough, the tent was being abused by heavy droplets.

"Let's do something," he said, and grinned an eager grin.

"What do you feel like doing?" I asked, feigning ignorance.

He placed his hand on my thigh and waltzed his fingers along my checkered jeggings. He searched my eyes for a reaction, an answer, a yes. I gave him one. I leaned in and sought his lips. He removed my clothes. I removed his. He threw himself on his side and guided me to lie next to him. He freed the long curls from his bun and told me to play with his hair. I obliged gratefully. I spread my fingers on his scalp to massage his silky roots, and traveled down along the coils that dangled at his collarbone.

I held him firm inside me and twirled my fingers around his curls, relishing his excitement when I tugged his hair. We were synchronized, running our limbs harmoniously along each other. I was delighting in that sage and onion funk dripping from his underarms. But something was biting me, meandering about my posterior thigh. I freed my hand from his curls to swat the intruder away.

"Keep playing in my hair," he said, and guided my hand back to his neck.

I felt the insect crawl onto my left butt cheek and weave aimless diamonds along my flesh. I tried to remain composed, sexy, stay in the moment. I didn't want to smack my skin every time I felt something graze me. I focused instead on the skillful tongue gliding along my lips, my neck, and my breasts. I wiggled and twitched in a sultry grind in hopes the bug would fall off, but wiggling disturbed the rhythm of our kissing, so I abandoned that trick. I unraveled his bountiful curls from between my fingers, lowered my hands, and gripped the slippery flesh of his sculpted lower back. I yanked my date off his side, pulling him flat on top of me. He enjoyed that move.

We rocked gently, my back pressed against the sleeping bag. I used this momentum to finally smoosh the insect beneath me. I was elated. I had thwarted the insect intrusion, and I didn't even feel icky about the remains of an unidentified bug being smeared across my rear. I was too absorbed in more pleasing sensations to mind.

I heard the rain grow wilder, knocking on the roof of the tent like a surly landlord looking for the rent. I looked up at the tent's ceiling, surveyed its structure to judge whether it would cave before I had the chance to climax. That's when I spotted an earwig positioned directly above our naked bodies. I moaned, partly in revulsion. My date moaned soon after me, likely in response to my utterance, figuring I was ecstatic. I was indeed, despite the creepy-crawlies. And I intended to keep my date in this position, clenched between my thighs, where I was shielded from the pincher bug possibly losing its grip and falling on my skin; a position where I could maintain surveillance on the insect. Soon, though, the thrill of light, determined kisses across my neck and shoulders, the breath and sweat of this alluring man, dissolved the tent ceiling into nothingness. Just me and my date.

The rain weakened to light pellets around us as we both climaxed, collapsing our exerted bodies wherever we could land. My arm dropped against his cheek. His hand landed on my rib cage. We giggled at the state of us. I shifted onto my belly and slid over to my sleeping bag, gathered it into a bundle and rested my head there. My date reached for the open Trojan wrapper and crawled over to his backpack. I heard him snapping, unzipping, crumpling, and zipping again. He crawled back to me, smelling like lemon, slid beside me and lay his head on my thighs, the cushiony part just under my behind. He gently kissed a cheek—the same one that had crushed the unidentified bug. I giggled, and promised myself I would tell him that secret a little later. But a moment later, from under my makeshift pillow, a stealthy spider whizzed across the synthetic floor and settled in the corner of the tent.

I squealed. My date jumped up, removing the warmth of his vast curls, which had been draped across my thighs and butt cheeks. I immediately regretted my reaction to the insect.

"What's going on?"

"Nothing! Yes, something. I just saw a massive spider."

"Where's it at?"

The spider had since sauntered off, but I figured this was the opportunity to get rid of the earwig on the tent ceiling. I pointed up.

"Spider's gone, but any chance you could smash that thing?"

"Sure." He reached up and flicked it with his middle finger. I watched the earwig bounce off the tent wall and land in the pile of our belongings.

I had told him to smash it, not flick it. This perturbed me. *I can't see this guy again,* I told myself. *He's just too outdoorsy.* I also wondered how it was possible, in the short amount of time we'd been on the campground, that we had already amassed such an infestation within the tent. Could I really make it through the night out there? As I considered how to make a graceful exit and head to the car, my date crouched beside me and pressed his forehead to mine.

"Thanks for being out here with me. You're amazing. And I get it, you hate camping."

"Did I give that impression?" I said, and we both burst into laughter.

"No more camping for us, I promise," he said.

He unzipped the tent and we sat, hugged up, sipping cold coffee and staring out at the wet trees. With the light breaking through the tent, I turned and studied those coffee-stained teeth, the rugged hair I had twisted into ice-cream swirls around his Adam's apple, the freckles on his nose. My date was downright gorgeous, and I reveled in the awareness that he was all mine at that moment. I smiled, imagining a bug-free date number two. But I was ready for a shower.

"It's stopped raining," he said.

"Let's get out of here," I replied, and gently swept the curls at his temple.

A Thousand Tiny Pieces

AMADEO CRUZ GUIAO

D ear One, close your eyes.
Close your eyes and think of the swashbuckling main character in my film script: a banjo-playing Filipina (BPF) who hitchhikes to Alaska to sniff out Mystery after her life falls apart, after everything she thought she knew became big question marks streaked with tears and soul-wrenching disappointment. No, it's not autobiographical.

Halfway up into the rugged Yukon wilderness—which is all sleeping bears, snow-blanketed forests that absorb all sound and memory of time, fast-moving storms that can kill you quickly if you're not paying attention, and gigantic moose—she scores a ride with a beautiful, wild-haired mama (WHM) who works part-time planting trees and drives an ancient, clunky fire-engine-red Ford F150 truck, which she drives with high heels 'cause it's the only time she can wear them, and whose heart has just been bro-ken by a callous jerkface. BPF knows this last part right away because her heart is broken too, and has been for a long time. It is taking our hero a while to put her heart back together because, first, she has to find all the pieces, which are scattered all over, in signs and riddles and on the open road.

They talk, telling stories and making each other laugh, and soon they are holding hands. They've only known each other for three hours, which seems absurd when considered in Real-World-Time, the place where the living dead pass their lives, a place where they try not to live, because it holds only death and dead ends. But they hold hands because they know there is no such thing as time, and that whatever this connection is, it is a Gift.

VERY SOON, IT IS PITCH-DARK, as there is no moon that night. WHM is in the middle of a story about Diana Ross when BPF gasps at a twinkling that appears in the middle of the sky, right in front of them. A flash of purple! Then red and green comes fast on its heels, and an audible crackling sound as if the ice that covers the earth all around them is breaking. Soon the whole sky is alight with undulating ribbons of color, and even the greatest painters could not imagine such beauty.

The dialogue goes something like:

WHM: Oh, wow. It's the northern lights. Aurora borealis. They weren't forecast for tonight.

BPF: Holy cow. Can we pull over and watch?

WHM: Sure, there is a lake in a couple miles.

They make sure to bundle up as it is a clear, frigid night, and they don't want to lose their noses or ears or hearts. When they finally find a place to spread the big down sleeping bag on the snow that covers the lakeshore, they are puffed out like humongous marshmallows in down parkas with big hoods covering their entire faces except for their eyes. They giggle as they plop down, their faces facing the heavens, and hold hands, which aren't actually hands but hands covered in huge mittens.

WHM: The Native folks around here say the aurora is actually a reflection in the sky of big bonfires in the far distant north, something to keep the humans warm when it's this cold out . . . they also say that it's a sign that our Mother still loves us.

[BPF can't hear her, because her ears are covered.]

BPF: We wear too much armor to enter into a place of such holiness.

[WHM can't hear her, because her ears are covered, too.]

Then a song plays (in the film scene) and God-art and human-art dance together.

[Cue "A Thousand Tiny Pieces," as sung by the Be Good Tanyas.]

Lyrics: Am I ebb? Am I flow? My lack of control . . .

There is no more talking, just quiet. The scene ends with a tender kiss, as the soundtrack poses another question, then yet another—

The All-Night Deluxe Tea Room

TEMIM FRUCHTER

T he shining star of the Shavuot resort is the All-Night Deluxe
Tea Room.

The room itself is not fancy. It's plain and wood-paneled like all of the other public-use rooms at The Pressman, which itself is more shabby relic at this point than actual resort. But the ivory-draped tables arranged in a U-formation at the front of the room are laid lavishly at all hours with seemingly bottomless platters of cake and fruit, which transform the room, lending it just a hint of majesty.

The cake, cut into serving-sized squares and stacked to towering heights on bright, white platters, is sorted by color: rich dark brown with a shining chocolate glaze; butter-colored vanilla with a pristine buttercream; and hibiscus-pink, overlaid with a layer of glossy, dark pink jam. Flanking the pyramids of cake are two large platters of sliced fruit, the strawberries and pineapples and kiwis gleaming like jewels. At the far ends of the display stand two tall golden urns—one coffee and one hot water—and next to those, little ceramic white cups and saucers stacked alongside small bowls of tea bags and sugar cubes and lemon slices and little creamers and a tiny tin of tiny spoons for stirring.

It is easy to imagine that, in the All-Night Deluxe Tea Room, something significant should happen. Easy, too, to imagine the room might grow into someplace beautiful, by wearing even just a touch of candlelight. That with just such a flourish, it might dim into something far more mysterious than a middling kosher hotel in Pennsylvania, even at the height of the glow of the afternoon sun. Easy, even, to imagine servers, slipping in through the side door handing out flutes of champagne, the room filling with the clinking, flirtatious sounds of a night just beginning.

The All-Night Deluxe Tea Room is often lying in wait—either sparsely populated or not populated at all. It's not that it's any kind of secret; it's just that Shavuot is a quick two days—three this year, with Shabbos tailing immediately behind—and there are other places to be. There is the large multipurpose room that functions as the sanctuary, where the guests will study and pray, with its temporary rows and its temporary ark robed in temporary velour. There is the sunny dining room, where they will gather at mealtimes to eat blintzes and cheesecake and drink intermittent glasses of the kosher wine the hotel has bought in bulk. They will kibitz and gossip and linger and take walks around the golf course and by the little stream out back.

It is late afternoon when Laurie and Rivky both breeze into the All-Night Deluxe Tea Room simultaneously and for the first time. The light is peak supreme, and the wood-paneled walls glow golden brown. It smells faintly, and as always, of coffee. Both women are still in their travel clothes. Laurie is wearing a blue button-down dress that falls to her knees and is cinched at the waist with a brown leather belt. Both Ralph Lauren, both on sale.

Rivky is wearing a long cotton skirt with a long-sleeved top, both black, as is generally her preference. On her head, a black scarf. The divorce is not yet finalized, so she still covers her head. Regardless, she can't imagine walking around bare-haired.

They meet face to face at the coffee urn. Laurie seems impatient, so Rivky lets her go first. Then Rivky fills her own cup, and they both attend to sugar and cream.

"It's going to be a long night," says Rivky politely. Her voice is huskier than Laurie might have imagined it would be. "I need to start with the caffeine now if I'm going to make it."

"Are you planning to stay up all night?" Laurie sizes up her companion, whom she might have pegged as too religious a woman to participate in the Shavuot tradition of staying up all night studying Jewish texts, a practice reserved for very religious men and for women more modern than this one appears to be. She must have a husband, Laurie figures, who will listen to the rabbis give talks for several hours and then pore over ancient tomes until dawn. She figures her own husband will make it until eleven thirty or so, at the latest, and then turn in. Respectability, not zealotry. Her husband, a generally respectable man.

"Probably not all night," says Rivky. "What about you?"

"I don't think so," says Laurie. "It's not for me, really."

They sip their coffees, testing. Then, they sit; not at the same table, but at two neighboring two-tops. They sit like women who only have a few minutes: each on the edge of a chair, each ready to catapult into whatever's next.

Laurie peeks at Rivky. She is dressed in head to toe black, like she's on her way to a funeral. Her clothing is very modest and she's not wearing any makeup, but she is striking. Her eyes are large and bright, her cheekbones enviably articulate, and her lips generous. From under the scarf, a few strands of wavy brown hair.

Rivky peeks at Laurie. She is smartly dressed, one of those Modern Orthodox women who looks like she has a breezy time of it all. She has long eyelashes and a sharp but delicate nose and her near-blonde-hair ponytail threaded through the back of a baseball cap. She reminds Rivky a little bit of someone famous she saw in a magazine once, but she can't remember who. The hoops that hang from Laurie's ears glint gold in the afternoon bright.

"Laurie," says Laurie, from the next table over, by way of introduction.

"Rivky," says Rivky.

They both nod at one another, now mutually licensed to look.

AFTER CANDLE-LIGHTING AND DINNER, THE Pressman hums with studious holiday chatter. The guests file into rooms to listen to talks about Deuteronomy and the Jewish laws of marriage. Some take matters into their own hands, sitting down with a study partner and a pile of donuts in the sanctuary to wrestle with biblical texts. In one room, the moderately alternative set goes to talk about feminist midrash and do some yoga.

Many of the women have transitioned into their Shabbos robes. Anyone who has a robe here also probably has a husband. If you have neither robe nor husband, you are probably at some other kind of resort, or at no resort at all. The robed women float past in an excess of fabric that swishes down past their ankles. Some Shabbos robes are fleece or velour, but many of the guests at The Pressman are wearing cotton or linen or silk, lighter fabrics for the summer holiday.

Rivky has a new robe, an eggplant-colored plush number she bought in Teaneck especially for this weekend. Hers is one of the fleecy ones, but she doesn't mind, in all that aggressive air-conditioning. She loves its intricate golden buttons and wears it buttoned all the way up to the top.

Laurie has also brought a robe, but it's more like a caftan. Plain, silky, aquamarine. Calvin Klein, she thinks, but she can't remember.

It is a little bit after nine when they find one another again in the All-Night Deluxe Tea Room. The fruit and cake, somehow, still plentiful and fresh.

"Hello," says Laurie.

"Hello," says Rivky.

In the air, inexplicably, the warmth of reunion, even though the two are complete strangers.

Laurie hesitates for only a moment. At dinner, Laurie and her husband sat with new friends, the Silberbergs. Laurie's children, teenagers, sat with friends at a different table. She'd been bored by pointless talk of real estate prices. She'd wondered, idly, about the black-clad Orthodox woman with the lips. Now, though, here the woman is. She can simply ask.

"Would you like to have some cake and coffee with me?"

Rivky looks only mildly surprised to be invited. "Okay," she says.

Laurie takes a slice of chocolate. Rivky goes for the pink. They sit.

It is hard, Laurie is embarrassed to realize, not to watch Rivky's mouth as she lifts her fork to it. She has rarely met someone with such a mesmerizing mouth.

"So," says Laurie, "is your husband burning the midnight oil in the sanctuary tonight?"

Rivky chews her cake for a moment before swallowing. "My husband," she says slowly, like she's considering the shape of the word. "We are divorced."

"Ah." Laurie masks her surprise the best she can. "I'm sorry to hear it."

"No," Rivky says. "No need." Her *o*'s come out soft and round, a pious affect. She offers nothing further.

"My husband is probably already winding down," Laurie chuckles. "He's a wimp when it comes to staying up late. Needs his beauty sleep, you know." She does not know why she keeps talking, but she does know that she'd like to talk to Rivky about something other than husbands.

Rivky takes care of this. She turns to Laurie. "You look familiar," she says in that voice of hers, so throaty it sounds like it's coming directly from the ground. "You look like somebody famous."

Laurie doesn't know if Rivky means she has a quality of celebrity—a quality, she admits, she tries dearly to channel every time she picks out new sunglasses—or that she looks like one celebrity in particular. It doesn't matter; she blushes, regardless.

"You look . . ." says Laurie. She does not know how to finish the sentence. She is not usually short on words. Something about Rivky unsettles her, but not in a bad way. She is disarmed; close to something she hasn't been close to before. It all feels vaguely embarrassing. She considers a bite of cake, but sips her tea instead. "I like your robe."

The truth is, Laurie does not much like Rivky's robe. But she really does like looking at Rivky in it. She likes, for example, how soft the fabric looks. Fleetingly, she wonders how soft Rivky must be underneath it, and is so alarmed by the thought she grows dizzy.

Rivky eats more of her cake until it is gone. She has made quick work.

"So," says Laurie, "you came alone?" It is uncommon, at The Pressman. There are singles weekends for religious Jews, but mostly The Pressman bursts at its seams with families. Parents, kids of all ages, the occasional grandparent or two.

"We had already booked the room, right when we got home after the last Shavuot. It was too late to cancel, and I wasn't going to let it go to waste." Rivky answers hastily, like she's been asked multiple times already. "What about you?"

"I'm here with my husband and my three kids. They're in junior high and high school. We've been coming for a few years now. My husband loves the food, and I mostly love not cooking." She chuckles politely, and then feels silly about all of it. She presumes Rivky doesn't have kids because none have been mentioned, but this, too, seems unusual for a woman who appears to be very religious and just past the prime of her childbearing years.

The sound, then, mundanely, of footsteps, and Laurie is overcome by an intense protectiveness. She isn't sure at what point the room has become their secret—hers and Rivky's—but it has. She feels suddenly, inexplicably, that if anyone else walks in, everything will be lost for good. She isn't even sure what *everything* is, but she feels terrified of this loss regardless. She must hurry. *Hurry?* Just hurry.

"May I take your plate?" She is already lifting Rivky's saucer off the table as she asks. On her way to the trash can to shake off the crumbs, she presses the pad of her index finger to the tines of Rivky's used fork.

The footsteps in the hotel hallway pass, growing distant. The room darkens, relaxing around them. They both fill mugs with hot water for tea and return to their table. Rivky can smell Laurie's perfume. Something grassy and modern. She runs her palm over her own robe under the table. She doesn't understand why she feels compelled to befriend this woman. The kind of woman who must while away a Sunday getting manicures and attending luncheons. Like no one she would ever befriend. But Laurie, she swears, looks like somebody famous. Rivky should leave, she thinks. She should go upstairs. She should read a little bit of Torah and then go to sleep. But Rivky can't seem to move from her seat.

Instead she leans in very close, close enough for Laurie to feel the wings of Rivky's soft breath on her ear. "Can I tell you something?" Her voice bending ever lower, whisperward.

"Please," says Laurie, more eager than she means to sound.

The All-Night Deluxe Tea Room doesn't bill itself as a place for trading secrets, but to visit it in this pocket of the night, a refuge away from the patter, you might understand why it feels like one.

It offers, in its implied opulence, and its parenthetical intimacies, a kind of protection. It offers surprise in a place that otherwise offers nothing of the sort.

Rivky leans in closer. She isn't sure why she feels compelled to do it. "It's something about Shavuot I always heard from my mother growing up. It's a little bit silly, so I actually never told my husband this, but I've always sort of secretly believed it."

Laurie's eyes widen of their own accord. She wants the childhood secret that isn't for the husband.

"What is it?"

"Every Shavuot, at midnight, the sky cracks open."

"What do you mean, cracks open?"

Rivky presses her lips together, thinking. "It's hard to say, exactly. It just . . . opens, for a split second. And then, so fast, it closes. My mother always said if you blinked you would miss it. So, we would stand outside a few minutes before midnight, she and I, and stare up at the sky without blinking."

"Did you see it? Did it open?"

"I don't know. At a certain point, when I turned, I don't know, fourteen, fifteen, I decided she was just being ridiculous. Once or twice, though, before that—I really did think I could feel it. Nothing I could really see or prove. But like something split open in me. Just a little. And everything felt more, I don't know. Allowed. Just for the night."

"Just for the night," Laurie echoes. She wonders what it must feel like to split open.

It is then that, unpredicated by warning sounds, a clamorous crowd spills into the tea room. Two tall men, both bearded, their white button-down shirts untucked. Several women, two in robes, two still dressed. A cluster of teenagers, loose-limbed and clumsy. The teenagers grab for the cake with their bare hands, not bothering with plates. It is all very noisy, and somehow brighter.

Laurie is disgusted by the din. It feels gauche. A desecration.

Rivky is jarred by the interruption. Where has she been, that she feels in this moment like the noise of these newcomers has woken her up?

The women sit up straight again, trying to shake the warm hum from their necks, the hushed haze from their eyes. The breath.

Laurie finishes her tea first. She has never been one to take her time.

"Well." She doesn't mean to be curt, but she can't help it. Something has closed now, ejecting her swiftly from wherever she's accidentally visited. "Nice chatting with you." She scurries out of the tea room with an urgency she cannot explain.

Rivky, never one to rush much, stays behind. The teenagers bustle around, eating their cake; the adults hover, guzzling their coffee, and leave again. Rivky sits, still, with her tea, thinking about the sky and about Laurie's sharp eyes, the way they'd darted back and forth, mirroring her hurry. Rivky isn't tired. She isn't lonely, quite, but she has a sharp awareness of her solitude, the sudden emptiness of the room buzzing bright around her.

LAURIE CAN'T SLEEP. SHE'S CLOSED all the curtains in her room, and she's wearing her lavender sleep mask, but still. Her husband remains downstairs. It must be after eleven, she thinks. She'll expect him back in the room soon, where he'll give her the cursory kiss he always does, whether she is sleeping or she isn't, and then turn away from her to fall asleep immediately. Her kids are either hanging out with the other teenagers or sleeping in their own room; she's lost track of them, and being able to fully lose track of them is one of her favorite things about being in the container of this hotel for the holiday.

Her evening had felt so strangely luminous, so brimming with potential, before it was cut off so abruptly. That gaggle of guests. The All-Night Deluxe Tea Room is for everyone, of course, Laurie knows this. But, just briefly, it had felt like it belonged only to them. Just her and the mystery Orthodox woman. *Deluxe*, she whispers. Even the word feels like an extravagance in her mouth.

She pulls off her sleep mask, gets out of bed, and walks over to the window. She pulls back the heavy curtain just a little. The sky is so much darker here than it is in the suburbs. No streetlights, no floodlights from driveways or lamplights from late-night living rooms. What would it look like for this dark to split? Would it simply split into more and more dark? Could something really split inside her, too?

She wants to cry with the stupidity of it. She should go back to bed, try to sleep. She feels like a child. She is queasy, but it is not her stomach, it is her everywhere. This mortifies her, which quickly leads to crying, and Laurie hates crying. Why is she crying? Why does it feel like something is lost to her now? She shakes her head hard, trying to loosen something stuck.

She looks at the bedside clock. Midnight, Rivky had said. It is nine minutes to the hour.

Laurie slips out of her pajamas, back into her caftan. She walks down the stairs, past the rooms of people still animated over their texts, past the couchfuls of slouching teenagers taking advantage of the lawlessness of the hour.

For Laurie, prayers are more habit than they are anything else. She does not consider herself a particularly spiritual person. She is pragmatic. She values repetition. But on her hurried way down the stairs, she finds her lips moving ever so slightly around some kind of wish, like a lyricless song.

When she gets to the All-Night Deluxe Tea Room, she crumples. There is no one here any longer. It is empty of its stupid magic. On one of the tables, an empty cup, dregs of coffee settled at the bottom, and a plate of nothing but pink crumbs. She sits, heavily. The platters of cake are full again, and the heaps of fruit, but none of this looks inviting to Laurie any longer. She wonders why she is here. In the tea room, at The Pressman, with her husband, in her silly house in New Jersey, in this life. Why is she here at all?

She will go upstairs, she thinks, her brain taking decisive and necessary control of the rest of her, and she'll take an Ambien. She brings it with her on trips for emergencies only. *This counts*, she thinks. She needs to stop wallowing at once. This nonsense. She doesn't know what's wrong with her.

It is when Laurie stands again that she sees what she sees. Something outside the window. Something moving. She moves toward it. When she gets close enough, she realizes that it is not an *it*. It is Rivky. The Orthodox lady is on the small fire escape outside one of the All-Night Deluxe Tea Room's large windows. Her fleece robe is bunched above her knees, allowing her lower legs to dangle between the metal bars. Undignified as a teenager. Her hair, Laurie is shocked to notice, is uncovered. The waves of it are generous, winding around her face. Laurie pushes open the window, and Rivky spins around, her face wearing an expression of genuine surprise. She grabs for her head scarf.

"Don't worry," says Laurie. "It's only me." She isn't sure what she means. They are strangers, mostly, still.

Rivky obliges, leaves her hair uncovered. "What are you doing here?"

"I." Laurie isn't sure what to say. She didn't have a plan, coming back here. "I . . . I was just wondering," she stammers, "about the sky."

The look that breaks across Rivky's face is giddier than a smile. It's something either childish or too adult. Something uncensored.

"Come," she says. She pats the tiny space next to her on the fire escape.

"I don't think this is meant for adults to sit on," Laurie says. As she sits. The metal is corroded, like it shouldn't be at a place they are paying this much to stay, and her legs, thin as they are, barely fit through the spaces between the bars.

It is indecent, Laurie thinks, the skirts of their robes split by the straddle, their thighs practically exposed. Their thighs practically touching.

Rivky looks at the delicate gold watch on her left wrist. She has freckles there, Laurie notes.

"Two minutes," Rivky says.

Laurie remembers excitement with her whole body. She remembers two scoops of ice cream and the sweet terror right before tipping over the edge of a mountain on her skis and the roaring expanse of the ocean stretching out before her on the first day of many at the beach.

Rivky's skin feels vibrant, her awareness of the late spring air on her exposed thighs perfectly attuned. She is shaky with anticipation. It is an old feeling, one she has not felt for many years. She remembers that ache in her young neck, craning upward.

Remembers wishing hard, wishing for nothing in particular, just something wild and wide open. Something she might disappear into, saturate with. Something she might let consume her wholly if she could.

Together, they are looking up.

"One minute."

Are they breathing?

"Thirty seconds."

Laurie's hand acts without her consent. It moves closer to the thick of Rivky's thigh, and only just barely touches the fabric of her robe. There is so much robe that Laurie is certain Rivky can't feel it.

Rivky can—very little is lost on Rivky—but she won't let on. Under Laurie's fingertips, Rivky's robe feels soft to the touch. So soft, it almost hurts.

"Five." Rivky breathes the word more than speaking it.

"Four," whispers Laurie.

"Three, two," they say together.

No one blinks.

No one needs to say *one*.

HERE IS HOW YOU CONSUMMATE a visit to the All-Night Deluxe Tea Room.

You wait until the hush falls. You'll know the one. It will come when the night arrives at a later chapter, past a bit late, past "Oh! It's getting very late," and squarely into too late.

You wait until the lights dim of their own accord. Somehow, the overhead lights are no longer themselves. The lights have been replaced with something far starrier, more dappled and warmer than anything emanating from a bulb.

You wait until the halls around the All-Night Deluxe Tea Room grow quiet, quieter than is natural for a building brimming with people. The kind of quiet so pronounced you start to feel like you can hear it.

You wait until the wood-paneled walls blur into something darker, then knottier, then thicker, then crowned by a sheen of green, as if you are being held by some kind of a thicket; a forest where, once, a room stood. The room camouflages itself entirely, no longer visible to anyone else.

You wait until the hour grows warm, a warmth that is at once sleepy and alert. A warmth that threatens to hypnotize you from the tingling skin inward.

You wait until anticipation. You wait until you are alive.

Five. Four. Three. Two.

And then you stop waiting. There is no waiting anymore.

No one has refilled the cake. No need for coffee anymore.

No more counting down.

On the other side, it feels like they are in another place.

No place that Rivky has ever been. Laurie either. They have tumbled back into the All-Night Deluxe Tea Room from the fire escape, flushed with the effort. Their eyes are wet from all the unadulterated night in them. They sit together, feeling glued in place, like they can't quite part ways yet.

"Water?" Rivky walks to the tables sitting in a U-formation, still impeccably set, and pours a glass for herself and a glass for her companion. She returns to the table.

Rivky drinks. She is too hot, and unbuttons her Shabbos robe. Not just the top button, but the top three. Four. Five. Her hair still uncovered.

"You are gorgeous," says Laurie, before she understands what she is saying. Her voice comes out hoarse, like it belongs to somebody else. She is so embarrassed, but that doesn't matter anymore. Her queasy skin doesn't care. The only thing she wants now is to help Rivky's robe the rest of the way off. Here in the thicket of this room, she allows the thought. In the low light, under these stars, past the split sky, she feels certain no one will ever find them.

Rivky, always even-tempered, flushes hot pink. Something about the way Laurie has complimented her feels unusual. She is bare at the chest, bare on the head. Here is a woman—a woman with a husband—who has spoken to her with the kind of hunger that tinged the voices of the men who most notably scandalized her in her otherwise chaste youth.

"Thank you." She all but growls the words.

The smell of coffee—still, always—mingles with the smell of the breeze from outside, neither of them having bothered to close the window. Whatever the cracked sky has released smells earthen, smells honeyed, smells floral, smells spicy, smells washed clean.

Rivky's body directs her now. She reaches for Laurie's hand. She takes it. Laurie turns her sharp eyes on Rivky. She does not shake her hand away from Rivky's. Rivky wonders if Laurie can see her trembling. In her mouth, Laurie tastes salt.

Their lips feel dry. Their hands, a bit clammy. It is hard to move. It is hard to do anything at all.

Laurie surprises herself by moving her face closer and closer to Rivky's, dizzy from the work it takes to convince her mouth to travel in the right direction.

Around them, the room grows thicker, all branches and fruit trees. *An orchard*, Rivky thinks, as Laurie approaches. Both women are standing now. Overhead, a ceiling of vines winds around the light fixtures, becoming chandeliers. The tall burnished urns glow attentive, like watchmen.

The satin of Laurie's robe under Rivky's fingers. Rivky's robe too soft, the kind of softness that could make a person forget herself entirely.

The robes don't matter anymore. Rivky's lips are the only thing, fat past comprehension, malleable under Laurie's eager teeth. Or Laurie's lips are the only thing, pointed and certain, searching the tender edges of Rivky's mouth as though for treasure.

The robes don't matter anymore.

They pull apart, perhaps in slow motion.

Rivky goes entirely silent, her golden world blank except for this feeling, the one rendering her voiceless, practically unconscious with pleasure.

Laurie, though, releases one long, low, moan. She can't help it. She is feral for this woman. She is gnarled with desire.

Rivky knows what's next. Somehow, even after this life she's lived—the humblest quiet, the most modest abiding—she knows. She is rid of the husband, the one who no longer cared for her, the one she no longer cared for. There were never any children. And even God, the God who she's known better than most members of her family, is a wily and mischievous stranger in this moment. This, she knows, is the furthest thing from what her mother meant. The splitting sky meant nothing so unholy. And yet, she knows, it is also exactly what her mother meant. Nothing—and of this, she is certain—has ever been holier.

Rivky unbuttons the golden buttons on her Shabbos robe. Every last one. She lets the robe fall around her feet. Laurie's mouth doesn't work anymore, but her feet do, and she stands, pulling the caftan over her head and letting it fall to the ground.

They are stunned. They are tearing at one another now with the appetites of the long-deprived. They are indistinguishable from one another. They are hair and arms and thighs and round and round and round. The thicket grows tighter, denser around them. The light, dimmer. The floor of the All-Night Deluxe Tea Room is soft; soft enough, now, that they forget it is a floor entirely. This is a surface made for pleasure. It is deluxe. A comfort dedicated to the exact opposite of sleep.

They know the way around one another's bodies. Now that they are here—braided like bread, wrapped and panting—there is no uncertainty. They know the way inside and then out. They know the way around and then through. They know the way across, the sticky trails, the soft breaths, the gasping way the skin rises and falls when it is touched in a way that is terrible and terrible and new. Laurie's thighs clench around Rivky's hand, and Laurie is screaming. At the tops of her lungs, Laurie is screaming, though she is unsure whether she's making a sound. She never wants to stop. Rivky rises and falls from some great height, hardens and softens and sings around Laurie's delicate and manicured fingers.

And then, it is quiet.

Softly, they kiss. Softly, and softly still shaking, each helps the other back into her Shabbos robe.

Softly, the trees begin to recede. They are no longer needed here.

Softly, the thicket of vines releases the chandeliers and Laurie blinks, wondering.

Softly, the regular hum. The hot water. The coffee. The tea.

All around them, just the wood-paneled walls.

All around them, platters of cake. Three colors. Still plentiful.

THE ALL-NIGHT DELUXE TEA ROOM is no prude. No stranger to what happens in the night's deepest pockets. No stranger to what happens in the lightning-quick chasm that tears across horizon, when the sky—once a year, and only for a brief moment—lets itself go.

The All-Night Deluxe Tea Room doesn't sleep, so it sees what most of us miss. It sees the stragglers who find their way back, and back again, and back to one another. It sees the unbidden and hypnotized. It sees sleepless and desperate and hungry. It sees wild and sad and unconquerably giddy. And all along it offers provisions for the way over. The way across. From one side of some chasm to the other.

ALL ALONG THE DARK HALLWAYS of The Pressman, men and women and their children sleep. It is still blue-dark outside the hotel as Rivky floats slowly to her room, the top of her robe still unbuttoned, and her head only barely covered. It is not quite morning as Laurie walks, as if through syrup. Her skin pulsing everywhere she can still feel she has skin.

Laurie doesn't know the language. Doesn't right now care. Doesn't. Her husband sleeps. She is wrecked. She kicks down the down comforter and slides under the white sheets. She doesn't know she is still shivering until she realizes how violently the bed vibrates underneath them both.

Rivky closes the door to her room. Blessedly alone. It is how she knows she can weep with abandon. How she knows she can writhe, still, around her own slippery core, her skin too alive to touch the sheets, or the blanket. Her skin too restless, now, for clothing.

In the morning, through the windows of the All-Night Deluxe Tea Room, the light is gentle. Changed. Things are always changed on the other side of the sky splitting open; the All-Night Deluxe Tea Room knows this. The buffet setup looks the same as it did yesterday. Only cake and then cake and then cake again, a refrain. Only fruit and frosting. Only tea and honey. Only the occasional visitor, hungry or thirsty or simply restless. Only the smell of coffee, the possibility of lower lighting, the implication of majesty. But also—the room glows today, the way an invitation glows if you look at it long enough. The subtle charge of a room that has held something too wild for holding.

It is seven thirty when Rivky and Laurie meet again in the All-Night Deluxe Tea Room. Both early risers, both in search of coffee. Rivky's hair is tidily covered, and she is wearing a dark blue dress that falls to right above her ankles. Laurie is wearing a green dress that comes to right above her knees, a belt that looks like a gold chain around her waist. They meet by accident, and move toward the coffee urn like people who aren't sure whether they will embrace with abandon or pretend politeness. Each wondering whether they should pretend their way, somehow, back into the pink-cheeked strangers they'd been the previous day.

But they are far too familiar now, decidedly unstrangered.

Rivky goes first, takes her time, lets the spout sing steaming coffee into her cup, and then blankets it with cream. Laurie's eyes on her so keenly she can feel it, like something hot at her back.

Laurie waits her turn, watching Rivky stir the sugar in, Rivky's plush, unmanicured fingers. Then she fills her own cup. She tries to stay steady, to look functional, but the bones in her feel like they might at any second give way, or just fully melt her into liquid. She tries to think words, but they are colors instead.

Rivky, aloft in her own body, moves toward the platters of fruit. The strawberries blush red, glistening, and plump. Rivky takes one and then two and then many, piling a small plate with them. She is not remotely hungry, but the fruit's sweet perfume entrances her. She is trying to stay on the ground. She has no idea how to behave.

Laurie follows. She wants to take Rivky by the shoulders and tell her everything. She isn't sure what *everything* is, but she knows now that it is for Rivky. She has a flash of some future morning, robeless and husbandless, in a crisp white bed, the two of them at some other kind of resort entirely.

Rivky still feels Laurie at her back, and wants to swivel around, to press the softest parts of her lips into the softest parts of Laurie.

She wants to say *we saw it. We didn't blink. We threw our heads back, and we waited, and we counted down, and then*—

Rivky understands that there is a before and there is an after. They both do. And they are in the great, wide, after.

The All-Night Deluxe Tea Room beams, its walls brushed with the early morning light. It breathes together with Laurie and Rivky—steady, steady. The wood panels pulse rhythmically, shaking the shimmer of the sun. Together, like a choreography they've rehearsed a thousand times, Laurie and Rivky sit. Rivky pinches one of the bright strawberries between her fingers and lifts it to her lips. Laurie watches, wondering how the fruit tastes in Rivky's mouth. Around them, the morning becomes itself. No one else is here yet. The room still theirs. Everything vivid with the hush.

Stunt Man

RICHARD SIKEN

A man fell out of the sky, and I took him home. He fell out of the sky a lot. He fell off roofs, robbed banks, lost gunfights, and died in the lousy dirt for a living. He was a cowboy, a scoundrel; a practitioner of the dark arts of the black hat. I was a waiter in a restaurant inside a downtown hotel. He wasn't a real cowboy, but I was a real waiter. He had spurs and a motorcycle. I brought him a beer. He didn't look me in the eye, he looked me in the mouth. He watched my lips. Outside, a crew was trying to figure out how to burn up a room on the second floor with fake fire. His regular gig was a Wild West show in a historic outdoor shopping center. It had a gazebo, an ice-cream parlor, and a steakhouse. The entrance was decorated with a real stagecoach and fake boulders. The steakhouse had a strict, casual-only dress code. If you wore a tie, they would ring a cowbell and make a big production of cutting it in half. Attachment is the root of all suffering. He wants to be a movie star, to be gigantic and perfectly lit, and I am no stranger to suffering. The wide smile, the low-down glow. The way he's looking at me now will make him famous.

Magdalena

V. RUIZ

Magdalena clicked on the gas stove and laid the comal over the flame. The air around her smelled of garlic, onion, and jaloro chile. She leaned over the pan and breathed in the sizzling heat. As usual, the carne molida was perfectly cooked. She checked her lipstick in the glass of the microwave, puckering her full bubble lips. Over in the living room, her husband was half-deep in his beer, jotting notes in his *Beer Connoisseur* journal. His friends were coming over later to talk hops, malt, and yeast, all while savoring sips of beer that—if Magdalena was being honest—tasted like fizzy dandelion root water. He got up from the couch and gave her a kiss on the cheek as she slipped on her jacket.

"You just need to heat up the tortillas, amor. I'm running late."

"Have fun, babe. I'll be up a while, so I'll see you when you get back." He stood by the door and watched her flutter out to the waiting ride.

This was Magdalena's once-a-month night out. The kids were out of the house. Carlos was probably smoking at the skate park (though she wished she didn't know that) before spending the night at his friend Tommy's, and Carla was at a slumber party a few houses down. Lena shook her head and tried not to think about where the kids were. This was her time to be alone. On these nights, she was free to clear her mind, and she often headed to the one place she could let loose without fear of predatory men watching: Gossip Grill. San Diego was one of the only cities in the country with a decent sapphic bar, and Gossip Grill had the best karaoke night. And that was where she ran; to women who understood her frustrations. To women who wanted nothing more than to be fully present in the sweaty pulse of '90s R&B, singing to whatever played-out song they all knew. It was only in a room with low lights and a mash of other bodies that she felt she could fully be herself.

Her husband was unaware of this detail. Mostly, he didn't question where she went. They had long ago established a routine—both went about their business, and neither expected the other to reveal each and every one of their movements. Sometimes she wondered why he didn't get curious about where she went. Was it a lack of caring or an assumption that she wasn't one to step too far outside what was expected of her?

Magdalena was a woman who found herself forty years too late for anything more exciting than karaoke nights. She was in a relationship that was just fine, just enough. Whenever she got frustrated with Johnny, she reminded herself he *should* be enough for her. He was a good man, a kind man, the type of man she could trust. Despite these truths, Magdalena could not ignore that he no longer gave her the *good* kind of hot flashes, nor did he seem to notice their lack of heat. He was the kind of man who thought talking over dinner was enough. Yet she stayed with him—fifteen years, so far. It had become a habit. She woke up with him, went through her humdrum of meal planning, of "when do we grocery shop" and "what bills are due," and completed all the tasks that only distracted her from knowing that he was *just* enough.

She had never been the kind of woman to ask for more than enough.

THE LINE OUT THE DOOR of the nightclub curved in waves. The driver had arrived earlier than expected, so Magdalena had been hopeful, but stepping out of the car she saw there was little chance she was getting in. She figured she'd line up anyways. If she didn't make the cut, she'd sneak off to the wine bar down the street and keep it mellow.

As she made her way toward the back of the line, someone called out, "Lena? Magdalena Ramero?"

Magdalena tried to find the voice, which was hauntingly familiar. A woman near the front of the line stepped out. She had smooth black hair, an undercut on one side, and sleeves of tattoos. What stuck out most, however, was her eagle feather earring, one Magdalena would have recognized anywhere. It hovered over a chocolate chip lunar on the woman's collarbone.

"Yatzil? It's been years."

"Lena, bonita? Give me a hug!" The two held each other for a few moments, Magdalena glowing with a smile wider than she'd felt in a while.

She pulled back and asked, "What are you doing here?" The line in front of Yatzil moved, forcing them to push forward.

Before Magdalena could get an answer to her question, Yatzil waved her in front, telling her, "We'll finish talking inside." They paid the bouncer their ten dollar cover and got their hands stamped. Once inside the nightclub, both women rushed toward the bar. Magdalena leaned over and ordered a paloma for each of them. She needed a drink if she was going to sing in front of so many women, especially now that she knew Yatzil was there.

"It's good to see you," Yatzil said, placing her hand on Magdalena's shoulder.

"Same, chica."

"You been here before?" Magdalena asked.

Yatzil shook her head in response. "No, I've only been back to SD a handful of times since leaving," she raised an eyebrow at this, "but I'm sure I'll get to know it soon enough."

Magdalena's eyes opened wide. "Oh! Me tienes que decir, what brings you here? It's been ages."

In the lights, Yatzil's hair was haloed with a zigzag of fluorescent pink. Her smile glowed white under the blacklights. "I'm going to be in the area for a few months. I'm doing a visiting teacher position at the uni a couple towns over."

"So, you're still teaching art? And at a university. Wow, que fancy."

They both laughed. "Yeah, it's a pretty cool thing I've got going. I get to travel to different schools. Meet different artists. They usually set me up with studio space, and you know, I've always loved teaching."

"I know. You like molding the kids into someone more like you, rebellious y todo." They were interrupted by two drinks placed in front of them.

"If my memory serves me right, I recall you had your own rebellious and creative side too." Yatzil smirked in a way that wrinkled her nose, something that had always made Magdalena's heart flutter, so many years ago.

She continued, "I think it's good for someone in their life to show them that their art is *their* way of seeing the world. And it's so rewarding when they realize that view makes them their own person, regardless of where they come from or where they're going." She blinked her eyes and looked up, "But I don't wanna get all cheesy and shit now, let's drink and cheers. To reunions, y encontrando lost time."

Magdalena clinked her glass against Yatzil's before taking a few gulps, her cheeks blushing from the music, the lack of air, and the space that seemed to be closing between them with each word.

THE REST OF THE NIGHT passed in a blur. Everyone danced, and Magdalena gave herself a sore throat from belting, "I Wanna Dance with Somebody." Drinks made their way into each of their hands, and before she knew it, the bartenders were shouting "Last call." The two moved outside the bar, Yatzil lit a cigarette, and they passed it back and forth just as they did decades ago behind the bleachers.

Magdalena had already ordered a ride and the driver pulled up as the two were starting to say their goodbyes. She wanted to stay. She thought about making an excuse to stick around a little longer, but found nothing other than her desire for the moment to continue. So, she got in the car.

As the driver waited for an opening in the passing cars, Yatzil stumbled up to the passenger door. "Wait," she smacked the window, lightly but drunk. When Lena rolled it down, Yatzil threw in a business card. "Estoy tan tomada, but call me, please? Tonight was nice."

She stumbled away before Magdalena could respond, dragging on the cigarette like she was Audrey Hepburn in front of Tiffany's instead of on the piss-stained, rainbow-flag-waving street.

THE NEXT MORNING MAGDALENA WOKE up with a headache so bad it was cliché. It was pinching and stabbing, and everything that was wrong with the world funneled into her temples.

"Morning, sunshine." Her husband leaned over her, smiling.

She could taste the desert on her tongue. She rubbed the crackle from her eyes and thought about sitting up, really thought about it, but instead lay groaning for a few minutes longer.

"Don't worry, I've got your coffee. And some Tylenol. The kids aren't back yet."

"Please, no words. Your voice is making the room spin." She pulled the pillow from under her head and placed it over her face.

Her husband laughed, shaking the bed. "You were a mess last night. The car dropped you off, you came inside, told me you were going to striptease, then you got your shirt caught on your neck, laid down, and said 'I'm giving up,' and you were out. Snoring like a fucking walrus." He paused, "It was cute, and I loved every minute of it."

"Stop it. I was not that drunk."

"You were. But it's all right. You had fun, though? Is the bar still doing that whole karaoke thing?"

"Yeah, I had fun. Karaoke night is always a hit. I keep going even though I always wind up with this sore throat."

"Seems like you're dealing with more than a sore throat," Johnny teased. "I might have to join you one day. Never seen you belt in front of a crowd."

Magdalena cringed internally at the thought of this. Yes, she craved more fun nights with her husband. Still, the idea of them together, in that bar, wasn't ideal. He didn't know it was a lesbian bar, or that "girl's night" was every night there. And it was her place. It was the only place she could go to be with people like her, who saw that part of her: the part that a husband and children seemed to paint over, hide from view. Those nights were her time to step out of her pretend, cishet-suburb mode, even if only for a few hours.

"Maybe one day. Or maybe we'll find our own place."

She threw the sheets off her body and reached for the coffee. There was a smear of brown cinnamon on top. Her husband had added too much as usual, and sipping it made her want to cough. Whenever she made their coffee, he praised it, saying the cinnamon brought out the sweetness. She had tried to explain her technique—she added little bits at a time, stirring and dissolving the cinnamon in the coffee and agave slowly—but in his mind, anything that took that kind of patience was simply delaying gratification.

She rolled her eyes at her own thought process. He had tried, and really, she just needed coffee in her blood. She wanted to go back to sleep, but the soda and tequila were trying to force themselves out of her body.

While in the bathroom, her phone buzzed, reminding her that her period was due in two days. She made a mental note to buy tampons at the grocery store. That was when she noticed the business card tucked between the phone and its case. It was pearlescent heavy cardstock with a metallic violet QR code. She recalled the drunken goodbyes from the night before and remembered how close they stood at the end of the night.

After washing her face and brushing the old hairspray from her hair, Magdalena went into the kitchen. She spent some time getting breakfast ready for her and Johnny, dicing quick and smooth even with a burning hangover. She added three different peppers to the onions and garlic, and sautéed two kinds of mushrooms that she'd chopped into fine cubes. She cooked this all with chorizo to lay in the center of the omelet. She pulled the comal out of the oven and placed it on the stovetop to heat. The round of it was dented and uneven. There were burn marks all over the silver, but its history served as seasoning and gave everything flavor. It didn't matter that the unevenness of it meant it took longer to heat. She didn't care that it took up a whole rack of the oven when stored away.

This was one of the first things her mother had bought when she came to the States. She had saved dollar by dollar from her checks until she could get one she knew would last. While her mother might have been cheap in other ways, she knew some things needed investment, and the comal was proof.

When the eggs were done cooking and plated, she diced fresh green onions from the can on the windowsill. She set the plates down on the table. At that moment, her children rushed inside from their sleepovers. Carlos went straight into the kitchen toward the cabinet.

"Mom, they don't—" he dug around looking for his favorite box "—have Pop-Tarts at Tommy's and I'm freaking starving, like I didn't even know they were vegan and his mom's a total almond mom," his hair hung over his eyes. He could have been blindfolded, and he still would have found what he was looking for in the crowded cupboard; nothing could stand in the way of him and his Pop-Tarts.

Carla went straight to her room: "I already ate," she shouted over her shoulder. "I gotta work on my science project."

Magdalena sat at the kitchen table, her eggs getting cold, while her son and daughter flew in a tornado around her. Her husband looked at his watch, "I'm so late! I forgot I was meeting Mike to talk about Monday's presentation." He shoved a few spoonfuls of egg into his mouth, "I'm sorry, love, I have to go." He scraped the rest back into the pan.

Everyone swept out of the room quickly, and Magdalena found herself alone, a plate full of food looking back at her.

THE WEEKEND PASSED AS IT usually did, doing things that ate away at her time and left her wondering what she had done for herself. Magdalena and her husband shopped for groceries, their children caught up on their never-ending piles of homework.

Everything seemed calm in a dangerous kind of way. Sunday night came, and Magdalena thought about what she would make for the kids, and what she would pack for lunch for herself and Johnny.

Last week she made guacamole, and this week she wanted to try something else with the cilantro that seemed to be overflowing with new leaves. A salad was perfect. Even though summer had just ended, the last of the season's watermelons were still round and full of juice. This had once been one of her favorite parts of the weekend. Thinking up new ways to use all that overflowed from her garden and windowsill. She didn't cook because she needed to—she cooked because it felt like magic. There was something about the alchemy of it all. She gained her skills from watching her mother all her life. Her mother always said a real chef didn't need "all that fancy stuff they show on TV." A real chef could make something out of nothing. And that was a proverb Magdalena continued to carry.

It wasn't just about cooking. Her whole childhood, Magdalena watched her mother struggle. Most weekends weren't spent connecting and resting, but working. As far back as her memories went, she remembered cleaning offices with her mother on the weekends. But her favorite office, the place her mother still worked to this day, was a place that made promotional items for movies. It was there she learned how easily white people tossed out things deemed broken because of a little scuff, a spelling mistake, or a slightly-off color. That used to be her favorite part of those days. At the end of a shift, Magdalena and her mother searched through the oversized boxes labeled "misprints." Sometimes her mother found unused glassware, and Magdalena would pick out watches, and pens, and shirts—an endless supply of shirts. The imperfect things were the most beautiful to her. The items that people thought a mistake, but she felt they were full of potential, ready to be made into new things. It all led to her now-forgotten passion: her art. She used to take broken glass and random fabrics and paste them to ripped pieces of cardboard. Sometimes she added photos and painted over them to make recuerdos. Other times she'd create vases out of cans with glued gears to fill her house with flowers.

When she was younger, before her marriage, she wondered what it would be like to do something like this full-time, to go to school and learn about other artists. But now she found herself twenty years too late for her dreams. Instead, she was an office manager in a body shop. She was a mother of two children who had never seen her craft. And a wife to a man who didn't know why she paid for a storage unit full of broken things.

This was why she had, for so long, bought groceries without a list. She'd buy items on sale and use every evening to challenge herself to make something out of whatever they had. Some days it was a machaca scrambler, other days tiny patties made out of canned tuna and one leftover potato. She wanted a challenge and to feel like an artist for one moment of the day. No one understood why she spent so much time in the kitchen or why she preferred to make things like salsa, guacamole, and sauces from scratch, why she played with recipes, changing ingredients little by little until she had perfected them. She'd sit and ask her husband and children what seemed different, what tasted brighter, or if they could find any of the ingredients from her garden in their plates. But her family rarely noticed.

Most of the time, her children looked at the meals with a strange curiosity. Her daughter asked why they always ate things with cacti and radishes while her friends got macaroni and cheese or pizza. Her son always devoured everything in a breathless manner. Her husband, likewise, would rush, always saying he'd wash the dishes, but instead, leave them soaking and forgotten, so they stood in the way of her coffee in the morning. Magdalena was used to doing things this way, but in the last few months, she found herself asking why she continued trying when no one appreciated this part of her. In those last few months, she started buying frozen pizzas. She minimized the nopales and the salsas and the carnitas. She bought meat that was pre-cooked from bulk stores. She continued trying new recipes on occasion for herself, because it seemed wasteful not to use the abundance of what she grew.

When she finished preparing the salad, she decided to heat up a tortilla with some butter and salsa. But when she went to grab the comal from the oven, all she pulled out was a handle. She looked inside and saw the metal round burnt with a bull's eye of black char. The handle sat on a completely separate rack. Upon closer inspection, it looked less like a handle and more like a lump of black clay. She was furious. And confused. She remembered it being fine just the other day.

It was at that perfectly timed moment that her husband chose to come in for some water. The look on his face showed her he meant to tell her; his wide eyes gave away that he had conveniently forgotten.

"I'm sorry. I was making a quesadilla the other night when I was working on my batch, but I started looking up hops drying techniques, and I fell into a loop of how-to videos. I forgot I had set the heat high, and then I smelled something burning, and I came in and—" He took a few steps toward her, "I'll go out first thing tomorrow, and I'll get you a new one."

She shook her head softly at this before letting out a long sigh. "I don't want a new one." Before she knew it, her eyes filled with tears.

Her husband tried to console her, "I know it was seasoned and all, but we can get a better one. One that's less bent, it'll heat evenly. I'll get you whichever one you want." Magdalena inhaled and held her breath while she wiped her eyes. For a second, she lived in this inhale. Before the breath left her chest, she set the comal down so slow it whispered as it touched the table.

"I don't want a better one. That one was perfect."

Her husband reached over and put his hand on her shoulder. He opened his mouth as if to say something, but Magdalena shook him off. She was done with the conversation, and when she was done, nothing that was said would ring in her ears.

WORK DRAGGED ON THE NEXT day. Magdalena was still angry at her husband. She was also exhausted, a kind of exhaustion she hadn't felt in years. Lately, things just seemed to slip her mind. It was as if all the days were bleeding together, and there was little that separated them. Though her distractedness wasn't usually a big deal, on that day it was. She had forgotten to order a specific shade of red paint for one of their biggest clients who restored old cars. He let her know he was furious. Because of the delay, he would be missing a show where that red car was supposed to be on display. Magdalena's boss chewed her out for it.

"You need to be on the ball with these kinds of things. I don't want to deduct your payroll, but if something like this happens again, we might have to. We had to take a big pay cut on this project just to keep him coming back."

Magdalena tried to say she would do better in the future. She apologized, but he kept going. At one point, she started rolling her eyes. She was getting overwhelmed. It was a mistake, something everyone had done. This was her first time to forget an order.

"I said I was sorry. I said it wouldn't happen again. Everyone here has cost the company money, you included. What do you want from me?" Her voice climbed in pitch.

Mark shook his head. "Lena," he said, mispronouncing her nickname even after years of working there, "It seems like you have something going on. Look, take the rest of the day off. Maybe you just need to rest."

Magdalena didn't want to say more. She had already said too much. This was the job she'd held for the last ten years. She gathered her things and left the office, unsure of what her husband would say, wanting to quit, but knowing at the end of the day that they needed the income. She needed to think of her family, regardless of how badly she was ready for some kind of change.

Once in her car, she unhooked the case from her phone and grabbed the heavy cardstock she'd reached for so many times in the last few days. She had tried not to overthink her reunion with Yatzil at the nightclub. It had been years since they'd seen each other. They were childhood friends—met back in grade school and grew closer each year. It wasn't until the summer before their last year of high school that both of them realized their feelings for each other. They had a fast but heavy relationship.

Truly, Magdalena thought they were going to be together longer. But when Yatzil made it into a university across the country, and Magdalena was forced to stay local, the two split. It was the one breakup that still made Magdalena nostalgic and curious about the what-ifs. She often thought about what it could have looked like to move across the country, both artists, both struggling but getting by.

She scanned the card and pulled up Yatzil's new phone number. Their last connection was too brief, and really, she needed to be around someone who understood that part of her: the part of her that felt like maybe life had passed her by. She sent a quick *hey. it's Lena. u free?*

And was surprised when a text back came almost immediately. *Lena! I'm so glad you messaged. I got a bit of time. Coffee?* They settled on a café close to the university.

. . .

BY THE TIME SHE GOT to the café, her heart was trying to perform its own drum solo. She felt clammy and sweaty, and she wished she had a moment to freshen up. She wasn't sure this was the best idea. But she didn't have time to think. It was then she noticed Yatzil was waiting for her outside, a cup of coffee in hand.

"I got you the dark roast, added honey, poquita canela, and milk. I'm guessing you still like it that way?"

"Gracias, mujer, yes. That's exactly how I like it, still."

They shared a smile before moving to a tiny table in front of the café. It was windy, so most people were inside, but both women had always preferred to sit outside. Rain, wind, or sun. It didn't really matter, as long as they could feel the fresh air.

After a brief silence, Yatzil started, "You know, I still think about you when I sprinkle the canela on my coffee every morning."

Magdalena looked down, blushing. "It *was* the best cup of coffee."

"I still can't believe you'd never had it in your coffee before we dated; you're fucking Mexican."

"Stop it. We kept it simple en mi casa, k? But doesn't matter, cuz I more than made up for it. I haven't had it any other way since."

"I'm glad something of me stuck with you then." She lifted one eyebrow before continuing, "Does your partner know how to make coffee for you?"

Magdalena stopped mid-sip. She hadn't mentioned Johnny, not that she had to. That was what rings were for, right? A symbol of who *should* be on her mind.

"Yes, he knows. He's a little heavy-handed sometimes. Adds too much, but he tries." She took a deep breath. "We met after my twenty-fifth. At a bar. Been together since. We got two kids too. Carla and Carlos."

"Wow," Yatzil pursed her lips and nodded softly, "Big suburb family. A lot of time has passed." She took a few sips of her coffee before continuing. "You know, I tried to look you up a few times, but you've never liked computers and social media and stuff. I gotta say, I was shocked when I saw you that night at The Grill. You were the last person I was expecting. You look good. The same, but wiser, ya know. I would have recognized you anywhere."

"I recognized you right away. You still got that earring too. And your pelo all long and straight, just like in high school. I've thought about you too, at times."

Magdalena wanted to say more about *how* she thought about her, how she felt after the breakup, and how it stuck with her all those years, but she said instead, "I can't believe you're teaching and still making art. I'm proud of you. You were good at that—going after what you wanted."

Yatzil tucked her long hair behind the ear with the feather. "I just think it's worth trying, at least trying." She bit her lip softly and blushed. "Anything you truly desire comes with a little bit of fear, no?"

The hour went by quicker than Magdalena would have liked, and she apologized for spending so much time talking about her job and the whole situation with Mark. But Yatzil repeated over and over that she didn't mind, she was just happy to see her again. Before the two parted ways, they set a time to meet up the next day. Yatzil was showing her work at a local gallery, and Magdalena was thrilled by the invitation to stop by and see it.

On the drive home, she thought a lot about her husband. She thought about how quickly their time together had passed, how their marriage had seemed a constant string of looking to the next moment and the next, rarely savoring the present or each other.

She remembered the day they met. She'd planned to go dancing with her girls that night. He had on one of those smooth silk button-ups in all black. His slacks were gray and held up by a leather belt with a buckle polished well enough that it reflected the neon lights. He smiled at her from across the room and sent the bartender to ask if she wanted a drink. She waited for him to approach her, but after buying her two drinks, he was still all the way across the dance floor. So, Magdalena decided to make the first move. She asked him to dance. He didn't say no, of course—they had been googly-eyeing each other all night.

It was salsa night. The minute they stepped on the floor "Suavemente" came on, and the two were on beat. He spun her in a way that made her feel everything but dizzy. She still thought back to that night every time they had one of their silent fights. Maybe she had set herself up for the kind of marriage in which *she* would have to walk up to *him* every time they found themselves at a standstill.

She knew she wasn't still mad about the comal. It was everything behind the comal, and she didn't want to have to explain this. She didn't want to tell him that throwing out her mother's comal was a loss so much smaller than the loss of everything she had already thrown away. All the years had passed by, and she found herself continually giving up pieces of herself. Her language: Neither of her children spoke Spanish. Her art: She put it on hold indefinitely to focus on raising their children. Johnny never asked her to let go of all that, not really. But she couldn't find any reason for all the ways she'd dimmed her light, other than him and her desire for their marriage to work.

She was worried that her history, the whole of who she was, was at risk of disappearing. She didn't want bits of her to become store-bought, replaceable. But this was all too much to tell her husband.

On the way to her home, she made a detour to the kids' high school. She texted them both, letting them know she was outside, and they didn't have to walk home.

Carlos texted back almost immediately, saying he was going over to his friend's house after school. Magdalena sighed heavily in her car. Her children wanted little to do with her these days. She tried to remember and understand that he was almost graduating, and she was once young too. But she had always been close with her mother—even now they talked often, and went out for dinner most weeks. Her mother was still someone she turned to when she needed direct and bold advice.

After a few minutes, Carla appeared at the passenger door. "Thanks, Mom. It's so hot out, and I have so many library books."

"No problem, mijita. How was school?"

"It was . . . okay." She sighed in a way that sounded much like Magdalena's own sighs. "I kinda need to talk to you about something. But I'm scared you'll get mad. Can we go get a cupcake?"

"Of course, mija."

Magdalena's mind ran through a thousand possibilities, but her daughter sat there looking healthy and mostly calm, so she tried to silence her worries. Carla was, after all, the one she worried about the least. She was always working on a science project or a paper or reading about scientific theories Magdalena could barely pronounce.

The drive to the cupcake store dragged in silence. Once inside, the two picked out a pair of frivolous and choco-loaded cupcakes.

"I don't know how to start." Carla started chewing at the skin on the edge of her thumb. "You know how sometimes I tell you I feel out of place?"

Magdalena felt her breathing slow. She nodded and waited for her daughter to continue. "Like sometimes it just feels as if everyone around me is one kind of person, and I don't think I'm like them. I feel my own way. You know?"

Magdalena put her hand on her daughter's. "Yes, I know exactly what you mean."

"And like," Carla continued, "I've thought a lot about finding a place where there are more people like me, and a place that wants to help me grow and follow my dreams. Mom, I'm just not happy here, being around people who make me feel so different."

Magdalena wanted to be as supportive as she could be. She made sure her expression was one of kindness and love. "I want you to always feel like you can be yourself, and feel like you can tell me these things."

"I was so worried. And like I know you know I study all the time, and, like, all the people at my school don't get it, Mom. They don't try as hard, and the classes are so easy. And, like, I really didn't think the school would accept me, but they even gave me a scholarship—"

Magdalena jumped back a bit in her chair, shocked. "Wait, what? What do you mean *school*?"

"Yeah, I applied to the University Preparatory School in LA, and they accepted me. *With a scholarship*. And I really, really want to go."

Magdalena was struck silent. This was not exactly the confession she was imagining. Her daughter had never talked about dating, and had never mentioned any boyfriends or crushes at school. On the drive to the cupcake shop, she'd thought back to when she first told her mother about her feelings for Yatzil. The awkward conversation about wanting to be herself and wanting to be honest. Her mother asked what a family of two women would even look like, asking how she would ever manage to have children. But this wasn't that conversation. And even if it had been, she hoped her daughter understood that her mother would always love and support her.

"So, what do you think?"

Magdalena hugged her daughter because she could see that was what she most needed. "I think you are brave for doing something so bold. I would never be mad at you for wanting to follow your own happiness."

After this big reveal, Carla was a lot more talkative than she had been lately. She talked nonstop about the science project that got her into the prep school, what the class offerings were, the book club, and everything she could spit out between bites of chocolate cupcake. And though Magdalena knew things were changing faster than she could comprehend, the excitement was enough to make her feel good about her choices as a mother.

BY THE TIME THE TWO of them made it home, Johnny was already there.

"You're home early."

Magdalena went straight for the cupboard, pulled out a new bottle of wine, and opened it.

"Rough day?" Johnny looked at the bottle, and back at her, back and forth as if the path between them somehow held an explanation. "What happened?"

"I got into a fight with Mark, and it escalated. I was tempted to walk away from that place today and not come back."

"I know it's not the best job, Lena, but it's steady, and the pay's good."

"I know. But I'm exhausted."

"Well, maybe call out tomorrow. Take a day off, tell him you were fighting a cold or whatever."

"Yeah. I don't know though. I think—I just think I'm not happy. I don't know how it happened, but I need a change, ya know? I don't want to be in the same job decades from now, like my mother."

"Just hang on a little while longer—we're building our retirement, the kids are getting older, and before you know it, we'll have all the time in the world." He stood behind her chair and began rubbing her shoulders in the way that always made her melt.

"This is just a rough moment," he said. "Things will work themselves out."

She put her hand over his, "I know. It'll all work out because it has to."

Johnny pulled away from her and grabbed a soda from the fridge.

"I'm going to be in the garage. I'm swapping beers with some of the other dads so I wanna make sure this batch is ready, but if you need anything just let me know, okay?"

She nodded and filled her glass with wine. "I forgot to mention something," she called after him. "I'm going out tomorrow night. To an art gallery."

He tilted his head as he stood in the doorway. "Oh, that's different. Alone?"

"No, an old friend from high school, Yatzil. She's teaching in town." She thought about how much she should say, whether she wanted to say anything at all. "We're going to catch up."

"I don't think I remember you mentioning her, but another night out might be good for you."

"I think so." She picked up her homemade recipe book from the table, needing an excuse to end the conversation.

She'd never told Johnny about Yatzil because she was never sure what to say—was she an ex? A best friend? Of course, she'd been both. For years she'd told herself it was out of respect for her marriage—no need to dwell on anything that existed before their love. But after seeing Yatzil the other night, she wondered if it was because nothing had ever fully measured up.

Not that comparing made sense. It was like comparing instant coffee and espresso from an Italian café. Unfair.

As Johnny left the kitchen, she sighed and browsed through recipes. It was almost time to prepare the garden for the next season. She focused on finalizing her plans for what she would grow, attempting to distract herself from thinking about Yatzil and the art show tomorrow night.

MAGDALENA ARRIVED AT THE GALLERY in one of the only dresses she owned. She didn't know how upscale the event was, but she knew it was an opportunity to get dressed up, something she didn't often do. She pulled out her phone and sent a quick text to let Yatzil know she had arrived. She wasn't sure she wanted to walk in alone.

When Yatzil stepped out of the doors, Magdalena was spellbound. Yatzil glowed in a sleek pantsuit that draped her body in ivory, giving her skin a contrast that made her appear golden. There were touches that made it a step above. The lapels were embroidered, likely by Yatzil's own hand, in vibrant teals, reds, and orange. It was a classic touch that reminded her of the Puebla dresses her grandmother used to make. She wanted desperately not to be so shaken by the sight of her.

"Lena, you look beautiful as always. I'll have to be careful they don't try to put you on a pedestal with a little label. You'll make all the paintings jealous."

Magdalena laughed from deep in her belly, "No seas ridicula. If anything they'll put me in a museum with a label that reads 'married and tired vieja.' But thank you. And you, mira que guapa. That cut fits you beautifully."

"Gracias, you know I had to add my own little touch to it." She gave Lena a wink and turned toward the doors behind her. "Shall we go inside then?"

Once again, Magdalena was blown away. Yatzil had always been a skilled painter, but there was more to these. She had truly found her calling. The paintings were all bright and vivid, full of intense pigment. Her new series featured portraits of women whose skins were rainbow and neon. Each had a background print that highlighted a specific color, and each color told a story about that woman's personalities. They both drank wine as they walked around the gallery. At times Yatzil would walk off and explain a color choice or technique to inquisitive viewers. Mostly, Magdalena hovered, taking her time to look at each of the paintings.

As she took in the whole space, one painting in the far corner stuck out to her. She made her way to the back of the room so that she could view it up close. This portrait was set against a daisy floral print that brought the eye to focus on the bright gold hues of the woman's skin. As she approached it, she started to recognize the woman: cupid's bow lips, the diamond-shaped face, a thinner frame, but still very much a reflection of herself.

"I wasn't sure what you'd think, and I couldn't find a way to mention it the other day." Yatzil placed her hand on Magdalena's shoulder, catching her by surprise.

"It's stunning, truly."

"I'm so glad you think so. I used a photo of us as a reference; I found it a couple of years back in a book you had bought me."

"I'm blown away. You made me look beautiful."

"You *are* beautiful. I didn't do anything, just shared the parts of you that I know."

Looking at the painting, Magdalena felt as if it was a portal: A mirror image both of who she used to be and who she could become. With the heat of the wine in her veins, she was overcome with bravery. She leaned in and kissed Yatzil. It lasted only as long as the flutter of a paloma's wings, but it was enough to awaken an old hunger. It was as if, in the breath they shared, she had given life to the buried parts of her heart.

THE GALLERY EVENT PASSED IN a quick montage of color and sound, music ringing in the background, Magdalena's mouth widening into a smile deeper than she had felt in years. By the time they left, neither could keep their hands off the other. Yatzil fumbled with the keys to her apartment, trying to peek through one open eye while she kissed along the curve of Lena's neck. Lena let out a soft sigh and felt herself ease into her body. It had been so long since she felt grounded in herself.

They tumbled in, Yatzil flipping the switch, lighting the room in ruby red. She peeled gracefully out of her pantsuit, then moved her hand along the length of Lena's waist.

"Is this okay?" She whispered into Lena's ear.

Lena bit her own lip, hard, enjoying the pressure and the reminder that all of this was real. After years of recalling this feeling only in sacred—and rare—private moments, she was finally back in Yatzil's hands.

"Mm-hmm," she said, her lips curving back into a smile, "yes, keep going."

Yatzil slid her palm into Lena's and pulled her along the studio apartment, moving toward the bed in the back corner. Lena felt the bed calling to her, the weight of the plush emerald comforter pulling her in. She fell backward, and Yatzil took this as an invitation to lean forward on her knees in front of her.

"I've missed this," Yatzil said between soft pecks on Magdalena's smooth calves, moving up to her knees. She let her tongue follow the curve of Lena's legs, alternating licks and kisses that felt like the graze of a feather.

Lena hiked up her dress, letting the cool satin rush shivers over her skin. Her heart raced. Her mind wasn't quite functioning, but her body remembered this—the exhilaration of being with Yatzil. She framed each kiss in her mind, not wanting the moment to end. Yatzil's hands gripped Lena's outer thighs, letting her grip move the satin dress farther and farther up her hips until red lace peeked out from underneath.

Yatzil went further still, sliding the dress up and up until it slid easily over Lena's head. A breeze blew in from the barely open window near the bed, and the pleasure of the cool air made her ecstatic.

"Yes, yes," Magdalena whispered.

She pushed herself onto her elbows, surprisingly confident, as if no time had passed between the last time the two had held each other. In just her underwear and bra, goosebumps forming on her skin, she looked to Yatzil.

"Is this what you want?"

Yatzil gazed up at Lena. "I have never stopped wanting this."

These were the words that Lena had fantasized about hearing, many times over the years, when she most needed to feel herself. She took a shaky breath, suddenly emotional. Yatzil's eyes shimmered, and it was as if they were back in high school, the night before Yatzil packed her bag before driving away with a piece of Lena's heart.

Their locked eyes parted and Yatzil returned to delivering kisses, moving closer and closer to the spot that most craved her attention. Yatzil's tongue slipped out from her round lips, running along Madalena's lace panties. Lena cooed, shutting her eyes and unknowingly pushing herself forward. Without missing a beat, Yatzil ran her nails along the hem of the lace, before slipping her fingers beneath them. She tugged them down with ease.

Lena had missed this, the feeling of being in her body in her most vulnerable state. In a flash she understood how often she left herself, how often she denied herself what she most wanted. Her legs parted slowly, shaking from anticipation, or shivering from the breeze—maybe both.

Yatzil moved her mouth back to the space between Lena's legs, fully exposed now. Lena moaned, letting out a deeply held sigh. Yatzil's tongue danced between her lips, her hand moving to part them farther. She started slowly, with the precision of an artist, dipping in soft before returning to her clit. Her tongue circled, moving quicker and quicker until Lena felt overcome by the sensation and the red of the room. She moved her hands to Yatzil's hair, pulling her in deeper as her body shook, the sensation building, moving like a wave of electricity up her entire body until it rested at the crown of her head.

"Please, don't stop," she cried, no longer quieting her voice. Yatzil slid two fingers into her, curving them up and in, urging her to come in more ways than one.

"Mi amor, come for me," she said, lifting her face to meet Lena's gaze.

As they locked eyes, Lena's body began to quiver. She couldn't hold it in and she didn't want to. "Yatzil! Yes, yes, yes!"

The orgasm felt like a long-suppressed volcanic eruption. Her entire body was lit like lightning against a dark sky. She collapsed back and let the sensation circle within her. This was what she had missed. Not just this moment, this orgasm—not just the pleasure of being with Yatzil—but being in her body, and back in a space where she was allowed to want, encouraged to desire without considering the consequences, without considering everyone else's needs.

"I love you." The words slipped out of her before she could second-guess them.

Yatzil slid onto the bed next to Lena, draping her arm across her waist. She placed a soft kiss again on the curve of Lena's neck. She kissed again and again, moving upward before her fingertips caressed Lena's cheek. She turned her face so they were locked, eye-to-eye.

"I love you too. Always have."

WHEN MAGDALENA WOKE UP, SURROUNDED by the emerald comforter, she was panicked—but not confused. She knew exactly where she was. The night rushed back to her in flashes. Her lips on Yatzil's lips. How their hands had roamed each other, over and over again. The way her back arched, the way she unhinged. The comforter pillowed in a tangle between them. Magdalena kicked her legs out from under the blankets and jumped up, looking for her phone and her bag.

Yatzil woke, startled, "What's going on?"

"I need to go—my family, I have to get back to them."

Yatzil sat up and scrambled to find some clothes, grabbing a robe from the foot of the bed. "I'll walk you to your car."

Magdalena wanted to say no, but she also wanted so desperately not to leave.

Yatzil stepped forward. She grabbed Lena by the shoulders and pulled her in, feeling her body quake from anxiety.

"Lena, I know it's been years. But I never stopped thinking about you. Not one day."

Lena felt a heat overcome her, she looked away from Yatzil as they separated.

Yatzil continued. "I need you to know: I don't want this to end. I need you to know that I want to be with you regardless of how we've changed, and all the time that has passed. None of it matters."

"I . . . I don't know what to say." Lena ran her hand through her hair. "I'm sorry, but I can't—" she glanced down, only to find her phone lit with at least a dozen missed calls and texts. She winced and clicked on Johnny's name.

> Johnny: Mag I'm worried

> Johnny: Where are you

> Johnny: I can't believe you'd be so irresponsible.

"I have to go. I'm sorry, but I need to think. Please, just stay here."

Lena rushed toward the door, throwing it open and feeling the August winds fall on her like a weight. As she walked, she sent a series of texts explaining how drunk and out of it she'd been. Her husband's response was nothing but a *i will cu here.* Aside from Johnny's frantic messages from last night, she had just one other unread notification. A reminder that she hadn't input her period in her tracking app. She was late by three days.

MAGDALENA STARED AT THE POSITIVE pregnancy test.

Her husband had been cold when she returned home yesterday, but ultimately accepted her excuses and brushed it all off as her having an "off week." Now time froze in a fog around Lena. They had been careful. Mostly careful. There were a few nights where they had, in a rush, started things off without a condom, but she thought she was nearing the age when pregnancy was unlikely.

What was she going to do? Her children were finally getting to that age where they were more independent than not. She missed them needing her, but she finally had time for herself.

And what about her marriage? After her night with Yatzil, she knew how unfair it all was to Johnny, not only the affair, but all Lena had held back in the marriage. She had made herself smaller over the years, afraid of admitting what she truly craved. While she loved Johnny, it was more a love of convenience than the love she actually wanted. Both of them deserved not only to be with those they loved, but to be fully loved from a space of knowing, not hiding.

It was so clear now to her that there had never been a love like what she had with Yatzil. With Johnny, the whole of their relationship was based on Magdalena giving up things so they—so he—could be happy. She wasn't sure she was willing to give herself away again, after all these years, just as she was beginning to find herself again. It was as if someone had finally shone a light on all the desires she buried.

She needed change desperately. After telling herself in the last few years that she was too old to return to her art, the night with Yatzil reminded her of possibility, reminded her that there was still so much life ahead of her. Hell, maybe she could write a recipe book. But none of these things would be in reach if she and Johnny had another child. They were financially stable enough to raise a child, but it would mean dipping into their retirement and pushing through longer. Remaining at her shitty job. And after years of being raised Catholic, in a family where there were no options but to "deal with the consequences," she didn't know if she had fully let go of those beliefs. She would have to start over. She had to question if, at the end of this, she would emerge empty of herself.

What would her children think if she up and left their father? They'd want to know why. What would she tell them—that she had simply changed? That she wasn't as happy as she once was?

She wouldn't tell Johnny about the test right away. She needed to make sure it was real, she needed to decide what she wanted, without the weight of everyone else's needs affecting her decision.

WHEN SHE CAME OUT OF the bathroom, she picked up the phone. She needed some reassurance, someone to help her understand. She wasn't sure she could tell her, especially with this lump in her throat, but she needed to hear a familiar voice.

Her mother answered on the first ring.

They exchanged their pleasantries, but her amá knew her well. She could hear that something was wrong, and she pushed Magdalena to tell her.

"I'm not happy, Amá. I don't know when it happened, but it's there. Eating away at me. I push it away only to have it rush up in my dreams. I have dreams of stones falling on me from the sky, until I collapse. I wake up. I look at myself in the mirror, and I see it in my eyes, Amá. I see all the time I ignored myself, deep in the lines on my forehead."

She took a deep breath and continued, "I once loved Johnny, Amá, truly. But now, me voy a dormir, lo beso, and suddenly it's like I don't know who moves my mouth. I don't know who is kissing him, but it's not me."

She went on, deciding to share the whole story—or most of it. She stopped short of sharing about the pregnancy test, but detailed her meeting with Yatzil, the way it felt when they kissed in the gallery, how easy it was to return to what they once were. How awake and fully *alive* she finally felt.

Magdalena laid her chin in her palms. She could feel the disappointment through the speaker. She hadn't meant to burden her mother with this; she knew how selfish she sounded. She was a woman complaining about her husband—a man who was alive, who loved her well enough—while her mother sat on the other line with a ring weighing her hand down from a man who was stolen from her too soon.

The wind moved the branches of the tree outside the kitchen window, and the scratches against the glass were the only sounds between them.

"Say something, Amá. Please."

"Mija, ay, mija." The two of them sat in the tension, Lena waiting for her mother to say anything.

"I know what I *should* tell you. That you have a marido who loves you. A faithful man. A good man. Un buen papa a tus hijos. You don't have to raise them alone like I did. You don't have to work two jobs just so you don't lose the roof over your head."

Lena began to regret the decision to call her mother. She knew her problems sounded frivolous to a woman who had traversed so much physically and emotionally.

"Pero, you know what I *want* to tell you. No. What I *will* tell you . . ."

Her mother's voice had a renewed ferocity. "Lena, you know I love Johnny, I do. But sitting here, thinking of your papa and all we worked toward. It was only ever for your happiness. We spent years of our lives siempre trabajando, doing what we thought we *had* to do. Pero tu, mija, you have a different kind of life. Mira, tus hijos are getting older, they're going to go to college, and where will you be? Sitting here like me, feeling alone. Even with a man by your side."

Lena's face curled into itself, her lower lip quivering and her heart racing.

"We only ever wanted you to be happy. Sometimes, Lena, I think back to you and Yatzil. Estava pensando, en ese tiempo, of all the hardships you two would face and, mija, I was scared. Pero, you're not a young girl anymore. You're a woman, with your own life."

Magdalena leaned back against the chair and felt, for once, like she was being given permission to be who she wanted to be.

"Mija, if Yatzil makes you happy, then you should follow this. It's been years that I've watched you slowly losing your wings, but I didn't know how to talk to you about it. I didn't know what it was."

At this point, Magdalena was in tears. "Amá, thank you," she whispered. "This was exactly what I needed."

"Good, I'm glad, mija."

Lena sat at the edge of her bed, long after her mother ended the conversation. This was the support she'd needed. She suddenly felt certain that she could do the unthinkable and still be loved.

LENA KNEW IT WAS UNFAIR to blame Johnny. She hadn't been up-front or vulnerable with him, not really, not in years. She also knew that this wasn't just about running into Yatzil. It was much more than that—she was exhausted from the work it took to hide the fullness of her sexuality, her creativity, her culture. She and Johnny both deserved to be wholly themselves. She found a pen and paper in the drawer of her bedside table, and settled in to write an honest letter to the man she'd shared her life with for fifteen years.

She did not know all it would take to change. She didn't have all the answers, but she didn't need them. She was ready to collapse her life. And from the rubble, she would build a new one. While it might have been years since she had called herself an artist, she felt the return of a belief she once held as sacred: It was possible to make something beautiful out of something broken, discarded.

THOUGH MAGDALENA INTENDED TO SCHEDULE a doctor's appointment when she picked up her phone, instead she found herself going straight to her texts. She found Yatzil's name. Her thumb hovered over the keyboard. She knew if she sent this now, she would make this real, setting in motion something she couldn't take back.

Before she could overthink it, she typed out a message and hit send:

LENA: you still think everything is worth one try?

Within moments, her phone lit up with a response.

YATZIL: Yes, everything. Even when it's scary, even when it's hard.

A moment passed and another message came in.

YATZIL: If you want this too, I will be by your side for every rough patch. We can make this work, Lena. We deserve to have our own happiness.

Magdalena thought about her mother's life: all the hard work, the endless jobs, the depression of losing her husband so early in their marriage. Then she thought about her daughter. A boldness many said she could only have gotten from her mother. Carla with her willingness to take risks. Her willingness to face the potential of disappointing others.

If her daughter could be so bold at such a young age, maybe it wasn't too late for Lena to embrace her own desires. Maybe what mattered most was that, for once, she followed her journey toward happiness, even if she had no idea what that meant in the long run. She was tired of avoiding the unknown.

Lena knew it was time for her to go after all she craved. Nothing would stand in her way—especially not her own fear, or self-imposed limitations. She had never stopped loving Yatzil, and she had never stopped loving herself.

Magdalena went downstairs, grateful that she was the only one home. She put on water for coffee, pulling the cinnamon down from the cupboard. She switched on the little radio on the counter and grinned as Whitney Houston's voice filled the kitchen. It was time for Magdalena to write her own long-awaited happy ending.

EPILOGUE

The Crossing

BRIONNE JANAE

There was a smaller crowd than usually showed for a broom jumping. Not everyone approved of two women jumping the broom together. The haters sat in the doors of their cabins sucking their teeth, while Momma Patty said the magic words that would bind me and Sarah together for as long as this life—or the master—would allow us to be.

Momma Patty waved her hands and one of the elders laid the broom before us with a flourish.

"May these two grow together like the roots of two loving trees tangled all up. Be you coupled through all time. You may jump the broom."

I took Sarah's hand and turned to look at her before we crossed over. She had put little blue flowers in her hair that circled her head like a crown. Her deep brown skin was shining in the sun, and her smile showed the cutest gap between her teeth. Her eyes were filled with so much love. For this one moment, no one could touch us.

We leapt in unison without a word between us.

. . .

WITH OUR FEET LIFTED IN the air, something happened. Time froze. The clapping hands of our friends slowed to a pause, and the world faded to black as I closed my eyes.

When I opened my eyes, we had left the plantation and were standing in our kitchen.

There was the smell of biscuits in the oven, light coming through the windows, and fresh flowers on the table. Without thinking, I moved to take the biscuits from the oven as Sarah poured coffee from the percolator.

We were in our home, not a one-room shack we shared with countless others. And we were laying the table for each other, preparing to eat on our own time, not in a rush before the overseer came to move us out into the field. It was a Saturday. We had all day to love and fuck and were taking just a moment to fortify ourselves with food.

MY EYES BLINKED AGAIN AND we were in a field. Laughing and running for no reason. Nothing chasing us but joy scratching like a kitten at our heels. We lay in the grass and I kissed Sarah deeply, sliding my hand beneath the hem of her dress.

I blinked again and we were at a carnival surrounded by free negroes, playing fair games and enjoying the day. I blinked again and again, and in each new landing Sarah was by my side, and we were free as birds stretching their wings across the sky.

The next blink was heavy, deliciously slow—Sarah and I were lying in bed, our bodies curled tightly against one another, falling asleep.

I OPENED MY EYES AS our feet touched the ground. On the other side of the broom, back on the plantation, we were surrounded by our friends, clapping and whooping with a joy that defied our enslavement.

Behind us, Mama Patty issued one last blessing, "May you run together toward your future with the stars on your side and the ancestors guiding the way."

Sarah and I locked eyes. On my wife's face was a look I knew she saw on mine, wild but also determined.

Together we had tasted our freedom.

END

Glossary

Each of the following words, phrases, and concepts is featured in one or more of the stories in *Someplace Generous*. The definitions are author-generated, not dictionary-defined, meant to spark curiosity, insight, and further research. If you hold a different definition than what you see here, wonderful—we revel in the various joys of interpretation. Enjoy!

ADIO' HABIBTI. *Mix of Spanish (slang, Dominican Republic) and Arabic.* Meaning "bye" (adio' from adios) and "my dear/love/darling" (habibti).

ALA-ALBEK. *Arabic.* "To your heart" or "I wish your heart good health." It is the appreciative response to when someone wishes you sahtein.

AMÁ. *Spanish.* A common nickname used by children referring to their mothers.

AMMA. *Tamil.* Mother.

AMOR. *Spanish.* Love.

ANDROID. A robot with a human appearance. In "Heart of Stone," Marqo is an android. May also be called an automaton.

AUTOMATIC WRITING EXERCISE. A generative and continuous writing exercise that allows you to write freely, openly, allowing a message to come through you.

AVATAR. Something that represents you when your body is not present.

BA'AL T'SHUVA. *Yiddish.* A Jew who has become extra religious; literally, one who returns.

B'NAI MITZVAH. A plural for bar or bat mitzvah; also used as a gender-inclusive singular term.

BDE. "Big Dick Energy," someone grounded in their confidence.

BEVERLY HILLS 90210. A '90s-era TV show about wealthy teenagers with tight jeans, a lot of bangs, banging.

BINAURAL BEATS. A binaural beat is an illusion created by the brain when you listen to two tones with slightly different frequencies at the same time. 432 HZ: Binaural beats music that is designed for sleep, meditation, and deep relaxation.

BONITA. *Spanish.* Cute, pretty.

BUENAS NOCHES. *Spanish.* Good night and/or good evening.

BUTCH-FEMME. An often-misunderstood historical category of sexual and emotional dynamic between queers. Misunderstood as an attempt to replicate heterosexuality and the gender binary, butch generally refers to "masculine-of-center" women and femme as more traditionally "feminine-presenting" women.

CANELA. *Spanish.* Cinnamon.

CAPTAIN AMERICA. A Marvel Comics and Marvel Cinematic Universe character with immense strength.

CARNE MOLIDA. *Spanish.* Ground beef.

CEREBRAL PALSY (CP). A group of neurological disorders, which can cause stiff and/or weak muscles, spasms, tremors, heightened reflexes, and difficulties with balance and posture, among other things. There are various types of cerebral palsy, which can occur at different levels of severity.

CHANNELED MESSAGE. A message conveyed from a spiritual guide. Usually received in a meditative state, but not necessarily.

CHERRY ANGIOMA. A benign skin growth made up of blood vessels. Looks like a bubble of blood.

COMAL. *Spanish.* A flat pan of sorts on which tortillas are heated.

CROOK OF AN ARM. The inside elbow area.

DAQQAT AL-OUD. A fragrant dark resinous wood used in incense. Known as "wood of the gods" for its spiritual significance.

DEXTERITY. The ability to perform tasks, especially with one's hands.

DTF. "Down to Fuck," someone open to casual sex.

EN MI CASA. *Spanish.* In my house.

ENCONTRANDO. *Spanish.* Finding.

ENTY ZAY EL AMAR. *Arabic.* You are like the moon, meaning "you're beautiful."

ESTOY TAN TOMADA. *Spanish.* I'm so drunk.

FEH! *Yiddish.* An all-purpose expression of disgust.

FODA-SE. *Brazilian Portuguese.* Meaning "fuck!" as in "damn!"

FOGO. *Brazilian Portuguese.* Fire.

FOUND FAMILY. In "Heart of Stone," Skba, Marqo, and Vin find family in one another.

G-D. Some Jews avoid writing out the name of the artist also known as "The Creator."

GAIT. A person's way of walking

GIF. Graphics Interchange Format. An animated image that can be inserted in a messaging platform.

GOLDSCHLÄGER. 107 proof cinnamon schnapps with very thin but visible flakes of gold floating in it. A '90s icon. Pretty poison beloved by alcoholic teenage girls. Unconventional romantic bouquet ideal for young queers and petty thieves to steal and present to the objects of their desire whose names also burn secret and delicious in the dark.

GONG GONG. Chinese grandfather, from mother's side.

GRACIAS. *Spanish.* Thank you.

GUT SHABBES. *Yiddish.* Friendly greeting used between sundown Friday and sundown Saturday.

HAFTARAH PORTION. *Ashkenazic Hebrew.* The section of the Torah that is chanted aloud each week in synagogue.

HAMSA. *Arabic.* The figure of a human hand, often worn as an amulet in Southwest Asian, North African, and Mediterranean cultures to ward off the evil eye.

HARRISON, VASHTI. Contemporary Black artist and illustrator.

HYPERMOBILE EHLERS-DANLOS SYNDROME (hEDS). A connective tissue disorder. Symptoms may include loose or unstable joints, chronic pain, fatigue, fragile, stretchy skin that breaks and bruises easily, and issues with internal organs, among other things.

KARAMBIT. A small, curved knife made for tearing skin.

KOSHER. *Hebrew.* Food that strictly adheres to Jewish dietary laws.

KRYPTONITE. A green rock that weakens Superman.

LEI-SEE. A red envelope with a monetary gift, given at holidays or special occasions.

LOIS LANE. Central character in DC/Superman Comics and film. Like Minnie in "Why Won't You Die?" she's a journalist.

MACHACA. A dried meat.

MANGO, LIMÓN Y SAL. *Spanish.* Mango, lemon, and salt.

MARIDO. *Spanish.* Husband.

ME VOY A DORMIR, LO BESO. *Spanish.* I go to bed, I kiss him . . .

MIDRASH. A creative mode of biblical interpretation.

MIJITA. *Spanish.* A nickname of sorts that uses the word "mija," which directly translates to daughter. Mijita literally means "little daughter," but it's a loving phrase used across ages.

MIRA QUE GUAPA. *Spanish.* Look how handsome (feminine).

MISBAHA. Prayer beads used by Muslims (also known as "tasbih").

MISS AMERICA. America Sanchez, a Marvel Comics character most recently depicted in *Doctor Strange in the Multiverse of Madness*.

MISTY KNIGHT. A Black Marvel Comics character with a metal arm and hand.

MODERN ORTHODOX. A Jewish practice that marries Jewish observance with attunement to the modern world.

MUJER. *Spanish*. Woman, but also used casually as a sort of nickname, similar to Bonita.

NO SEAS RIDÍCULA. *Spanish*. Don't be ridiculous.

NUDNIK. *Yiddish*. A pain in the ass.

OH, COMMUNITY. You know how the queer world can just be so small?

OLD FASHIONED. A classic cocktail made by muddling simple syrup, bitters, and orange and adding bourbon, soda water, and a cherry. On ice, preferably one large cube.

PELO. *Spanish*. Hair.

PERO TU, MIJA. *Spanish*. But you, daughter.

PLAGUE. Referring to COVID-19.

PLATANO FRITO. *Spanish*. Also known as "tostones," fried green plantain.

POQUITA. *Spanish*. A little bit.

POR POR. Chinese grandmother, from mother's side.

POWERCHAIR. An electric or motorized wheelchair.

REBBETZIN. *Hebrew*. A woman who is married to a rabbi.

RECUERDOS. *Spanish*. Directly translates to memories, but recuerdos are also a type of art that honors a deceased person, made with mixed forms of media and often shadow boxes.

"RHYTHM NATION." A Janet Jackson song from the 1980s. In the video, Janet and her dancers wear all black, including a black baseball cap and black gloves.

RUMMANIYYA. A Gazan dish made up of unripened pomegranate seeds, eggplant, tahina, garlic, hot peppers, and lentils.

SAHTEIN. *Arabic*. "Double health" or literally "two healths." It is a blessing offered at the start of a meal.

SANS. *French*. Without.

SÉANCE. A ritual in which a psychic medium or someone with the ability to or experience with communicating with spirits attempts to assist a person or people with contacting a deceased loved one.

SERIAL MONOGAMIST. Someone who moves from one serious/monogamous relationship to the next without much time to be single in between.

SHABBOS. *Ashkenazic Hebrew/Yiddish*. The weekly Jewish day of rest, from sundown Friday to sundown Saturday.

SHAVUOT. A Jewish holiday that happens in the summer, translated as "the festival of weeks." It commemorates the ancient Jews receiving the Torah. One tradition to mark the holiday is to stay up all night studying Jewish texts.

SIEMPRE TRABAJANDO. *Spanish*. Always working.

SPADES. An ultra-competitive card game that is played in pairs. There are major consequences for errors in judgment.

SPASM. A sudden, involuntary movement or muscle contraction.

STEAMPUNK. A subgenre and aesthetic incorporating retrofuturistic technology. In "Heart of Stone," the creation of Marqo is based on steampunk principles.

STONE SOUP. The folktale that inspired "Heart of Stone."

SUAVEMENTE. *Spanish.* A popular song but also directly translates to softly.

SUBLUXATE. To partially dislocate (a joint or other part of the body).

SUPERNATURAL. A television show about two brothers who hunted demons and other supernatural beings, eventually having to repeatedly save the world.

TATO'. *Spanish (slang, Dominican Republic).* All right, okay, that's it.

THE EQUALIZER. A television show on CBS starring Queen Latifah.

THWACK. The sound of contact made by a moving object forcefully coming down on a stationary object.

TICK. A relative of spiders and mites that are parasitic, known for carrying Lyme and other bacteria.

TOUCH-ME-NOT. Someone who prefers not to be stimulated, or touched, during sex.

TU SI ERE' LINDA. *Spanish (slang, Dominican Republic).* You're beautiful.

U-HAUL. A term used in Lesbian parlance to indicate the quick move from sex to falling in love and suddenly living with a new lover.

UN BUEN PAPA A TUS HIJOS. *Spanish.* A good father to your kids.

VEDIC ASTROLOGY. A traditional Hindu system of astrology.

VIEJA. *Spanish.* Directly translates to old woman.

VONNEGUT, KURT. A satirical writer enjoyed by teenagers and others.

WINTER SOLDIER. A Marvel Comics and MCU character with a metal arm and hand who is also an assassin. It's discovered that he is also Captain America's oldest friend, Bucky.

YARMULKE. *Yiddish.* You know, a kippah.

ZA'ATAR. A Palestinian spice mix including variations of za'atar/wild thyme, caraway seeds, sumac, toasted sesame seeds, cumin, allspice, and salt.

Content Descriptions

SYMBOL KEY

🕯️Candlelight glow—There is no sex scene in this story. Which doesn't mean it's not *sexy!*

🔥 Bonfire heat—Contains NSFW content, but depictions are not graphic, up-close, or detailed.

🚒 Call the firetruck—May include "open-door" sex scenes, kink, or detailed physical interactions.

🖤 Shadow work—These stories artfully address trauma or violence in a character's backstory.

For the Love of Sky and Smoke, by Mavis L. Johnson
Conjuring the night her grandparents met, Clove retells a story that honors Black love, celebrating spice and sweetness across

generations. **Could be compared to:** The taste of good whiskey in a highball glass and the rich spicy smell of home. **Subgenres:** Contemporary.

HEAT LEVEL: 🕯️

Sofia, by EJ Colen

A queer woman on a quest to have fifty first dates—determined to keep from getting attached too quickly—falls in deeper than expected. In any version of the story, she wants Sofia. **Could be compared to:** *Sliding Doors* meets a hot queer dating show on Netflix. **Subgenres:** Contemporary, Speculative.

HEAT LEVEL: 🔥

How to Open a Door, by Sammy Taub

Two players of an online werewolf video game—a traumatized agoraphobe playing as a woman, and an unknown person playing as a wolf—meet online and fall anonymously into a relationship. **Could be compared to:** *Looking for Group* by Alexis Hall. Or: some older short stories of Amy Hempel or George Saunders. **Subgenres:** Contemporary, Romcom, Dark, Cyber-Romance. 🖤

HEAT LEVEL: 🔥

The Boiler Room, by Max Delsohn

Frank is a trans guy working the front desk of a reform Jewish synagogue. He's thrilled when he's asked to help Lucas, the cute new cis guy on the facilities team, move a bunch of old music stands to a remote corner of the building. Frank would be happy staying down in the boiler room with Lucas all day. Does Lucas feel it, too? **Could be compared to:** *Heartstopper* meets Andy and April from *Parks and Rec.* **Subgenres:** Contemporary, Romcom.

HEAT LEVEL: 🔥

The Séance, by Mystery Post
On a hot Southern day in a Mississippi hotel, a nonbinary sex worker with psychic abilities helps a rich widow reconnect with her long-lost lesbian lover by performing a séance of both body and mind. **Could be compared to:** *Upright Women Wanted* by Sarah Gailey meets *The Master of Djinn* by P. Djeli Clark, with a dash of *Supernatural*, The Dresden Files, or *Ghost*—but make it queer AF. **Subgenres:** Fantasy, Historical, Speculative.

HEAT LEVEL: 🔥

Why Won't You Die? by Jessica P. Pryde
D is a skilled assassin on a job, but the woman she's been sent to kill just won't die. When she finds herself cornered by her own mark—an irritatingly adorable, seemingly indestructible journalist named Minerva—D can't help but ask the question: *Why won't you die?* **Could be compared to:** DC Comics and Marvel Cinematic Universes. What if Lois Lane was Luke Cage? **Subgenres:** Contemporary, Speculative, Superhero. 🖤

HEAT LEVEL: 🕯️

True to Your Heart, by Brittany Arreguin
For Daphne, dating always came secondary to her job and her family. But when someone knocks on the door to her grandmother's apartment, her luck might just turn right around. **Could**

be compared to: *Lunar Love* by Lauren Kung Jessen. **Subgenres:** Contemporary, Romcom

HEAT LEVEL: 🕯️

Luna × Noura, by Ayla Vejdani

When Luna met Noura, they made moonlight. Luna met someone who helped her heal, Noura met someone who set her free. This modern entanglement depicts self-discovery in middle-age and love after divorce. It is both a celebration of the type of romance that makes us lose sleep, and a love letter to the friendships we could never live without. **Could be compared to:** Where *Sex and the City* meets *The L-Word: Generation Q.* **Subgenres:** Contemporary.

HEAT LEVEL: 🚒

Jess & Daya, by Pamela Vaccariello

Jess has chronic pain, but what hurts worse than her knees or shoulders is the shame and self-hatred she feels regarding her disability. Daya hates seeing Jess in pain but loves spending quality time with her. Can Daya's care help Jess find love and acceptance for herself? **Could be compared to:** Mia Mingus's essay "Access Intimacy: The Missing Link" meets Red's allyship and admiration for Chloe in *Get a life, Chloe Brown* by Talia Hibbert. **Subgenres:** Contemporary, New Adult.

HEAT LEVEL: 🕯️

Waves, by Anis Gisele

A glimpse into what love looks like when queers of color choose and invest care in each other. This is a story about learning that you can be accountable to your own pleasure. **Could be compared to:** A really good Hayley Kiyoko music video. **Subgenres:** Contemporary.

HEAT LEVEL: 🚒

Desperate for a Good Time, by Corinne Manning
Clarice and Angela are strangers, until suddenly they are not. Set off the gloomy coast of Washington—fraught with tick bites, colonial histories, and a modern-day plague—this is a darkly humorous tale about the sapphic and vampiric urge to merge in the first few months of quarantine. **Could be compared to:** The TV show *First Kill*, the film *Vampyres,* and Jewel Gomez's *The Gilda Stories.* **Subgenres:** Contemporary, Horror, Magical Realism. 🖤

HEAT LEVEL: 🚒

Unstoppable, by ronni tartlet
Everyone's gathering at the synagogue for Evan's bar mitzvah party, and baby trans-masc Kasha is packing a special secret under that dress. Will Kasha succeed in sparking the right kind of trouble? **Could be compared to:** *You Are So Not Invited to My Bat Mitzvah* but make it queer. **Subgenres:** YA, Romcom, Autobiomythography.

HEAT LEVEL: 🔥

Something That Only Shines in the Dark, by Britt Ashley
Punk chivalry, an American muscle car, and the need to keep the night from ending push two teenaged friends toward a delicious and dangerous new desire. You'll be hoping Angie and Helen get away with absolutely everything. **Could be compared to:** One

part "Swing Low" by Gossip mixed with a shot of the TV show *Trinkets* and just a dash of *My So-Called Life*. **Subgenres:** Contemporary, YA, Flash Fiction.

HEAT LEVEL: 🕯️

Heart of Stone, by Sophia Bahar Vaccaro
Skba thinks she is destined to runs with dogs and sleep each night alone until she runs into two mysterious travelers—including the boy called Marqo—who need her help with an unusual task. **Could be compared to:** *Spinning Silver* by Naomi Novik, and the folktale Stone Soup. **Subgenres:** Fantasy, Folklore, New Adult.

HEAT LEVEL: 🕯️

Runner, by Rachel McKibbens
A grieving neurodivergent woman, fixated on a series of news stories about murdered women, finds surprising refuge in the velvet den of an amputee. **Could be compared to:** *You Made a Fool of Death with Your Beauty* by Akwaeke Emezi, (Ab)*Normal People*. **Subgenres:** Contemporary, Speculative, Dark. 🖤

HEAT LEVEL: 🔥

Forest Bae, by Amber Patton
A short erotic scene about the joys of expectation—that feeling when something seemingly innocuous sends a thrilling chill down your spine. **Could be compared to:** *Secretary*, but make it outdoorsy, Black, and joyful. **Subgenres:** Contemporary, Erotica, Flash Fiction.

HEAT LEVEL: 🚒

The Camping Date, by Sabrina Stuart Smith
On an adventurous first date with a guy she believes to be out of her league, our heroine is determined to curb her abhorrence for the outdoors while achieving the ultimate romantic conquest. When a series of unwelcome encounters arrive to thwart her goal, she must redirect her fears. Can she turn a potentially irksome experience into a delight? **Could be compared to:** *Falling Inn Love* starring Christina Milian. **Subgenres:** Contemporary, Romcom.

HEAT LEVEL: 🚒

A Thousand Tiny Pieces, by Amadeo Cruz Guiao
A Filipinx nonbinary person is hitchhiking in an Alaskan winter. They set out to find answers to their big questions, but when a wild-haired Mama in a red truck offers a ride, they encounter wonder and magic instead. **Could be compared to:** *Eat, Pray, Love,* but not as basic, and in two pages. **Subgenres:** Contemporary, Romcom, Flash Fiction.

HEAT LEVEL: 🕯️

The All-Night Deluxe Tea Room, by Temim Fruchter
It's just a regular hotel in the Poconos, but The Pressman, host to throngs of Jewish holiday observers, has a special feature: the All-Night Deluxe Tea Room. Lavishly laid with tea and cake at all hours, the room seems, despite its humble wood-paneled contours, like a portal to elsewhere. And for Laurie and Rivky, who meet one another there at the edge of the holiday, it just might be. **Could be compared to:** *Disobedience* meets *Where the Wild Things Are.* **Subgenres:** Contemporary, Romcom, Speculative

HEAT LEVEL: 🔥

Stunt Man, by Richard Siken
In an epic story told in a flash, two men meet and consider what's true. **Could be compared to:** *Crush, War of the Foxes,* and *I Do Know Some Things* by Richard Siken. **Subgenres:** Contemporary, Western, Flash Fiction.

HEAT LEVEL:

Magdalena, by V. Ruiz
After nearly twenty years, Magdalena—now a married mother of two children—runs into her high school sweetheart. Yatzil is an artist and teacher who remembers exactly how Magdalena likes her coffee. Magdalena's life begins to transform as she allows herself to crave more than the suburban way of life she's grown accustomed to. **Could be compared to:** *The Notebook*, if Allie was queer and Latinx, Noah was a woman, and Lon was a beer-brewing dad. **Subgenres:** Contemporary.

HEAT LEVEL:

The Crossing, by Brionne Janae
Two lovers jump the broom and are transported into a world where they are free. **Could be compared to:** *The Underground Railroad* by Colson Whitehead, or *Kindred* by Octavia Butler, in poetic flash fiction. **Subgenres:** Historical, Fantasy, Magical Realism, Flash Fiction.

HEAT LEVEL:

About the Authors

Brittany Arreguin *(she/her)* is an author from Oakland, California, who loves stories with happy endings and reading about characters who share her Asian, queer, and neurodiverse identities. Her debut novel, *Waking Up in Vegas*, released in January 2024. She lives with her husband and cat, Princess Peach.

Britt Ashley *(she/her)* is a queer femme from Texas who makes poems and biscuits. Her writing and artwork have appeared in *Tammy Journal*, *Southern Indiana Review*, *The Pinch*, *Cream City Review*, *Juked*, *Winter Tangerine Review*, *The Offing*, and elsewhere. She lives and writes in Seattle with her handsome husbian and a bossy miniature dachshund named Waffles.

EJ Colen *(she/her, they/them)* is a queer artist/teacher/editor/writer whose books include *What Weaponry*, a novel in prose poems, poetry collections *Money for Sunsets* (Lambda Literary Award and Audre Lorde Award finalist) and *Waiting Up for the End of the World: Conspiracies*, flash fiction collection *Dear Mother Monster, Dear Daughter Mistake*, book-length lyric essay *The Green*

Condition, and fiction collaboration *True Ash*. Nonfiction editor at Tupelo Press and freelance editor/manuscript consultant, she teaches at Western Washington University.

Amadeo Cruz Guiao *(she/her, he/him, they/them)* strives to live into the meaning of their name, which means "Lover of God." Born into the mystical Catholic tradition of their Philippine ancestors, Amadeo channels most of their creativity into their work as an organizational healer, facilitator, and spiritual teacher, working nationally and internationally to facilitate transformative change. When they're not exploring the world(s), they live on the shores of the sacred Salish Sea/Puget Sound in Coast Salish/Duwamish territories known as Seattle, in close proximity to their partner, Rose, and their menagerie of brilliant children and unusual animals.

Max Delsohn *(he/him, they/them)* is a trans and anti-Zionist Jewish writer. Their prose has appeared in *McSweeney's Quarterly Concern*, *VICE*, *Joyland*, *The Rumpus*, *Triangle House*, *Nat. Brut*, *Passages North*, *Moss*, and the Graywolf Press essay anthology *Critical Hits: Writers Playing Video Games*, edited by Carmen Maria Machado and J. Robert Lennon. They have been awarded residencies and fellowships by the Constance Saltonstall Foundation for the Arts, Mineral School, and Hugo House. Their debut short story collection, *CRAWL*, is forthcoming from Graywolf Press. Learn more at www.maxdelsohn.com.

Temim Fruchter *(she/her)* is a queer, nonbinary, anti-Zionist Jewish writer who lives in Brooklyn. She holds an MFA in fiction from the University of Maryland and is the recipient of fellowships from the DC Commission on the Arts and Humanities, Vermont Studio Center, and a 2020 Rona Jaffe Foundation

Writers' Award. She is cohost of *Pete's Reading Series* in Brooklyn. Her debut novel, *City of Laughter*, was published by Grove Atlantic in winter 2024.

Anis Gisele *(they/them)* is an artist, a slow burn, a summer babe. They'll flirt with you all night.

Brionne Janae *(he/him, they/them)* is a poet and teaching artist living in Brooklyn. They are the author of *Blessed Are the Peacemakers* (2021), which won the 2020 Cave Canem Northwestern University Press Poetry Prize, and *After Jubilee* (2017) published by Boat Press. Brionne is a 2023 NEA Creative Writing Fellow, a Hedgebrook Alum and proud Cave Canem Fellow. Their poetry has been published in *Best American Poetry 2022*, *Ploughshares*, *The American Poetry Review*, The Academy of American Poets *Poem-a-Day*, *The Sun Magazine*, *jubilat*, and *Waxwing*, among others. Off the page, they go by Breezy.

Mavis L. Johnson *(she/her)* delights in hearing, reading, and creating stories that honor and center the diverse experiences of Black communities. As a storyteller, she helps others discover the hidden gems in lived experiences to create and document stories that celebrate legacy. She loves happy endings that inspire new beginnings. Mavis is a proud descendant of brave Georgia-born people who were part of the Great Migration of African Americans from the American South to the Northeast. She was born with a disability that has sparked her creativity.

Corinne Manning *(they/them)* is the author of the story collection *We Had No Rules*, published by Arsenal Pulp Press in 2020 to starred reviews from *Booklist* and *Publishers Weekly*, the latter noting it "exquisitely examines queer relationships with equal parts humor, heartache, and titillation." They have received fellowships from The MacDowell Colony, Artist Trust, Hub City Writers Project, and The Banff Centre. They are based in Seattle and teach writing locally and nationally. www.corinnemanning.com

Rachel McKibbens *(she/her)* is a queer Chicana poet and author of three full-length books of poetry, *blud* (Copper Canyon, 2017), *Into the Dark & Emptying Field* (Small Doggies Press, 2013), and *Pink Elephant* (to be re-released on Button Poetry). In 2012, McKibbens founded The Pink Door Writing Retreat, an annual retreat held exclusively for non-men writers of color. In 2022, McKibbens was the subject of the podcast *We Were Three*, from *The New York Times* and the creators of *Serial*.

Amber Patton *(she/her)* is a Jill-of-all-trades. An actress, novelist, voice actor, screenwriter, producer, director, and avid film watcher, Amber loves to be creative. Recent projects include a short film, *After Forever*, out on YouTube; a podcast about actors for actors, *Catching Up with You*, and a steamy novella, *What I Wouldn't Do: Where It Started*, available everywhere e-books are sold. More at www.amber-patton.com/novelist.

Mystery Post *(they/them)* is a queer, nonbinary writer born and raised in Utah. In 2020, they earned a BA in English & Creative Writing from Westminster University and, in 2023, an MFA in Creative Writing from Vermont College of Fine Arts. When not chipping away at their novel-in-progress, an Industrial Revolution ghost story featuring cannibal gods and magic textiles, they enjoy spending time with their cat and playing TTRPGs.

Jessica P. Pryde *(she/her)* is a Black reader, writer, and librarian living in Southern Arizona with her husband and a creamsicle rosy boa named Rainbow. She is a contributing editor for *Book Riot*, where she cohosts the *When in Romance* podcast, and the editor of the nonfiction anthology *Black Love Matters*.

V. Ruiz *(they/them)*, author of the poetry book *In Stories We Thunder*, is a writer, artist, and astrologer living in Los Angeles. They are a Queer Disabled Xicana who works as a publisher for Row House Publishing, helping elevate voices that matter. When they aren't writing or reading, they are feverishly studying astrology or trying their hand at a thousand new hobbies.

Richard Siken *(he/him)* is a poet, painter, and filmmaker. His book *Crush* won the 2004 Yale Series of Younger Poets prize, selected by Louise Glück, a Lambda Literary Award, a Thom Gunn Award, and was a finalist for the National Book Critics Circle Award. His other books are *War of the Foxes* (Copper Canyon Press, 2015) and *I Do Know Some Things* (forthcoming, Copper Canyon Press, 2024). Siken is a recipient of a Pushcart Prize, two Lannan Fellowships, two Arizona Commission on the Arts grants, and a fellowship from the National Endowment for the Arts. He lives in Tucson, Arizona.

Sabrina Stuart Smith *(she/her)* is a Canadian poet and fiction writer born in Toronto to a Jamaican mother and Bajan father. Her work centers on Black love, sensuality, Caribbean culture, multiculturalism, and motherhood. Find her new and forthcoming work in *Volume Poetry*, *Aunt Chloe: A Journal of Artful Candor* and *Pink Panther Magazine*. She is a graduate of York University, where she received her BA in English, and Toronto Metropolitan University, where she studied book publishing. When she is not writing, she is likely out walking the vast multicultural corridors of Toronto, often with her two kids by her side, absorbing inspiration for her work.

ronni tartlet *(they/them, squee/squir)* is an anti-Zionist Jew rooted in diaspora, with ancestors from both Ashkenazic and Sephardic lineages, and they are okay with complexity and contradiction. They live on a big rock in the Salish Sea, where they harvest fruit, build stuff, feed kids, and respond to medical emergencies. Their nonfiction writing has been published in *Real Change* newspaper, *Fifth Estate*, and numerous zines, including 2001's *The Missing Peace: Truth & Justice in Israel/Palestine*. Their lifelong goals include undermining structures of oppression and contributing to cultures of joy and liberation.

Sammy Taub publishes anonymously.

Pamela Vaccariello *(she/her)* is a disabled writer from Montreal, Quebec, currently pursuing a BA in creative writing from Concordia University. She writes both prose and poetry, with an affinity for focusing on the everyday—likely because her disability, cerebral palsy, forces her to move slowly, allowing her to appreciate life's smallest, simplest pleasures. Her work often depicts what it's like to experience life in a disabled body—both the struggles and the immense joys. When not writing, she can be found watching romantic comedies or reading. Her work has previously been published in *SPACE* magazine and *Creations* literary journal.

Sophia Bahar Vaccaro *(she/her)* is a writer living in Los Angeles, California. Her love affair with music has been marked in equal parts by both scandal and romance, but her long-standing partnership with writing has been one of constant support and the warm and fuzzy feeling of knowing someone out there sees you, truly sees you. While it is extremely difficult for her both physically and emotionally not to feature a giant worm in every single thing she writes, she has done her best for you in her *Someplace Generous* contribution, "Heart of Stone."

Ayla Vejdani (*she/her*) is a storyteller, holder of space, curator of experience, and creator of beauty. Her current projects include a QBIPOC contemporary romance novel and a QBIPOC children's series. Raised and educated all over the world, she has a master's in human rights, and is an inclusive leadership consultant. She speaks four languages and laughs in all. Ayla is a queer Iranian/Canadian living in Tiohtiá:ke/Montréal, Canada, raising her two young children. She is an insatiably creative, hopeful romantic who believes in magic.

About the Editors

Editors Elaina Ellis and Amber Flame are longtime friends and creative collaborators.

Elaina Ellis *(she/her)* is publisher and cofounder at Generous Press. She owns and operates A Trusted Reader, providing literary book editing services for brilliant writers of all stripes. For ten years she worked at the Pulitzer Prize–winning publishing house Copper Canyon Press where she served as editor. She is the author of *Write About an Empty Birdcage*, and has received support from Artist Trust, Mineral School, Vermont Studio Center, Jack Straw, Tent, 4Culture, and Seattle Office of Arts & Culture. Ellis is a queer, disabled Jew who envisions a free, safe, and just future for all people, from the US to Palestine.

Amber Flame *(she/her)* is deputy publisher and cofounder at Generous Press. She is a multi-genre writer, educator, and arts administrator serving as program director for Hedgebrook, a premier writing residency for women-identified writers. She has served as a copyeditor, developmental editor, and general "fluffer" for all manner of texts. Her mission is joy. Flame is the author of the poetry collections *Ordinary Cruelty* and *apocrifa*; her writing has earned awards from Hedgebrook, Vermont Studio Center, Jack Straw, Seattle Office of Arts & Culture, and YEFE NOF.